An excerpt from
A Proper Lord's ...

"Perhaps I think about these things too much."

"Not at all." He cast about for a proper response and hit upon a remembrance from his school days. "According to Socrates, an unexamined life is not worth living."

"Ah, Socrates." Her smile returned. "He believed nature was akin to divinity. It's telling that so many philosophers have concerned themselves with nature's mysteries. It's endlessly interesting, don't you think?"

I think, Lady Jane, that Lord Hobart probably lost his nerve after just such a conversation as this. He'd met Hobart on a few occasions, and remembered him as a small-minded fellow, unlikely to bear much interest in the mysteries of nature. For Townsend, the most interesting parts of nature revealed themselves in the bedroom. One found mystery and divinity indeed, if one bedded down with an adequately voracious woman.

A dangerous line of thought, that, as he strolled with his maidenly fiancée. She was still going on about Socrates, God save him.

"I suppose I am talking too much and behaving like a bluestocking," she said, as if she'd heard his thought. "There, I shouldn't have said that either." Her ladylike mask fell away, revealing more honest anxiety. "I must admit I'm not the best at..."

She paused, biting her lip, and glanced back toward the house.

"What are you not the best at, Lady Jane? Vapid conversation? Have you studied philosophy when you ought to have been perfecting your witty banter?"

He was teasing, but she answered with a serious frown. "I was meant to marry a family friend, so I haven't had much practice with courtship." She gave him a sideways look. "I suppose you're used to more well-spoken women."

"If by well-spoken, you mean capable of prattling on about absolutely nothing for the better part of an hour, then yes. That's not a difficult art. You can learn to be better at it if you like, Lady Jane, but when we're alone, you may speak as you wish…"

Copyright 2020 Annabel Joseph/Scarlet Rose Press

* * * * *

This book is a work of fiction. Names, characters, places, and incidents are products of the author's imagination or are used fictitiously. Any resemblance to actual events, locales, or persons living or dead, is entirely coincidental.

This work contains acts of punishment and discipline. This work and its contents are for the sole purpose of fantasy and enjoyment, and not meant to advance or typify any of the activities or lifestyles therein. Please exercise caution in entering into or attempting to imitate any fictional relationships or activities.

All romantically involved characters depicted in this work of fiction are 18 years of age or older.

A Proper Lord's Wife

by

Annabel Joseph

Properly Spanked Legacy, Book Two

Other books by Annabel Joseph
Mercy
Cait and the Devil
Firebird
Owning Wednesday
Lily Mine
Disciplining the Duchess
Royal Discipline
The Royal Wedding Night

Fortune series:
Deep in the Woods
Fortune

Comfort series:
Comfort Object
Caressa's Knees
Odalisque
Command Performance

Cirque Masters series:
Cirque de Minuit
Bound in Blue
Master's Flame

Mephisto series:
Club Mephisto
Molly's Lips: Club Mephisto Retold
Burn For You

BDSM Ballet series:
Waking Kiss
Fever Dream

Properly Spanked series:
Training Lady Townsend
To Tame A Countess
My Naughty Minette
Under A Duke's Hand

Properly Spanked Legacy series:
Rival Desires
A Proper Lord's Wife
Book Three: Marlow's story coming soon
Book Four: August's story coming soon

A Guide to the Properly Spanked Families
(and the characters you'll meet in this story)

The Marquess of Townsend
(the hero of this book)
eldest son of the Duke and Duchess of Lockridge,
aka Hunter and Aurelia from
Training Lady Townsend
He is called Townsend or Towns by friends, but his future wife calls him Edward in private.
Townsend's sisters Felicity and Rosalind also appear in this book.

Viscount Marlow
eldest son of the Earl and Countess of Warren
aka Warren and Josephine from
To Tame A Countess
His given name is George, but he goes by Marlow due to his inherited title.

The Earl of Augustine
eldest son of the Marquess and Marchioness of Barrymore
aka, Minette and Augustine from
My Naughty Minette
Now that the previous Lord Augustine has inherited his father's title of Barrymore, his oldest son now bears the name and title of Augustine. His Christian name, Julian, is rarely used.

The Marquess of Wescott
eldest son of the Duke and Duchess of Arlington,
aka Arlington and Gwen from
Under A Duke's Hand
In book one of this series, *Rival Desires*, Wescott and Townsend fought over a woman, Ophelia. Now happily married to Ophelia, Wescott is the only one of the four friends who isn't single.
Wescott's sisters Hazel and Elizabeth appear in this book.

Chapter One: Revenge

December, 1822

Edward Lionel, Marquess of Townsend, strode across St. James Street feeling incredibly smug about his afternoon's work. One day home from the continent, and he'd already engineered a satisfying act of revenge against his former friend, Lord Wescott.

It involved getting married, yes, but sometimes sacrifices were warranted.

He stopped in the doorway of his preferred gentlemen's club, taking in the familiar scents of tobacco, smoke, and leather. Ah, it was good to be home, even if London was a cold, muddy mess in the thick of an early winter.

He handed his cloak and hat to the attendant, smoothed his dark hair, and went to the dining room in search of his closest friends, Viscount Marlow and the Earl of Augustine. He'd barely entered when the two men stood, calling his name in a boisterous fashion more suited to a boxing emporium.

"Is that Townsend I see?" Marlow said.

"Look at him, in the flesh!" Augustine strode to him, grinning. "He found his way back to London after all."

He'd been gone so long their noisy breach of decorum didn't bother him. He'd drifted around the French countryside for three long months, devastated that Wescott, one of his best childhood friends, had stolen the love of his life. The loss would always hurt—Lady Ophelia had been meant for him, he knew that—but at least he'd been able to pull off a satisfying counterblow.

"Come and sit, Towns," said August, his black hair messily tousled, as customary. "Are you hungry?"

"We're drinking more than eating," Marlow confessed, pale blue eyes glinting beneath his famously white-blond hair. "We've missed you. How was the hunting in France, my friend?"

He meant women, not wildlife. "*Très bon*," Townsend answered, although, in truth, he'd been too heartsick to respond to any advances that came his way.

He glanced around the half empty room. Things weren't as busy at White's outside the Season. Come spring, there'd be no empty tables, as married gentlemen returned from their countryside haunts. Speaking of married gentlemen… "Wescott's not here, is he?"

"No," said August. "But if he was, we'd have to broker a peace between you. You can't hold that grudge forever."

"I certainly can." He poured himself a glass from the spiced brandy on the table. "He stole the woman I loved."

"I don't know that he stole her so much as saved her life in a fire," said Marlow.

Townsend glared at him. "Even so, I can't forgive him. You don't know the whole story. The man is no longer my friend."

"The two of them are happy, anyway." August ignored his obvious anguish to deliver the cursed update. "They're content as lovebirds, now that they're over their rough start. He took her to Wales and everything. Taught her how to fight with swords."

"He taught her swords?" Townsend found the idea preposterous. "She's not strong enough to wield a sword. She'll end up maiming herself."

"She's not your worry anymore," said Marlow. "You've got to face that. Lady Wescott's happily married, and you've got to make amends with Wescott before Christmas, anyway, so the four of us can be friends again."

Townsend did his best to hold back a smirk. He generally tried to be a proper fellow, not the smirking sort, but his recent victory was too great not to gloat a bit. "He won't want to be friends again when he learns what I've done."

"What have you done?" Marlow and August asked at once.

"I'm going to be married," he announced, raising his glass of brandy.

"Married?" Again, both his friends spoke in unison. They both sounded displeased and ignored his invitation to toast.

"It's bad enough Wescott caught a leg shackle," said Marlow. "Why are you getting married now?"

"That's fifty percent of us, right out of commission," grumbled Augustine.

"You're supposed to ask me whom I'm to marry," said Townsend.

Marlow threw up his hands. "Fine. Who are you marrying, Towns? Who's the unfortunate innocent?"

"The Earl of Mayhew's daughter," he said triumphantly. "The woman Wescott was meant to marry before he lost her by ruining Ophelia's life. Isn't it capital?"

"The Earl of Mayhew's daughter?" Augustine echoed. "Isn't she—?"

"In the country right now? Yes, but I've spoken at length with her father. We talked about how difficult a time she's had since Wescott jilted her."

"But...Townsey..."

"Of course, I didn't mention Wescott's name when I brought it up," he continued over his friends' protests. "That would have been unseemly, to confront him with the whole debacle, so I went about it delicately. Her father was instantly agreeable to a contract. He said, considering her situation, that Lady Jane would be happy to wed me right now. A Christmas wedding in Berkshire! I understand it, really. Wescott left her in a terrible lurch when he dropped her in favor of Ophelia."

"Townsend, dear fellow—" Marlow tried again to interrupt, but he held up a hand.

"I don't want to hear any scolding," he said in a strident voice. "If Wescott can steal my intended away, I can steal his." His friends would never understand how deeply Ophelia's loss had wounded him. He took a drink of brandy, savoring the heat on his tongue. "The idea came to me halfway across the Channel, and I couldn't get home fast enough. Thank God her father was in town or I'd have had to slog all the way to Reading. I would have done it, though, to pull this off."

"So, Towns, you're engaged to Lady Jane, then?" said August.

"Yes, and I'll thank you not to argue about the civility of it. I do like Jane, from what I know of the woman. I'm not only marrying her for revenge. She's quite pretty, isn't she? I saw her at the balls last season, dancing with Wescott." He smiled. "No more dancing for those two."

He finished his drink and put the cup back on the table. "Be happy for me, fellows. This is all working out exactly as I'd hoped. Jane and I won't have much time to get to know one another before the wedding, but by the first ball of the Season, we'll make a handsome figure together, and I'll consider Wescott paid back for his perfidy in kind."

"His *perfidy*?" August shook his head. "Wescott didn't even know you were in love with Ophelia when he rescued her."

"Don't defend him." He poured himself another drink, draining the already much depleted bottle. "At least not until I'm drunker."

His friends might believe he was acting hastily, or unreasonably, but in time they'd come to understand what he'd realized on his way home from France—that this was the only way to even the score between him and his former friend. It would torment him to see his lovely blonde Ophelia on Lord Wescott's arm about town, it always would, but it would sting a tiny bit less when he was wed to Wescott's beautiful Lady Jane.

"What is it?" he asked his friends, as the waiter delivered a new brandy bottle. "Why must you look at me like that? I'm behaving more honorably than he did. He nearly ruined Ophelia, while I'm rescuing a recently jilted lady with a very generous marriage contract. Her father was so pleased by my offer, so surprised by my generosity he could barely speak."

"Oh, I imagine he was surprised, all right," said Marlow. "You're about to be surprised, too."

"What do you mean?" He looked from Marlow to Augustine. It was August who finally spoke.

"Townsend. Dear friend. It was Lady *June* to whom Wescott had promised marriage. Lady *Juuuune*." He drew out the name, emphasizing the vowel. "The same Lady June who married Lord Braxton a couple weeks after Wescott married Ophelia."

"Lady June?" Townsend blinked at his friend. "Are you sure?"

"You utter boff. You've betrothed yourself to the wrong woman," Marlow said. "Not only that, but Lady Jane—"

August held up a hand, silencing him. "Be careful what you say now, Marlow. He's going to marry her."

"He ought to be warned first, don't you think?"

Townsend's brain was in a muddle, and it wasn't from the strong drink. "What are you saying? Go back, please. There is a Jane *and* a June?"

"Not very creative of the Mayhews, but yes." Marlow blinked, half frowning. "It's like naming your daughters Margaret and Murgaret, isn't it?"

"Or Agnes and Ugnes," said August.

"Charlotte and Churlette," Marlow offered, warming to the game.

"Shut up, would you?" Townsend waved a brusque hand. "Are you having me for a joke? I've never heard of this Jane, never seen her at any balls or gatherings."

"It's no joke," said Marlow. "June is the elder sister, the one Wescott was meant for. Jane is the younger. They're not at all the same."

Townsend narrowed his eyes. "But when I spoke to Lord Mayhew of the way she'd been jilted, he agreed it had been a terrible thing."

"Because Lady Jane suffered the same misfortune," said Marlow. "She'd been meant to marry the Earl of Hobart as soon as Lady June was situated with Wescott. They'd had a marriage contracted for years, because those two families are thick as thieves, but Hobart broke the engagement. Not for another woman. Just because. He'll not be received by many families next Season because of it."

They all fell silent at the cruelty of such a maneuver.

"Hobart refused to marry her, then?" Townsend pushed his drink away. "For what reason? What's wrong with her?"

Marlow and Augustine exchanged a woebegone look that did nothing to soothe his rising anxiety. "Tell me," he insisted. "Tell me what I've done."

"I can't believe you don't know about Lady Jane," said August. "She's a frequent subject of gossip."

"I don't listen to gossip. It's rude and unmannerly."

"And informative," Marlow muttered, "when it comes to prospective brides."

"Gossips are petty and tend to exaggerate the smallest flaws. Is there truly a problem? Don't tell me she has lost her reputation somehow?"

"No, nothing like that. I don't know her very well," said August. "She's loosely acquainted with Wescott's youngest sisters. They met while he and June were considered an item. Not to put too much a panic on it, but in some circles the sister has been called...Insane Jane."

"Her kinder nickname is 'the naturalist,'" said Marlow. "Apparently, she's been banned from the Exeter menagerie for protesting the animals' captivity. She..." He swallowed hard, flushing. "She has apparently walked about in front of the building with a lettered sign."

Townsend gaped at him. "She has not."

"I believe she also snuck into a Royal Zoological Society meeting by dressing as a man. It's not a well-known fact," he added, as Townsend's insides roiled in horror. "It hasn't been proven or talked about much."

"Then it can't have happened. Mayhew wouldn't have allowed it, would he?" Townsend asked, hating the plea in his voice. "These tales about her can't be true. I would have heard."

"Would have heard?" August scoffed. "You lunkhead, you couldn't even figure out Wescott's intended was June, not Jane."

"I haven't paid attention to this season's marriageables," he said. "I meant to marry Ophelia. She was, and always will be, the love of my life."

"You can't keep talking that way," said Marlow sharply, looking around. "She's married to your friend now, and Wescott won't have you spouting off about your lost, unrequited love, especially in a public room like this. As for your hunger for revenge, I hope you're happy. You've revenged yourself right into a disastrous engagement."

"Come, that's an awful thing to say to him." August turned from scolding Marlow and patted Townsend's hand, perhaps in an effort to stop him drinking more brandy. "Look at it this way. You enjoy disciplining women, Townsey, and now you've got a good project to take beneath your wing. I'm sure it'll only take a week or two for you to set this Lady Jane straight as an arrow. Why, she'll thank you for developing her into a more proper lady. Surely she hates being maligned by gossips all the time."

"All the time? I can't have a peculiar wife." Townsend drew a ragged breath, then bent to rub his temples. "I have to find a way to escape this engagement or she'll make me the object of ridicule. I didn't realize to whom I was offering marriage."

"And how will you explain this error to her father?" Marlow drew himself up into a mocking example of Townsend's stature. "I'm terribly sorry, Lord Mayhew, but I thought I was engaging myself to an entirely different sister for vindictive reasons."

"No, I won't tell him that. I'll tell him I didn't understand..." He stopped, realizing how impossible such an explanation would be. "Bloody hell. I must go see my parents. Perhaps they'll have some ideas, some way to undo this mess. My father has a persuasive way of speaking."

Marlow and August stared back at him, their expressions communicating doubts they were too considerate to express. To break an engagement for such a ridiculous reason, because he misunderstood who she was...and the poor woman so recently rejected by Lord Hobart?

Oh God, what had he done? He hadn't the least desire to marry an insane naturalist known for picketing outside the Exeter Exchange.

"You'll excuse me for quitting your company, friends," he said, pushing away the brandy. "My life seems to have taken another turn for the worse."

"Tell your parents we said hello," said Marlow. August continued to grimace at him, mirroring the sense of doom he felt.

*****

Townsend checked in at his house to be sure his luggage had arrived, then dressed to go to dinner at his parents'. He thought of hiring a gig to their Regent's Park mansion but decided to walk instead to disperse some of his panic, not to mention the smell of brandy on his breath. The Duke and Duchess of Lockridge normally would have been in the country by now, preparing to celebrate Christmas amid the wooded beauty of Oxfordshire. It was his fault they were still in London, awaiting his return from the Continent.

He ought to have gone to them first, as soon as he'd arrived in London. He ought to have consulted them about his plan, proposing to Lady June, or Jane, whichever one Wescott had been meant for. His parents could have told him she'd already married another man. His sister Rosalind would have known, at least; at seventeen, she was an astute observer of the marriage market.

When he arrived at the Lockridge home and greeted his mother and father, he put on a cheerful face. His mother embraced him, bringing the first sense of comfort he'd felt in a while, and he held her close an extra moment. Rosalind appeared, sweeping down the stairs in a demure white gown, her chestnut locks piled up in an intricate chignon for dinner. She was his only remaining unmarried sister, and she looked more grown up each time he saw her. He teased her about her fanciful hairstyle only to avoid his mother's searching gaze.

From a mere hug and a kiss on the cheek, she knew something was the matter. His mother had always been that way.

They proceeded to dinner at once, the servants having planned a special feast in honor of his homecoming. His favorite dishes were brought out: curried parsnip soup, roasted rack of lamb, swiss chard with leeks, and au gratin potatoes. It was comforting to be with his family in the gilded dining room, though he could feel his mother's eyes on him.

"Did you have a pleasant journey home?" his father asked. His hair, dark as Townsend's, barely showed any gray. "I suppose it can get choppy, crossing the Channel in winter."

"It was sunny, with calm waters," he assured them. "And France was peaceful and enjoyable, for the most part."

"After so much upheaval," his mother said. "I'm glad. And how do you do, Edward?" she asked gently, using his Christian name.

She feared he still nursed a broken heart over Ophelia. And yes, his heart was a wasteland since he'd lost her, but the entirety of his problem was so much worse. He put down his fork and faced his parents. "I've done something rash, I'm afraid. Something foolish."

"That's unfortunate," said his father. "I hope it's easily fixed."

"I don't know. I don't think so." He glanced at his sister, whose eyes had gone wide. "I've asked someone to marry me, but I think, now, that I ought to have consulted with both of you first."

"A French woman?" his mother asked. "Has there been an…entanglement?"

Rosalind's eyes went wider. His sister was known for being demure and polite, but he knew a secret part of her enjoyed mayhem. Her puppy-dog crush on his friend Marlow was proof enough of that.

"Not a French woman," he assured her. "I visited the Earl of Mayhew as soon as I arrived in London. I don't know why, but I thought it would be a wise and just course to propose to the young woman Wescott jilted. I had this idea that it might fix everything…everything that happened between us." *And exert a measure of vengeance.* He didn't admit that part out loud, but feared it was obvious enough.

"Oh, but Lady June has already married another," said Rosalind. "Lord Braxton, a longstanding acquaintance. They left recently for his country estate."

"I realize that now. Unfortunately, I didn't know she'd already married when I arrived at her father's home. And I thought…" He sighed. "I thought her name was Jane."

His parents stared at him. The food on his plate, so recently warm and delicious, seemed less so as he forced a forkful of lamb into his mouth.

"So, you see," he continued after he chewed it, "I have engaged myself to Lady Jane, the younger sister, by accident."

"When did you discover this…accident?" his father asked. Townsend had the sinking feeling he was trying not to laugh.

"I met with August and Marlow just afterward and told them I'd become engaged to Wescott's former marriage prospect. They let me know I was mistaken."

"My goodness," said Rosalind, her delicate whisper too loud in the quiet room.

His mother blinked rapidly. Rosalind had gained her commendable polish at the Duchess of Lockridge's knee. His mother disguised her surprise—her dismay?—but the blinking said everything.

"I wonder now, in hindsight, if we will suit one another," said Townsend. "I find myself in a situation."

"I'd say so." His father leaned back, resting his elbows upon his chair. "Didn't you speak to the girl herself before you set forth your proposition?"

"No, sir. She's in Berkshire, in Reading with her mother. I spoke to her father, though, and put my name to an extensive marriage contract."

"Ah." The faint hint of laughter faded from the man's dark brown eyes. "It is, indeed, a situation. You are legally engaged to Lady Jane, then. And she is of an age...?"

"She is my age," offered Rosalind. "A few months older, perhaps."

"Lord Mayhew said he wished for a quick wedding, a holiday wedding, and I agreed." He could feel the flush rise beneath his tanned skin. "But, learning later that I had proposed to the wrong woman, I wish I had not."

"Oh, my dear." His mother's words were soft but full of feeling. "Of all the things to do impulsively."

"I know. I regret it."

"But you have done it," his father pointed out. "You offered marriage, and your suit was accepted."

Townsend took another bite of food, forcing himself to chew it. His mother fidgeted with her silverware. Rosalind waited, watchful and still.

"Lady Jane is of excellent birth," his mother finally said. "The Mayhews are a fine family, even if their youngest daughter is a bit...out of the ordinary."

"Have you met her?"

She paused a moment, considering before she spoke. "I've heard she is a great lover of nature."

The naturalist. That's what Marlow had called her. Even his mother had heard the gossip, and she was not one to seek it out.

"Lady Jane is very interested in plants and animals," Rosalind said. "I've never met anyone like her, man or woman."

When neither parent moved to silence her, she took it as permission to go on.

"From what I understand, she spends far more time in the gardens and forests of her family's country estate than the drawing room. Hazel met Jane while June and her brother were courting; she told me Jane took tea at Arlington Hall once with a great streak of mud staining her gown's hem."

"You mustn't repeat gossip," the duchess chided. "I'm sure if such a thing happened, it was a mistake."

Rosalind bowed her head, gently but duly chastened. Still, she met her brother's gaze, expressing the reservations she wasn't allowed to voice.

"I'm sure this young lady is kind-hearted, if she cares so for the natural world," his father said. "It's best to look for the good in everyone."

"Especially since you have to marry her," said Rosalind.

This time his father gave Rosalind a warning look. Few mortals had the courage to stand up to the exacting Duke of Lockridge. In fact, everything Townsend had learned of propriety and discipline, he'd learned at his father's hand.

Which made it that much more difficult to imagine marrying an irregular sort of wife. Why, his own mother had flawless manners, had been held up to countless contemporaries as the very model of decorum.

"I can't help thinking Jane and I won't suit," he murmured, draining his wine glass. Goodness, how much had he drunk today? Too much. "I fear we'll have a disaster of a marriage."

"Your father and I believed the same thing when we were engaged," his mother said with a faint smile. "Things have a way of working themselves out."

"Yes," the duke agreed. "It's hard to know if you're suited to someone you haven't even met. You must give this young woman a chance, and not depend upon other's opinions of her character."

"Lady Jane has been recently jilted, has she not?" His mother clicked her tongue. "Poor woman."

"By Lord Hobart, for no cause at all," said Rosalind. "That is not gossip," she added, when her parents both turned to her. "It's something that really happened. It's hard to believe any man could be so heartless."

Heartless. Townsend supposed he was heartless, because he wished he could jilt her too.

"Our engagement cannot be well known yet," he said, grasping at any possibility of escape. "I have only told Marlow and Augustine."

"At their homes?"

"At White's," he admitted.

His father rolled his eyes. "Then it's well known."

"Perhaps if I visited Lord Mayhew at once...right now...and explained everything." It took all his courage to meet his father's dark gaze. "Do you think I could...?" His shoulders slumped at the message he read there. "I'm trapped, aren't I? There is nothing to be done."

"Unfortunately, there is not." The Duke of Lockridge didn't temper his words or soften his frown. "You signed a contract, driven by vengeful intentions rather than regard for the lady in question. Sometimes the mistakes we make carry heavy consequences, son. There's nothing to do now but welcome this Lady Jane into our family and accord her our affection and respect. Your mother and I must call on the Mayhews tomorrow to begin forming a deeper acquaintance. Don't you think so, Aurelia?"

"Indeed," she said, with reluctant finality.

"Lady Jane is in the country at the moment," said Townsend. "Lord Mayhew is summoning her and her mother to London."

"Then we shall await their arrival and pay a call."

His father's tone was immovable. Townsend's satisfaction with his perfect act of revenge had ebbed into a haze of self-loathing, for he'd done this to himself. No matter that he still adored Ophelia; this strange Lady Jane would be his wife a few weeks' hence because of his utter stupidity, and he couldn't help feeling it was exactly what he deserved.

Chapter Two: Such a Prospect

Lady Jane McConall, the Earl of Mayhew's youngest daughter, toiled patiently in her private garden, trying to undo the previous season's damage to her spindly winter hollies. She was probably ruining her boots in the muddy snow, but she wished to save the shrubs if she could.

"These dastardly leaves," she said, brushing them from the sparse branches and tucking them over the roots. "They blow here from the east meadow, as if we want them." She was not sure what the word *dastardly* meant, but she'd overheard a gentleman using it in London, with the sort of vehemence that matched what she felt. "They'll do better for you there, won't they? Keeping your roots warm and protected from the snow?"

The plant didn't answer her now, but it would, eventually, by growing healthier. As she picked off the sodden, smothering leaves, she could practically hear her holly breathe a sigh of relief.

"There, you see," she said, finally exposing the knee-high bush to the winter sun. "That will be better for you, and you can grow up big and strong." She stroked one of the deep green, pointed leaves. "And in the spring, the worms will come and work your soil, and make you oh, so happy."

"Jane!" Her normally refined mother leaned from the parlor window and shouted her name. "Jane, what are you doing?"

She squinted up at her, hoping she wouldn't see the mess she'd made of her boots. "I'm cleaning up the garden, mama. Is everything all right?"

"Goodness, what are you wearing? Is that Spencer's coat?"

"Yes, one of his old ones. He said I could have it."

Her cousin's hunting coat was a lovely shade of brown, just right for disguising the mud she got all over herself, no matter how carefully she gardened. To that end, a great many of her gowns were shades of brown, too. It had become her favorite color, although her mother begged her to wear ivories and creams, and the pale pastels so popular with the ballroom debutantes in London.

Pastels had not kept Lord Hobart from breaking his engagement to her.

"You were told never to wear men's clothing again," her mother reminded her. "And what are you doing out here in the wind? Think of your complexion."

"The hollies have been covered in oak leaves since autumn."

She clicked her tongue. "You're gardening? It's freezing out. The ground is covered in snow."

"Plants grow in every season," she called back. "Even winter."

"Jane, you must come inside at once. Your face will be chapped to a cherry. Please, this is not the time to worry about holly bushes. You won't believe the letter your father's just sent."

With those words, her mother pulled shut the window. Jane sighed and moved toward the garden gate, wondering if it was a good or bad letter. Since June had married, only Jane remained at home, a future spinster, no doubt. She would have loved to marry and have a family, but she'd known for some time that men did not find her an attractive marriage prospect, with her gawky stature and horrid carrot-hued hair. Oh, her disastrous hair! It was the color of pale, overboiled carrots, thanks to some random Scots ancestor on her father's side.

If only she'd gotten her looks from her mother's side. The Countess of Mayhew was thoroughly English, blonde, petite, and elegant, and good at everything. She was good at society, good at balls, good at manners, good at fashion, good at being a proper lady, and June took after her so readily.

Jane had gotten none of those graces. It was a bitter shame.

Her mother rapped upon the window, beckoning her in, and Jane walked faster through regrettable amounts of slush. She brushed as much of it off her boots as she could on the flagstones near the side patio, then handed her coat and soiled gardening gloves to a footman by the door. The laundry women hated her, understandably. Perhaps that was why her father had written. Perhaps the laundry women were once again threatening to quit.

"In here, Jane," her mother called. "Come quickly."

She hurried to the green drawing room, passing another pair of silent footmen. Was she in trouble for something? Would the stone-faced servants hear her berated again for some petty crime? She thought of some of her more recent, secret transgressions. She'd added another pet to her menagerie, a juvenile rabbit too lame and small to be out in the cold, but her father wouldn't know about that. She'd also written to a natural science professor at Cambridge with a question about diet and hibernation in reptiles, using the false name of Josiah McConall...

"Jane," her mother said, as soon as she entered. "What do you know of the Marquess of Townsend?"

She blinked at her. "The Marquess of Townsend? I've seen him a few times."

She tried to sound casual, although his name made her heart race a little bit. He was one of the few gentlemen she'd really noticed the past season. Tall, elegant, classically handsome...

She'd become aware of his appealing attributes while her sister was holding court upon the marriage market, and after that, Jane's eyes had searched for him in every ballroom, finding him only a handful of times. She remembered that Lord Townsend danced with a sort of powerful grace and had striking black hair and piercing eyes.

Well, to her, they seemed piercing, although she'd never had the opportunity to feel his gaze close up. No, he only danced with breathtaking women, diamonds of the first water. The way Lord Townsend held them and guided them had excited her in some way, then made her feel silly, because such an impressive man would want less than nothing to do with a plain carrot-top like her.

"Isn't he one of Lord Wes—" She stopped herself from saying the name. It was not to be uttered in their household anymore, since he'd gone back on his expected offer of marriage to her sister. "Isn't Lord Townsend one of Lord W's gentleman friends?"

"I believe he's part of that group, but it can't be helped." She waved the letter as Jane settled into a chair by the fire. "The marquess has asked for your hand in marriage, and your father, assuming your agreeability to the match, has told him yes."

Having barely sat down, Jane jumped to her feet again. "He has asked— Lord Townsend has— What?"

"Lord Townsend has visited your father and put forth a marriage proposal. You are going to be wed," her mother exclaimed. "And to such a prospect."

"That cannot be. The Marquess of Townsend has asked to marry me? The Duke of Lockridge's son?"

"Really, Jane, would there be another? Yes, he's asked to marry you. Your father wishes us to return to London at once, so you may meet your future husband and his family." She fluttered the note in agitation. "He hints at a holiday wedding, but that is surely too precipitous. We must find you a wedding gown, manage invitations, arrange a proper breakfast..."

Jane sank back into the chair before the fire. A gown? A reception? Lord Townsend could not truly intend to marry her. It made no sense. He was one of the most sought-after bachelors in London. "Are you sure you read it correctly? May I see it?"

Her mother handed her the letter, and indeed, in her father's own handwriting, it said very shortly and urgently that the marquess had proposed marriage and that they must come. A contract had already been signed.

"Jane, look at your hem." Her mother gazed mournfully at the wet mud splotched upon the bottom of her skirt like some ill-conceived painting. "That's practically a new gown."

"It's a day gown, not hard to wash. If you would let me wear trousers, just in the garden—"

"No. Proper ladies don't wear trousers. If you're to wed this man, a duke's son, you've got to take more care with your appearance and reputation, young lady."

"My reputation?" She cleaved to this argument, for otherwise she must think about this shocking marriage proposal. "I'm perfectly virtuous. I always have been."

"That's not the reputation I mean. I'm talking about your propensity to muck about in meadows and forests, and collect those godforsaken monstrosities you house in the kitchens and barns."

"They're animals, mother, not monstrosities. They are natural beings just as we are."

"Of course you would say so, you exhausting girl. This is why that horrible man broke his vow to marry you and fled to Spain."

Jane pushed down her hurt emotions because they wouldn't move her mother. Why, she'd cried buckets of tears over that "horrible man" who'd jilted her, the man she'd barely known, and it had accomplished nothing at all. Now she was to be married to a different man who'd never spoken the first word to her?

It had to be some mean-spirited joke.

"Why would Lord Townsend propose to me?" she asked. "Do you think father is telling the truth?"

"I don't imagine he'd go to the trouble of ordering us to London if he wasn't. My dear..." She took back the letter she'd been clutching. "Your father writes that Lord Townsend offered with great passion for your hand."

"But mama... It must be a mistake. I've never spoken to Lord Townsend, not once. We've never been introduced."

"Mistake or not, the contract is signed, unless you're foolish enough to refuse him. The Duke of Lockridge's oldest son, dear girl!" She softened her voice and lifted her daughter's face with a finger beneath her chin. "What, not even a smile? This is joyous news."

"What if it isn't true, though?" Her stomach wrenched with fear of mockery. "What if it's a prank? Some sort of nonsense?"

"Nonsense? Why would you think so? Remember how quickly all the gentlemen came calling for June when she became available for marriage?"

"I'm not June, mother. I'm not as pretty or vivacious, or light on my feet."

"Pish posh. You're a fine marriage prospect. It may be this Lord Townsend has admired you from afar, and learned you were recently...unengaged to that awful scoundrel."

Lord Hobart, the other name that was not to be mentioned in the Mayhew household. Jane sighed, trying to imagine Lord Townsend "admiring her from afar." It was impossible. He was too handsome and lofty, too untouchable. She could not feel excited because she worried none of it was true. How could she even speak to a man so dashing and worldly? Much less marry him?

"I can't believe he would 'passionately' offer for me," she persisted. "Why?"

"The why doesn't matter. Good families seek out other good families. Perhaps it's because his rapscallion friend has married, so Lord Townsend wishes to as well. Let's take it for what it is, a blessing." Her mother said *blessing* as if she meant *miracle*.

It was a sort of miracle, and that frightened her. What if Lord Townsend met her, merely looked upon her, and broke the engagement—her second? At that point she'd have no choice but to move to some haunted, windblown cliff and never show her face in society again. She could not believe such a fine, wealthy man—a duke's son—would stoop to beg for her hand in marriage.

"What if it doesn't happen?" she asked her mother. "What if he meets with me and changes his mind?"

"Oh, Jane," she replied in a tone that was mostly a scold. "Go to your room and pick out some lovely, unstained gowns to take to London. Colors, not drab brown. And leave your animals here with Davis. Don't dare try to smuggle some fawn or lizard in your trunks."

* * * * *

Jane stared in the mirror as her lady's maid smoothed her hair into an ornate twist atop her head. Where her sister's hair shone with depths of gold, her own color was flat and orange. Where June's hair sprang naturally into pretty curls, hers flopped with shagged edges. It was hopeless.

"You must smile," Matilda chided, persisting with the curling tongs. "If you smile, you will look beautiful to him."

She tried to smile at her reflection, but nerves twisted her lips into a grimace that was worse than a frown. Her amber-gold eyes, just as strangely colored as her hair, did nothing to soften her expression or make her appear "prettier." The truth was she'd been tired and worried for days, for the entire journey to London to meet her new fiancé.

She took a deep breath, her rib cage straining against the stays pulled especially tight for this meeting. When her hair was finally curled and smoothed to perfection, Matilda helped her put on her most stylish gown, a delicate blue toile print with a satin sash and ruffled hemline. It was something she'd never wear in the garden, so there was no fear of mud stains or tears along the bottom. No, she couldn't meet him that way.

Jane would not feel like herself in such an elegant gown, but it would be better to not be herself around Lord Townsend. She caused controversy with her behavior at times. Did he know it? The letter from the Cambridge scientist to Josiah McConall had arrived at her father's desk and caused a row only yesterday. He'd not allowed her to read the professor's reply until he'd scolded her soundly, shouting that Lord Townsend would not wish to wed a bluestocking, an overly intellectual woman. Why was that a bad thing?

Oh, she must stop thinking that way. She supposed, now, she must discover what Lord Townsend preferred in a wife, and act in that way so he would find her agreeable to marry. It was too much to wish that he would like her as she was, prone to rescuing wild animals and mucking about in gardens and woodlands, not only for science, but because she found them magical. She wouldn't mention any of that until they were married. And then...

And then she probably still better not mention it. Too much to hope a lofty Duke's son would understand.

Her maid clucked about her, adjusting the gown, handling it carefully to prevent wrinkles. It was light and flowing, empire-waisted in the current style. Once Matilda tied the sash and fastened the tiny pearl buttons at the back, Jane looked at least fifty percent a fine lady. She tried another smile and failed.

"Will you wear the pearls, my lady, or the locket?" asked Matilda.

"What goes better with the gown?"

"The pearls, I think."

A string of luminescent pearls was fastened about her neck, along with matching earrings that pinched her lobes. She took in the full effect. Well, she looked far better than she looked on a normal day, even if she wasn't as naturally stunning as June. June was married off, so she wouldn't be in the parlor beside Jane making her look so plain in comparison. Marriage suited her sister; June was quite happy, simpering on about Lord Braxton whenever she wrote.

Maybe Jane would have some of that luck too. Maybe Lord Townsend would be such a grand and devoted husband that she herself would be improved. Perhaps their marriage would make her more normal and accepted in company. This thought, finally, brought a smile to her face, a hopeful smile that did much to make her more appealing.

"There you are," said Matilda. "He will like you, my lady. You mustn't fret."

It was difficult not to fret when you were about to be introduced to the stranger you were to wed, even if he was a handsome gentleman you'd admired from afar. *Especially* when he was a handsome gentleman you'd admired from afar.

"I suppose I'll go down then," she said.

"Yes, my lady. Mrs. Barton is preparing a lovely tea for the visit."

When Jane entered the parlor, she found her mother and father in their formal clothes, awaiting Lord Townsend. His parents were expected as well, along with his remaining unmarried sister, Lady Rosalind.

"How fetching you look," said her father.

The words were complimentary, but the look he gave her told her she was to behave with fetching manners too, or lose his approval entirely. She went to the window overlooking the courtyard and square.

"You mustn't gape out of doors," her mother said. "Come sit down and be ladylike."

"I'm too nervous to sit down and be ladylike."

"Yet you must."

"I would like to see them arrive."

She had an unreasonable fear that the Lord Townsend she remembered was not the one who had proposed marriage to her. In fact, the past few days, the trip to London, even preparing for this meeting carried an air of unreality. *How could it be?*

Then a fine, gilded carriage with the Duke of Lockridge's crest upon the side turned into the front drive, and she jerked back from the window, knowing there was no mistake.

"They are here," she said.

It was a task to sit and compose herself, knowing her future husband was about to walk into the family's opulent parlor. Indeed, her father's house was one of the loveliest in town, spacious and sprawling, done up in a timeless, elegant fashion. There was no worry the Lockridge contingent, or Lord Townsend, might find the Mayhew family wanting.

No, it was only *her* he might find wanting.

Jane curled her toes in her pale blue slippers and straightened her spine, and tried to relax her expression so she might be able to smile—delicately, of course—when their guests were announced at the door. But when they were finally announced, minutes later, her whole face seemed to go numb.

The Duke and Duchess of Lockridge entered first. Townsend's father was tall and dark-haired like him, and his mother voluptuously beautiful in an emerald green visiting frock with pearl buttons and lace.

Why had Jane worn toile? Why couldn't she have shining honey-colored hair like Lord Townsend's mother rather than the orange straw she'd been cursed with?

Lord Townsend entered behind them, along with his sister. She could sense him there, could sense his great height and presence, but could not summon the courage to look at him yet. First she went with her parents to greet his parents. The duchess reached out and took Jane's hands, with a smile so warm and sincere that Jane's face unfroze enough to return it.

"This must be the young lady my son has told us about," she said to Jane's parents. "How wonderful it is to meet you, Lady Jane. Look at your beautiful frock. Toile is my favorite, and the blue perfectly suits the shade of your hair."

"Thank you, Your Grace." The knot in Jane's stomach eased at the woman's kind words. She offered her hand to the duke, then greeted Lady Rosalind. After that, there was nothing to do but turn to Lord Townsend as his father introduced them.

She watched this stranger—her fiancé—as he acknowledged her parents first. Yes, he was the same dauntingly handsome man she'd seen at the balls last season, the ones he'd deigned to attend, at any rate. Up close, he was even more striking. His hair was glossy black and full, his lips well-formed, and his nose straight and aristocratic.

His eyes were large and wide set, framed by strong brows and dark lashes. When he turned them on her, she felt caught beneath a spell. And their color...

My goodness. Lord Townsend's eyes were the same color she saw each time she looked in the mirror. Jane had always been at a loss to describe the exact color of her eyes. They were mostly brown, but slightly gold and amber as well, a strange, in-between color she'd never seen on anyone else.

Until now.

She realized she'd been staring and offered her hand. His fingers seemed huge. Even with their gloves between them, his grip felt strong and affecting, and she felt a twinge of excitement to be touching him at last.

But she was not smiling. Goodness, she'd forgotten to smile. She tried to force a quick smile and it came out crooked, and those eyes so like her own regarded her with a veiled scrutiny that made her want to run away and hide. He barely smiled either. He had a reserved manner at odds with the easiness of his parents.

"Won't you sit and join us for tea?" Her mother turned about, directing the guests to various chairs, making sure to seat Lord Townsend in the armchair adjacent to Jane's. "It's so pleasant to have visitors in the winter, when it's so quiet in town."

"Indeed, most of our friends have left for their country homes."

While the parents spoke of niceties, and Mrs. Barton and her parlor maids distributed tea and cakes, Jane was hotly aware of Lord Townsend sitting mere feet from her. He bore little resemblance to his sister, Rosalind. She looked more like her mother, her hair a shining golden brown, while Townsend clearly took after his father. Jane remembered, though, that Lord Townsend had an older sister who was as striking and dark as he, who had married an Italian prince. It had been the talk of society when it happened. Jane had been young then, perhaps seven or eight years old, beguiled by fantasies of becoming a princess.

"Felicity is well," answered the duchess, to some question of her mother's. "She and her husband are planning a trip to London in the spring, in fact, with our grandchildren. We've been brushing up on our Italian."

Yes, Lady Felicity. That was his oldest sister's name. She must be Princess Felicity now, and of course Jane's parents would inquire after her right away, excited to have a connection, however tenuous, to Italian royalty. Lord Townsend himself might be an Italian prince, in his finely tailored coat and shining riding boots. She imagined he must ride very well. He seemed the sort to do everything very well.

She did nothing well, except for things young ladies weren't supposed to be interested in. She slid a look at him, wondering if he regretted his proposal now that he was sitting so near her. He followed the parents' conversation politely, contributing when required. His voice was very deep, rumbling and masculine, rich with personality. As for Jane, she could not seem to summon a word. She could only think, *why? Why are you here? Why do you wish to marry me?*

Soon, talk turned to their new engagement and impending wedding.

"How pleased I was to receive your son's petition for marriage," said her father. "So many young men these days aren't of a mind to wed and settle down into family life."

"Indeed." The Duke of Lockridge smiled at his duchess. "I remember how unhappy I was when this one dragged me before the parson."

The duchess returned his smile and blushed in a way so girlish Jane could only stare. Her mother and father never teased one another, especially in front of company. That was what they were doing, teasing, like a pair of courting birds. Lord Townsend caught her eye with a faintly embarrassed half-smile.

She did not know how to respond, whether she ought to smile back or shyly glance away. She'd had little experience with marriageable gentlemen, especially the dashing, mysterious type that made up Lord Townsend's circle of friends. Some said they were the scandalous sort, but Jane imagined it was unfair gossip. June's association with Lord Wescott hadn't had a whisper of scandal associated with it. Well, until he jilted her to marry an operatic singer.

"We're pleased about this engagement as well," the duke continued over his wife's blushes. "How exciting, for our two families to unite behind an excellent match."

They shared lemon cake, cream fingers, and wedding plans, although Jane felt too shy to eat, drink, or say a single word unless prompted for an opinion. What day? Any day. Which church? Any church with an altar and parson would do. She could not bring herself to plan too excitedly. What if Lord Townsend changed his mind about a wedding before this polite tea was over? She would have liked to converse with Rosalind, who did not seem so threatening, but she wasn't sitting here in her special toile dress to spend time with Rosalind...

"Jane, dear." Her mother's voice interrupted her jittery, anxious thoughts. Jane glanced at Lord Townsend. Had she offended him because she was too hapless to address any conversation to him? "The sun is out today," her mother went on, "and the conversation of elders can be tiresome. Why don't you show Lord Townsend around the courtyard gardens?"

"What a lovely idea," said the duchess. "I'm sure the young people would enjoy some fresh air."

"Go fetch your cloaks," her mother pressed, as Jane's heart beat faster. "And a bonnet, Jane. You'll need it for the sun."

"I'd love to see your gardens, too," said Townsend's sister, putting down her plate and rising to her feet.

"Rosalind, why don't you stay?" The duchess's tone was kind but firm.

Lord Townsend's sister resumed her seat, polite enough to almost hide her disappointment. Jane, on the other hand, rose with some reluctance. A walk in the gardens brought to mind every soiled hem, every scolding she'd received for mucking about in the dirt.

Lord Townsend indicated that she should proceed before him, and she did, feeling the weight of five pairs of eyes as they left the parlor. Why could she not do anything easily, with grace? *Why do you wish to marry me?* she thought. *How could I possibly become your wife?*

They were being sent out into the gardens because they were engaged to wed and must get to know one another. As much as she wanted to get married, as much as she admired the intriguing Lord Townsend, she had not pictured courtship being as nerve-wracking as this.

Chapter Three: A Walk in the Gardens

Townsend accepted his overcoat and hat from the butler, then waited as his future bride donned a pale blue pelisse and bonnet. *Lady Jane.* She looked exactly like her name, prim and unobjectionable. Not ugly, not at all, but no raving beauty either.

Plain Jane.

The unkind moniker came to mind, but he stifled it. She was not plain. Her hair was an odd color, yes, a very pale orange that could not pass for blonde, but her face held a quiet animation even when she was silent. Her eyes were a graceful shape, and her pert nose and rosebud lips too dignified to ever be plain.

She led him out a pair of back doors to a vast stone palazzo, surrounded on all sides by slumbering winter gardens.

"There's a pretty archway this direction," she said, gesturing down the wide stairs to the left, "if you'd like to go there."

"Of course." He offered his arm, but she hesitated, glancing toward the doors.

"How strange to walk off alone. Perhaps your sister ought to join us?"

He nearly laughed, remembering how quickly Rosalind's desire for fresh air had been rebuffed. "I think our parents prefer us to go off alone, to become better acquainted. It's hard to get to know one another in a parlor, having tea."

She bit her lip, a frequent mannerism. "I suppose that's true."

At last she accepted his arm, barely leaning upon it as they traversed the palazzo's grand staircase and descended into the Earl of Mayhew's manicured backyard. It was a large garden for a city manor, certainly larger than the fenced patch of nature behind his town home, which suited him well enough, since he wasn't the gardening sort.

Now, he appreciated the space. It felt good to take a breath. Such a farce, to listen to the polite banter in the parlor, as the two families planned a wedding embarked upon by accident. It had taken all his discipline not to bury his head in his hands. That would have been rude, of course, and hurt the feelings of his future bride.

His *bride*. For God's sake, things were moving quickly. Upon first impression, the lady was sweet, if awkward. He could barely see her face beneath her bonnet's brim. Just a bit of delicate nose and that prim, dainty chin.

"There are benches over there, if you'd like to sit." She led him from the stairs toward an Italianate arch. "Or we could walk beneath that arch into the back gardens. There are paths, and a fountain."

"Which would you prefer?"

The question seemed to fluster her. She stopped and turned, her eyes searching his as if to divine what he wanted. Then, as he watched her, a corner of her lips turned up in surprise, or delight. "Do you know, our eyes are the same color? Just exactly the same."

It was unexpected, this artless outburst. She was right. Her eyes were the same pale, gold-flecked brown color as his, perhaps even golder now that she'd lifted her face toward the sun. His mother had once described them as having a copper cast. His sister Felicity likened them to amber. He thought it was probably some chance mixture of his mother's grey eyes and his father's dark brown ones.

And here now, yes, was a young woman with the same unusual gaze.

"If we're still, we might grow too cold."

It took him a moment to realize she was answering the question he'd posed earlier. "You'd prefer to walk then?"

"Yes, I think so."

After her exclamation about his eye color, she turned shy again, facing away from him although she still rested her hand upon his arm. She was a bit taller than most women, so he didn't have to lean down to escort her. He was learning all these things about her now, a mere week or two before they were to wed. He tried hard not to compare her to his memories of Ophelia. There was nothing but misery down that pathway, for he'd adored Ophelia with every fiber of his being. Poor Jane could hardly be expected to measure up.

Do not obsess over Ophelia now, he scolded himself as they passed beneath the stone archway into a neat, landscaped garden of low shrubs and limpid winter flowers. There was, indeed, a grand fountain a little farther on, with a stately Roman maiden holding a pitcher. Lady Jane gave him a small, sideways smile.

"Water flows out of her pitcher in warmer months. There's a clever pressurized pump beneath, but it's turned off in winter so it won't be damaged if the water freezes to ice."

"Yes, it's the same at my parents' manor. The pump is turned off at the first hint of frost."

They stood and stared at the water, which was clean and clear. "No fish?" he asked, teasing.

"Not here. The groundskeeper treats the water to keep it free of mold and odor, and the fish wouldn't survive that type of poison very long. Well, I say it's poison, but it's not that, it's only unnatural. When bugs fall in, they die. Frogs used to jump in and die, but I asked my father if we could create a sort of barrier to prevent that and so, you see..."

She leaned to show him the pale line where the fountain's edge had been extended several inches with decorative marble work.

"It's far enough out that frogs can't hop in anymore. If they try, all they do is hit their heads on the underside, and decide to go somewhere else."

"That's amazing." It was amazing, really, to hear a young woman speak at such length about frogs. At least she was looking at him now.

"It was too sad before, to see them floating about the fountain belly up." She shuddered, then brightened. "As for the fish you mentioned, we have three great, massive ponds at our country home in Reading, and there are ever so many fish in there."

He hadn't the heart to tell her he'd only been joking about the fish, so he was obliged to listen to her list off the numerous varieties that made their homes in Lord Mayhew's ponds. He tried to look interested, while picturing, for his own entertainment, how horrified her parents would be to know their daughter was chattering to him about frogs and fish in this beginning stage of their acquaintance.

Marlow and August would howl at this story later. The naturalist, indeed.

"Shall we move on?" he asked when she came to the end of her fish monologue. "See more of the gardens?"

"Of course."

"Are you cold?"

"No, the sun warms me well enough."

He offered his arm again, and she took it more readily this time. They walked in silence for a moment or two, then Jane let out a small sigh. "I'm sorry I went on about the fountain," she said. "And the ponds. It's just that I know so much about fish."

He must not laugh. He would not laugh. If he did, it would be the maniacal laughter of a man who'd mistakenly engaged himself to the most bizarre woman in England.

"You may speak of whatever you wish," he said. "I have heard from some friends that you're a great lover of nature."

He felt her fingers tense upon his sleeve. Well, she *had* spent the past ten minutes going on about aquatic animals. She hadn't scrabbled about in any of the garden beds yet. Perhaps she wished to, and barely restrained herself.

"I do enjoy nature," she said at last. "I find it very interesting."

"In what way?"

She turned toward him, thinking. "In the way that it never stays the same. There's always a mystery to it. Nature is connected to life. It *is* life, don't you imagine? And look how complicated that can be. Life, I mean."

Her face grew animated as she warmed to her topic. There must have been some surprise on his face, no matter how he tried to hide it, for she followed up weakly.

"Perhaps I think about these things too much."

"Not at all." He cast about for a proper response and hit upon a remembrance from his school days. "According to Socrates, an unexamined life is not worth living."

"Ah, Socrates." Her smile returned. "He believed nature was akin to divinity. It's telling that so many philosophers have concerned themselves with nature's mysteries. It's endlessly interesting, don't you think?"

I think, Lady Jane, that Lord Hobart probably lost his nerve after just such a conversation as this. He'd met Hobart on a few occasions, and remembered him as a small-minded fellow, unlikely to bear much interest in the mysteries of nature. For Townsend, the most interesting parts of nature revealed themselves in the bedroom. One found mystery and divinity indeed, if one bedded down with an adequately voracious woman.

A dangerous line of thought, that, as he strolled with his maidenly fiancée. She was still going on about Socrates, God save him.

"I suppose I am talking too much and behaving like a bluestocking," she said, as if she'd heard his thought. "There, I shouldn't have said that either." Her ladylike mask fell away, revealing more honest anxiety. "I must admit I'm not the best at…"

She paused, biting her lip, and glanced back toward the house.

"What are you not the best at, Lady Jane? Vapid conversation? Have you studied philosophy when you ought to have been perfecting your witty banter?"

He was teasing, but she answered with a serious frown. "I was meant to marry a family friend, so I haven't had much practice with courtship." She gave him a sideways look. "I suppose you're used to more well-spoken women."

"If by well-spoken, you mean capable of prattling on about absolutely nothing for the better part of an hour, then yes. That's not a difficult art. You can learn to be better at it if you like, Lady Jane, but when we're alone, you may speak as you wish."

What a kind and husbandly thing to say. He was warming to her strangeness, against all odds. She'd never have the grace or beauty of Ophelia, but she wasn't unpleasant. They would rub along together well enough if she wasn't a bore.

"What beautiful gardens," he said, as they strolled past a ruthlessly manicured hedgerow. "Did you have a hand in any of the planning?"

"Not this section, no. The head groundskeeper won't let me touch it, but I have my own garden nearer the house, one I've planted myself."

"How wonderful."

"I'm sure you won't wish to see it, not at this time of year. It's more colorful in spring."

"Everything is more colorful in spring, isn't it?"

Was his answer too curt? She was silent for long moments, then she said, "I suppose we'll be wed by then. By spring."

"It seems your father wants us wed at the earliest opportunity." He didn't say it meanly, or with sarcasm, but beneath her bonnet's brim, he could see her delicate jaw go tight.

"Don't you wish to wed?" she asked.

It was tempting to tell her the truth, that this had all been a terrible accident, that he did not wish to wed any woman but the one

Wescott had stolen from him. But to admit he'd meant to offer for her sister, not her, in some quest for petty revenge...

He couldn't do it, not after the tremor he'd heard in her voice.

"Of course I wish to wed you," he said. "I wouldn't have offered for you otherwise. I hope you didn't find it impertinent, that I didn't seek an introduction first."

"Impertinent? Oh, no. Just a little surprising. If I may ask..." She stopped on the path, and he stopped too as she drew her arm from his. "Why did you choose to marry me, Lord Townsend? Is that too rude a question?"

She was not flirtatious, this one. She was not glib and teasing as other society ladies were. She was awkward and sincere in a way that unsettled him. He cleared his throat and removed his hat, turning the brim in his hand.

"It's not rude, Lady Jane. I'm sure you're due an answer."

"No, you needn't tell me. I shouldn't have asked."

It was a silly, pointless argument they were having, but it gave him time to frame a plausible lie to spare her feelings.

"If you must know, I heard of your plight during the events of last season, when your expected fiancé decided... Well." He turned his hat again. "I heard you were poorly treated, and it incensed me. I felt the need to come to your rescue, to play the hero, perhaps."

Her eyes were wide, amber-gold and utterly trusting. What a liar he was, and she believed every word. He looked across the gardens toward the fountain, returning his hat to its proper place atop his head. "It was forward of me, yes. I hope you don't mind."

"Oh." She turned away, biting her lip again. "No, I don't mind."

"As a proponent of decency and honor, I saw an opportunity to come to your aid and I took it. Why, I had been looking for a prospective wife for some time when I heard of your plight." Such lies. Unctuous, flowery lies, while his fiancée was guileless to a fault.

Another thought came into his head. Did the poor woman wish to marry him? He'd assumed, because of her desperate circumstances, she'd gladly accept his offer, but maybe she preferred to remain unwed at her country home, cataloguing fish, gardening into her spinsterhood, surrounded by the nature she loved so much. If *she* were to break their engagement, no one could fault him.

"Jane. I must ask you something now, in private, before we return to your parents' parlor." He took her delicate hands and squeezed them gently when he saw the panic in her gaze. "No, it's nothing worrisome. It's only that...this has all been so sudden. I didn't speak to you before offering for your hand as I should have, and your father seemed to feel you did not need to be consulted about a marital agreement."

A spot of color rose in her cheeks. "No, he didn't consult me. But he knew I wished to marry. When Lord Hobart decided he didn't want me after so many years of expectation, oh..." Her voice trembled before she steadied it. "It piqued my feelings very much."

From the tears in her eyes, he'd done more than pique her feelings. He'd hurt her badly. She could be so easily damaged, this one. The union which had seemed merely inconvenient to this point began to seem perilous. Lady June would have been so much safer. She was shining and confident, and would have helped him exact revenge on Wescott. Lady Jane was a crystal vase at the mercy of his brutish, selfish fingers.

He resisted the urge to drop her hands, but it was she who pulled away, to brush at the corner of one eye. He reached into his coat to remove his handkerchief and held it out to her in silence.

"I don't know why I'm going teary," she said, accepting it and then waving it as if to banish her emotional display. "I was so pleased to learn you wanted to marry me. It made the other situation easier to bear. To forget even. I worried, after what happened with Lord Hobart, that I might be untouchable. Wouldn't that have been a terrible thing?" She glanced away, frowning. "And perhaps you know that around that same time, June was jilted by your friend Lord Wescott."

"He's no friend of mine." Now he could, at last, tell the truth about something. "When I heard what he'd done to your sister, after raising her expectations, he ceased to have my regard. Gentlemen should not behave so."

"Yes, June was very hurt."

"Lord Wescott has a habit of acting selfishly, even if it hurts others. You may be sure I'm not that type."

Her eyes met his. Amber-gray. Brown. Copper. Whatever they were, they were full of sincere emotion.

"Do you want to hear something amusing?" she asked.

"Yes, of course."

"When I heard you'd asked for my hand, I feared it was some kind of prank. I thought..." She shook her head. "When your heart is broken once, you fear it will be broken again. How relieved I am to know you're not the heart-breaking sort."

He said nothing, caught in a spell of guilt and longing. He wanted to be the fine man she thought he was, not the scheming, uncaring man who'd asked for her hand. Curse it all. He couldn't go back and change how things had begun between them. He could only move forward.

"I did not propose to you as a prank, Jane," he said, holding her gaze. "You needn't worry about your heart being broken anymore."

She smoothed his handkerchief across her gloved fingers. "Very well. I won't." Her smile was bright, sudden, almost tremulous. "Instead, I shall look forward to being your bride."

"Just as I look forward to becoming your husband," he replied politely.

She had a way of looking at him, a sort of adulation bordered by fear. It affected him more than he liked.

"Once we're wed, I'll believe I'll take you to Somerton," he said, leading her back along the path. "It's my country retreat in Berkshire, very wild and wooded. Considering your devotion to nature, I'm sure you'll like it there."

"I can't wait to see it. It must be a very fine place."

It was a fine place to get away from town and throw wild parties. As for marriage, that remained to be seen.

"And I've a large town house here in London, a place we can call home during the Season. How does that sound?"

"It sounds wonderful, my lord." She paused a moment. "I've been meaning to ask you... I have a few pets which are very special to me. If you don't mind, I would like to keep them with me after we're married."

Of course this nature-loving woman-child would have pets to bring to their marriage. She probably had dogs, cats, rabbits, all the furry, smelly things. Well, he wasn't a monster. He wouldn't separate his naturalist from her beloved animals. The busier she kept with her pets, the less she'd bother him.

"Yes, you may bring all your belongings to your new home, Jane, and that includes your pets. If you'll write out the necessary requirements and measurements for kennels, I'll send them to my groundskeeper at Somerton so he can get to work."

"How generous of you, Lord Townsend. I'm so pleased." She said this with real joy, not the nervousness that had afflicted her up until now.

"Prepare the instructions as soon as you can, so he can have everything ready upon your arrival after our wedding."

Her eyes shone with a new, fond regard. "Thank you so much, my lord. Truly, thank you. I desperately hoped you would allow me to bring my animals. They mean so much to me."

"I wish you to be happy." He held up a finger in warning. "However, I must set a rule. No pets in the house. I prefer a calm, orderly household, and pets can be a nuisance, always getting under your feet."

"Of course, my lord. As long as they have a secure, warm place to stay, I'm content. Oh..." She placed a finger upon her pointed little chin, tapping it twice. "Have you some dependable mousers at your estate?"

"Mousers?" He modulated the amusement from his voice. "Yes, I believe we've three or four excellent mousers at Somerton."

"Perfect. Then I can leave my cats at my family's home, where they're happiest. They're older, you see, and set in their ways. They've always had the run of the estate."

"That's settled then. Anything else you require, just add it into the instructions. The Somerton staff is excellent, and I'm sure they'll be anxious to help you feel at home."

She turned shy again, just like that, giving him a crooked smile. "Do you want to know something else amusing?"

"Certainly."

"I was so afraid to meet you today. I saw you only a few times last season, from afar, and you seemed...intimidating."

Was this, now, an awkward attempt at flirting? "Intimidating?" he repeated.

"I feared you might be a cold-hearted type because you are so handsome. Oh, I don't know why. I suppose sometimes I expect the worst for no reason at all, maybe so I won't be disappointed if things go wrong. But you don't seem cold-hearted. You seem very warm and kind."

He met her gaze, looked into those eyes that were just like his own. He had cold-heartedly thought of every possible way to escape this engagement, but here he was. "I was raised in a loving home and taught to be a proper gentleman," he said. "If I'm ever cold-hearted to you, well, then, you must let me know."

She laughed at that, her eyes curving up just like her lips. "It's strange to think you'll be my husband soon, and that we might talk about these sorts of things."

Yes, it was very strange. Here was this unfathomable woman, soon to take up residence in his home, as well as his bed. He could not imagine making love to her. He still ached for Ophelia in his weaker moments, even though she was married to his damned faithless friend. Perhaps some magic would happen at the altar to make him forget Ophelia and lust for the woman before him. Perhaps not. He had no idea how things might square out between them, but he understood one thing for certain: it was his fault the two of them, two perfect strangers, were getting married this holiday.

She still clutched his handkerchief; by now, it was quite rumpled by her fingers. "I'll try to be a very good wife to you, Lord Townsend, if only to thank you for rescuing me. I think if you hadn't come along, I would have had a very sad and lonely life."

She was making herself so vulnerable to him. He could hardly bear it. He didn't want it. *I worry I will destroy you, poor little Jane, all by accident.*

"Come now." He tilted his head to catch her gaze. "Someone would have come along and swept you up. You're too charming to live a lonely life, don't you think?"

"I don't know. Even if someone else had come along, I doubt they would have been as dashing as you." Her blush deepened to epic proportions. "It would have been one of my father's widowed friends, or some dissolute rake looking to marry money."

"You find me dashing, do you?"

She didn't giggle or bat her eyes. No, she gave up without trying, and handed over his handkerchief, mute with her odd, admiring anxiety. She glanced longingly toward the house, and he took the hint.

"We ought to return, I suppose, before your flirting makes me kiss you."

She looked shocked. Well, she could not have been kissed before. There was something appealing about an absolutely pure woman. And something appalling too, of course.

"I shall kiss your hand, if you don't object." He winked at her. "That's what I meant, naturally."

She offered her gloved hand and he pretended not to notice her trembling as he lifted it to his lips. He placed a delicate kiss upon the back of her palm, holding her gaze as he did. She did not have the glorious elegance of Ophelia, nor her older sister's sparkling ebullience, but there was something there that compelled him. Her deference and vulnerability, maybe. He could win her over easily—

and ask her to do just about anything in the bedroom once she was his.

That was how his dastardly mind worked. She found him "dashing," but he was thinking about bedding her, and exploiting her purity and fear to his advantage.

Ah, well. Perhaps marriage would reform him. Why not? Nothing, to this point, had made reasonable sense. He matched his stride to hers as he led her back through the gardens. Once, she reached out to trail her fingertips along the top of a manicured shrub. His naturalist, as yet unknowable.

Back in the parlor, the parents were drawing up invitation lists for a wedding to take place two days before the New Year.

Chapter Four: How Lovely

Jane drifted amongst the guests at her wedding breakfast, feeling like a princess in her ruffled, dove-gray bridal gown. Her parents' ballroom had been transformed into a winter wonderland of flowers and lace, with delicate glittering snowflakes hanging from the chandeliers. This elegant holiday wedding had been the best Christmas present she'd ever received. Between the lovely church service, her friends' well wishes, and the shining weather, the day had been perfect in every sense. Well, except for one.

Lord Townsend didn't seem very happy to be wed.

She told herself it was nerves as they stood at the altar. She'd been nervous too. The church had been full to the rafters, as just about everyone still in town had attended. He'd stood so straight and tall beside her he could have been a prince. His sister Felicity was married to a prince, but Jane couldn't imagine that man, her new brother-in-law, being any finer than Lord Townsend in his tailored black wedding suit.

She feared she might stumble upon her vows, but his steady manner gave her the confidence she lacked. Now, as they rode together to their wedding breakfast, his mood remained sober. Almost *somber*.

Well, she supposed most men looked on marriage as a loss of freedom, though she believed they'd have a marvelous union once they came to know one another. She'd do everything in her power to make him a happy husband because she admired him so. Every time their eyes met across her parents' ballroom, she felt a shiver of amazement. *I'm his wife now. He's my husband.*

It wasn't that she didn't feel deserving of marrying such a fine, handsome lord. She'd just never imagined it would happen after the heartbreak of the previous year. How quickly one's circumstances could change.

"Jane, dear, come sit with us."

Her sister beckoned her over to a table decorated with winter greenery, and Lord Braxton jumped up to seat her. Speaking of changed circumstances, how lucky her sister had been to find such a doting husband after Lord Wescott left her in the lurch. Lord Townsend's sister Rosalind sat at the table too, along with her friends Hazel and Elizabeth. They were Wescott's younger sisters, and Jane was pleased they'd come to wish her well, though Wescott himself had wisely decided not to attend. "Braxie," as June called her husband, probably would have flattened the man.

And of course, Wescott was no longer Lord Townsend's friend.

"My dear, how radiant you look." June took her hand with sisterly affection. "And now you are a married lady, like me. It's wonderful growing close to your husband and setting up your own household." She smiled at Lord Braxton, the picture of newlywed bliss. "I cannot express how comfortable it is to be at home with someone you adore."

"You flatter me, darling," said Braxton. "And I adore you, too."

Jane envied their easy camaraderie. How long would it take to feel comfortable with Lord Townsend? "I'm glad to be married, especially to such a distinctive gentleman. I very much admire your brother," she said to Rosalind.

The sable-haired beauty took her hand and squeezed it. "Townsend is happy you accepted his suit. Honestly, I think marriage is just what he needs, and I'm glad we are to be sisters now. We'll have to visit as soon as you and my brother are settled."

Jane felt grateful for the warmth in Rosalind's eyes, but a little deflated about the idea they would need to "settle." There was so much weight within the word, so much expectation. They would need to get to know one another better if they had any hope of matching June's happiness. They'd need to talk, and touch. Kiss perhaps. Do other things, which Jane vaguely knew about.

"Hazel is to be married soon," said Elizabeth, her polite voice breaking into Jane's thoughts. "She's ever so in love."

"Mama and Papa told you not to say anything about it yet," scolded Hazel in a hushed tone. "Not today. This is Jane's special day."

"It's all right," said Jane. "It's hard to keep such news a secret. Has someone asked for your hand?"

"Yes," said Hazel, blushing pink. "It's not to be announced until the spring, but the Marquess of Fremont came to visit my father. We met at a ball last season and instantly knew we were meant to be together."

"How wonderful for you, to be able to marry someone so dear to your heart."

As soon as she said the words, she regretted them. Rosalind would think Jane was disappointed in her brother, and June...well, she had wanted to marry Lord Wescott for the longest time.

"It *is* wonderful," said Lord Braxton gallantly, to cover Jane's gaffe. "There is a precious value in sharing your life with another person, a value in knowing they will be there for you. Marriage isn't always easy, but it's always worthwhile, wouldn't you say so, my love?"

June met her husband's gaze with a giddy smile. "Absolutely. You've a way of expressing just how I feel. Oh, I'm so happy for you, Jane. You have so much to look forward to as a new bride."

She tried to return her sister's smile, but hers had a bit of a wobble. "I'm excited, but nervous as well."

"Nervous? Whatever for? Your Lord Townsend is the top of the heap as far as marriage prospects. Not to talk about your brother as a mere prospect," she said to Rosalind in apology, "but you must admit he's been pursued by dozens of ladies over the years."

Rosalind nodded. "Too many ladies. Lord Townsend this, Lord Townsend that. To me, he'll always be Edward, my bossy older brother. I hope he's not too bossy with you, Lady Jane. Er, I mean, Lady Townsend."

"He'll be bossy sometimes," said June, with a teasing glance at her husband. "Men make a habit of it. But I'm sure he'll also be sweet."

"Townsend is more bossy than sweet, in my opinion." Elizabeth gave Jane a sympathetic look. "But I'm sure it's as Rosalind says, that he only needs a bit of marriage to round out his edges."

"His edges?" Hazel giggled. "He's not a table, silly."

"No, he's not a table," said June. "He's a gentleman, he's your husband, and he's looking at you right now. Smile at him," she said, squeezing Jane's hand beneath the table. "Don't behave as if he's a stranger."

He is a stranger, she thought to herself. The wedding had come upon them so quickly, they'd only had time for a couple of outings together, one of which had been cut short by rain. In their limited time together, he'd told her more about Somerton, the manor they'd call home. She'd sent over the plans for her beloved pets' kennels, a sturdy cage for Bouncer, and a cozy den for Mr. Cuddles, who needed plenty of bedding to curl up in. Townsend had told her she could have all the space she wanted for her pets in Somerton's stables.

He was all that was kind, and yet...he maintained a distance from her, an indefinable space that felt too wide to bridge just yet. When she summoned the smile she ought to give him—considering it was their wedding day—his answering smile didn't quite reach his eyes.

Well, they only needed to *settle*, as June so wisely put it. Jane intended to start today, this very afternoon, trying to get to know Lord Townsend better. They couldn't stay strangers forever, especially with the wedding behind them. She held his gaze as long as she could, until she blushed self-consciously and turned back to her friends.

*****

"Have you lost your bride already?" August joined Townsend beside a beribboned pillar, staring with him into the ball room.

"Lost her? He doesn't even know how he found her in the first place," teased Marlow, taking up a place on his other side.

"You're both tiresome." Townsend was nearly drained of patience by this point in the proceedings. "And I know exactly where she is."

His friends knew, too. They were only making idle conversation, knowing he needed some mindless banter to shore up his defenses. He'd survived the wedding, and this reception too, speaking politely to the guests and pretending to be the most satisfied of bridegrooms.

Now, he watched as Jane conversed with her sister. It was startling to see them together, especially when June was the one he'd imagined as his wife.

"How sweet your bride is," said August, smiling at Townsend. "Just sweet as a new bride can be."

"She is sweet," he said, shrugging. "She seems pleased to marry me. There were no tears at the altar, no protestations."

"Only the ones ringing in your head," said Marlow in a low voice.

"What am I to do about it now, but make the best of it? I don't think she'll be a difficult wife, and if she is, I'll know how to handle it."

"Spend more time at Pearl's?" August suggested, alluding to their favorite brothel.

"Not now that I'm married. I don't wish to run around on her unless it's necessary." When she stood and moved across the room, he found himself focusing on her curvacious figure, and what he imagined to be a shapely bum. "I'll try to have my needs met at home."

"If you're speaking of your need to discipline naughty ladies," said August under his breath, "then I hope she's a handful and a half, and ever deserving of spankings."

"Spankings upon spankings," added Marlow in an amused whisper. "A good birch rod is sure to bring your headstrong naturalist into line."

"I won't menace the poor girl. Well, not unless she deserves it. From what I've observed, she's a very even-tempered young woman." *Even if she's not the person I intended to marry when I came home from France.* "Perhaps her infamous days are behind her."

"Er, speaking of infamous," said August, clearing his throat. "I stopped in to see Wescott and Oph—" He didn't say her name when Townsend turned blazing eyes on him. "And his wife. They regret they could not attend and send their sincerest wishes for a happy marriage."

"They 'regret' they couldn't attend?" Townsend scoffed. "More like the man didn't dare show his face, not with June here. That's one good thing about marrying a Mayhew daughter, even if I proposed to the wrong one—those families will never mend fences, so Wescott needn't be part of my life."

"Aw, Towns." Marlow's pale blue eyes flickered in disappointment. "You won't relent? Not yet?"

"Not ever."

"You have to let it go at some point," said August. "You don't always get to marry the person you want."

Townsend frowned at his dark-haired friend. Who was August, to lecture him about letting go? The man had been mooning over Felicity for almost two decades now. Never mind that she was long married to someone else—a prince, no less.

Still, his friends were here to support him, unlike Wescott, who was to blame for everything that had gone wrong in his life. "Will you go to Pearl's tonight," he asked the two of them, "now that you're back in London?"

He only said it to lighten the mood, but saw they were both considering it. Pearl's highly skilled courtesans were up for anything when it came to erotic discipline. He would miss his visits there. Probably. He wasn't sure. He felt numb and confused, surrounded by the celebrating families and all the flowers.

"We might go," said Marlow, raising a brow. "What about you, old man? Heading to Somerton this afternoon?"

"Indeed. Jane's things have already been moved there, and she's excited to see it."

"I have so many happy memories of Somerton," said August, and Townsend wasn't sure if he was pining for Felicity and the togetherness of their childhood, or remembering the bachelor parties that came later, that had sometimes stretched on for more than two weeks. For God's sake, he'd had a long and enjoyable bachelorhood. Getting married wasn't the end of the world. He only wished he might have married Ophelia.

That was why today had been so difficult, because he'd imagined a wedding with Ophelia, who was elegant, polished, talented, the most perfect of women. Guilt churned in his stomach as Jane turned to seek him out in the thinning company.

"You'll come to love her," said August, ever the romantic. "I'm sure you have much more in common than is obvious right now."

"Yes, and even if you don't become the best of lovers, you'll have her to look after your gardens and woodland creatures," added Marlow with a smirk.

His jests were growing tedious. "If I have my way, the only creature she'll be attending to from this point forward is me."

"May she do it well," he replied, then sobered. "Honestly, congratulations. August is right, you don't always get to marry who you want." His gaze darted toward Rosalind, then away. "But you can make the most of things as they are. Lady Townsend seems very fine today, without a hint of dirt about her wedding gown's hem. Do keep in touch with us and let us know how your situation is going in a week or two."

He nodded to his friends, then smiled at his mother as she came to take his hands.

"My darling," she said, "you must go to your bride. It's not good to spend the entire reception apart from each other."

"Didn't you and father—"

"Don't bring up our wedding, not today of all days." She grimaced, then took his arm. "Jane is going to love you once she knows you as we do, darling. Your father and I are so proud of you today, we truly are. We're pleased to see you married so well."

She meant they were pleased he'd seen this through.

"Give your bride as much love as you can," she continued, tears shining in her eyes. "Never let her question that you care for her."

"Of course, mama. Everything will be fine."

He patted her hand, took leave of his friends, and made his way across the ballroom to Jane's side. She stood with a group of Mayhew cousins, none of whom he knew. She greeted him with a smile, a pure, welcoming smile that sparked conflicting emotions within him. Guilt, possessiveness, pride. Confusion that she would like him so much when they barely knew one another. *Never let her question that you care for her*, his mother had said.

"How lovely it is that we're finally married," he whispered in her ear, so no one else could hear it. He would care for her, of course. He'd be a cad otherwise.

Love? That might take a while longer, if it happened between them at all.

* * * * *

Jane sat up straighter on the carriage seat, looking out the window to watch her new husband riding alongside. He certainly had a handsome stallion, large and dark like him.

Goodness, Townsend was large, wasn't he? She hadn't noticed until he was close to her, very close to her, how much he towered over her. At the wedding, when she placed her hand in his, it was almost comical how much larger his was. It was the difference between a dove's claw and an eagle's talons, as she stood there in her pale dove-gray gown, and he in black wool and cream like a bird of prey.

For some reason, she feared he would ride ahead and leave them behind. Leave her behind. He'd been a little too pleased there was no room for him in the carriage, after the last of her things had been loaded into the traveling compartment.

Well, he was still there. He hadn't flown off yet. No, for they were to spend tonight together at an inn, and then arrive at Somerton tomorrow. Would she have her own room at the inn? She wasn't sure and had been afraid to ask. Either tonight or tomorrow night would be their wedding night when he'd come to bed with her. She'd insisted to her mother and sister that she needed no education on that account, that she knew all there was to know of mating from her animal studies. Her mother had said, "Jane, really!" Her sister had smiled and laughed and said she would certainly be fine if she left the hard work to her husband.

The hard work?

It was possible she didn't know as much as she thought, but Jane prided herself on her practicality. Whatever she did not know, she would learn, either tonight or tomorrow night. She would be the best, most blameless wife to Lord Townsend, the sort of wife he would be proud to accompany in a carriage, when said carriage was not full to bursting with wedding gifts, last minute personal items, and two wild animals in traveling crates.

Bouncer, her bunny, was a comfortable traveler. All he needed was a cozy box, some fluffy bedding, and a full stomach to fall asleep in the bump and sway of the journey. Mr. Cuddles, her four-foot-long albino *python regius*, was not used to such close quarters, even though his box was bigger than Bouncer's. She had rescued the exotic python from a filthy barrel at the Exeter Zoo Exhibition, the poor reptile half-mad and stunted by starvation by the time a sympathetic keeper warned her of his imminent demise.

Over the past year she had nursed him back to health, soothing his mind with gentle caresses and fattening him up with fresh-caught mice from the kitchens. She hoped Somerton's cats were as talented as the prolific mousers at her parents' estate.

Now and again she peeked in on Mr. Cuddles to be sure the journey wasn't upsetting him too much. A couple of pats on the head, a soothing rub along his coiled body went a long way to helping him relax. "Soon you will be warm and safe in your new enclosure," she said. "I've told them to put in nice, deep soil and branches, and a big water bowl just as you like."

She could not have sent her pets ahead with her lady's maid, although it would have been easier. Only she knew how to care for them properly, after much study and consultation with books. Hers was a small menagerie, but well-loved. Without her care, Mr. Cuddles would have died in his miserable zoo, and Bouncer would have been long snatched up by predators due to his malformed back foot.

Jane wondered if there were any animals in need of rescue at Somerton. Townsend said it was a wooded, wild place, and she looked forward to exploring the grounds once they arrived, if Lord Townsend would let her. She closed her eyes and leaned her head back upon the high seat. His carriage was a lovely conveyance, soft and plush, well cushioned for the bumps along the road. She held Mr. Cuddles' box upon her lap and set one hand near the ventilation holes at the side, because snakes smelled by flicking their tongues out, and her scent might bring her pet some comfort.

She had not told her husband yet that she owned an albino python—or a lame bunny, for that matter. He'd invited her to bring her pets to their marriage, and promised them a warm, dry corner in Somerton's stables. She had decided not to explain the sort of pets they were, for fear he'd rescind his permission. Nor did she challenge his requirement to keep them outside the house. Eventually, he'd come to love them as much as she did and perhaps allow them to stay in closer quarters. Until then, she'd make sure to visit them in the stables a few times each day.

Yes, she was just at the beginning of a grand adventure. She drowsed through some of the journey, having daydreams about a lovely, romantic married life. In the spring, how proud she would be to attend balls and entertainments on Lord Townsend's arm. All the unkind ladies and crotchety old widows who'd gossiped about her broken betrothal would have to take their words back. She was not unmarriageable after all and would not be a spinster. The engraved gold ring upon her finger made her a marchioness, the new wife of a prominent aristocrat...

"But I will still make time for you," she told her pets.

The tedious journey had her talking to herself, more or less, for the animals couldn't answer. If Lord Townsend had found a way to crowd into the compartment with her, what would they have talked about? What would they talk about tonight during dinner?

Would he come to bed with her at the inn? Would they talk then, or move straight to the mating?

She must remember that it was not called mating in polite society, among people. It was not called anything, or talked about, but her mother had alluded to "the bedding." Jane had also read an illicit passage in a romance novel once, about lovemaking. Making love sounded beautiful, even if the passage had been too flowery to impart any real information.

When they finally stopped at the inn, he said she must be tired and that she ought to have her own room so she could rest. What choice did she have, but to go along with his suggestion and spend the night alone? Again, she had the feeling he might leave without her in the morning. It was silly. He was polite and kind, and saw that all her parcels were taken upstairs during dinner, so she would be able to refresh her pets' food and water before bed, with the kitchen's help.

Perhaps that was why he took his own room, because of her pets. It was hard to know his mind, for he was a reserved sort of gentleman, speaking to her of general things, like whether she was comfortable in the carriage, and whether she preferred the roasted or sauced meat.

All through the inn's delicious dinner, she stole glances at him and thought about *lovemaking*. He would be good at it, wouldn't he? June had assured her he would know what to do. He did seem to be good at a great many things.

The next day seemed interminable, for she was anxious to get to Somerton and settle in, and smell some fresh, bracing country air. They arrived late in the afternoon, so when the carriage rolled into the courtyard, the grand country mansion was outlined in the rich, golden fire of a setting sun. It was majestically designed, with imposing columns and a tiered Romanesque fountain in the courtyard. She drew in a breath as she noted the surrounding fields and forests. Though the trees were bare and the fields wintry gray, the property seemed as wild and beautiful as he'd promised.

As she peered out the window, great numbers of household staff emerged and stood on a grand set of stairs to greet them. She felt tired and travel worn, but when Lord Townsend helped her down the carriage stairs, she forced a smile for the smartly attired servants.

It became a real smile at their welcoming applause. Her husband introduced her as the new Lady Townsend—which would take some getting used to after spending her entire life as Lady Jane. Her personal maid, Matilda, was there, having arrived days earlier with the bulk of Jane's trunks and luggage. She came forward with the housekeeper, a Mrs. Loring, who invited her to come inside and have a hot cup of tea while her husband supervised the unpacking.

And oh, she wanted to go inside and see if it was as grand within as without, but she needed to tend to her animals. "I must go to the stables first and help move my pets into their new enclosures," she said.

"You've brought your pets?" asked Matilda, eyes going wide.

"Lord Townsend said I could, as long as they weren't in the house." Jane set off after the carriage, feeling a bit less than a proper lady in front of the assembled staff, who'd probably expected her to float inside and collapse on a fainting couch.

She was not the fainting-couch type, and they might as well know it from the start. When she arrived at the large, domed stables, she scanned the spacious interior to see horses being groomed and fed, and luggage disembarked by the light of stolid iron lamps. She saw her pets' new enclosures ready and waiting near a warming stove, each cage crafted of glass, wire, and polished, shining wood. What a beautiful job they'd done following her directions!

Then she saw a stable boy peer into Mr. Cuddles' traveling box and drop it with an alarmed cry. The lid popped open and her startled snake slithered out.

Chapter Five: Setting Expectations

The uproar happened so fast, Townsend hardly knew how it started. A man yelled, "Snake! Snake!"

Another yelled, "Adder! Viper!"

"No," his wife cried. "It's not a viper, it's a python. Don't hurt it. It's my snake."

Her snake? He saw a dash of yellow and white, a curving streak shooting across the stable's center aisle. If it was a snake, it was unlike any he'd seen. For a moment, everyone froze and stared except for Jane, who ran after the thing, arms outstretched. "It's mine," she said again. "He won't harm anything. He's only looking for a place to hide and be safe."

The snake darted under the door of the last stall, the largest one containing his most rambunctious stallion. Whether from the shouting or the sudden appearance of a slithering reptile, the beast began to stamp about.

"Oh, no," said Jane. "No, no, no."

He shouted as she ran toward the stall. "Stop, Jane. Take care!"

A Proper Lord's Wife

Between his yelling, the groom's exclamations, and the stallion's agitated snorting, the noise rose to a fever pitch as his harebrained new wife yanked open the stall door and entered to try to retrieve the snake.

"Jane, come out of there at once." By the time he reached her, she was alongside his horse, bending down, combing through the straw. "You'll be injured. For God's sake, he'll trample you. Are you listening to me?"

"Mr. Cuddles will die if I don't catch him. He can't survive winter weather."

She was in tears, oblivious to the stallion's increasing agitation. Townsend grabbed for reins that weren't there, trying to settle the horse. "There now, Gallant. Down. Please."

The damned snake darted between the corner walls, trying to find a way out of the stall. As he watched, helpless, his wife fell to her knees to trap the snake just as Gallant reared up.

"Jane, watch out!"

It happened in seconds, but it seemed an hour that he stared at his wife's delicate back and his stallion's great hooves hovering just over top of it. She caught the snake with a panicked sob and stood, oblivious to Gallant's right foreleg passing inches from her head. The horse twisted sideways as he pulled his wife to the stall's door. She slipped out ahead of him with the snake held in a knot against her breast.

The entire stable had gathered to watch this drama play out. Now that she was safe again, a new uproar of chaos burst forth, with grooms yelling, the stable master coughing, and a lone stable boy crying where he stood. Jane cried too, cradling her snake. Her *snake*!

Townsend didn't know where to begin unraveling his feelings. He reeled from anger, fear, shock, and a delayed sense of panic that burst forth in a furious scold.

"You brought a *snake* here?" he bellowed at Jane. "That is your pet?"

"His name is Mr. Cuddles."

Her quietly reasonable response piqued him even more. She tutted at the creature, the cursed reptile that might have gotten her killed, checking it over for injury. When she was satisfied it was unscathed, she set it into a glass-faced box near the wood stove. As she closed and latched the box's lid, he turned to his stable master.

"You knew my wife was bringing a snake? You built a cage for a snake?"

"Yes, my lord," said the servant, abashed. "You said I was to follow the directions she sent."

"He built it expertly well," Jane said, taking his man's defense. "It's got the greenery, soil, and water I requested for the snake's health. Now Mr. Cuddles will be safe and warm, and there will be no more danger from ill-behaved horses."

"Ill-behaved horses? My horse is well behaved, my lady, when snakes aren't being set free in his stall."

"That was a mistake. Mr. Cuddles surprised that young man, and he dropped his enclosure."

The stable boy cried harder, until one of the groomsmen led him away.

"*Mr. Cuddles?*" shouted Townsend, who couldn't seem to control his temper. "You have a pet snake named Mr. Cuddles and you didn't think to inform me of this before you brought it into my stables? Where is it from?" He peered into the enclosure. "Is it venomous?"

"Goodness no, my lord. He is a *python regius* from the grasslands of Africa. Well, from the Exeter Zoo." She pushed back a lock of her orange-blond hair which had come undone in the fracas. "I adopted him when he was sickly and likely to die and nursed him back to health. He needed a home."

Townsend glared at his wife. "His home is in the wild, not in Somerton's stables."

"He cannot be released into the wild, not unless I take him back to the African continent. He cannot survive England's forest climate, especially not with his albino coloring." Her lower lip trembled as she faced him. "Please, he'll do no harm."

"Only get you killed beneath the hooves of my goddamned stallion. Do you even realize what you did? Do you realize how close you came to disaster chasing that damned snake?"

He'd shouted curses at her twice now, because he didn't know how to feel or how to take a full breath after watching his new wife almost get her head caved in by a panicked horse. She burst into tears, gripping the sides of her gown, now ruined with dirt and stains from grubbing about after her blasted African python. *Mr. Cuddles?* Of all the ridiculous, outrageous pets for a young woman to have. Did she cuddle the thing? He wanted to throw something.

"Go to the house," he told her, modulating his voice with effort. "Go to your rooms now, as you ought to have done when you arrived, and change out of that muddied gown."

"But my other pet—"

"There's another?" He asked too loudly. He was still shouting. "Another snake?"

"No, my lord." Her voice wavered as she took a step back. "Only a rabbit—a very small one—with a malformed foot."

"A malformed rabbit." He threw up his hands. "Of course."

"That is all, my lord. All my pets, just those two. I ought to have told you about them. You see, I care for things, for miserable creatures that I find."

"You care for them more than your own life? My horse could have snapped your spine or crushed your skull."

"It was an accident," she said, as if this might make everything that had happened—her near death—acceptable to him.

He could not bear to stay in the stable another moment. He turned on his heel to leave before he cursed at her again. "I will speak with you, Jane, as soon as your pets are settled," he said over his shoulder. "You may await me in your rooms."

He would not live this sort of life. He'd been married to her for less than two days and already felt his sanity slipping. He did not like chaos and uncontrolled situations, and having nightmares about pythons and trampled women. She must understand this was not acceptable.

He would explain it to her in no uncertain terms once he was calm.

* * * * *

Jane settled her pets into their enclosures with shaking hands, and left feeding instructions with the head groom. Tomorrow, she'd bring each of them a treat to make up for all the upheaval. Poor Mr. Cuddles. What a fright he'd had, and now her husband was furious with her. Livid, honestly. She didn't know how she could ever face him again.

For now, she would do as he said and retreat to her room. In fact, there was nothing she wanted more than to hide away in shame and change out of her soiled traveling cloak and scuffed slippers. She put a hand to her head. Yes, her hair was disarranged too. Why wouldn't it be, after she'd scuttled about on the ground in her new husband's stable?

She walked past the restless stable hands, attempting to appear dignified even in her dirty, bedraggled state. Beyond the stable, the great house rose against the now-dark sky like a pretty holiday cake, with rows of windows for decoration. Her faithful maid waited within the entryway to show her to her rooms on the second floor.

"My lady...?" Matilda's voice trailed off when she saw her disarray.

"There was a snake escape," she replied, her voice tight.

"Mr. Cuddles escaped?"

"Yes, and was almost trampled by a horse. He's fine now, but I'm feeling rather frazzled."

"The servants have already drawn a bath for you," the maid assured her.

A bath sounded like just the thing. She looked around as she went up the stairs, admiring her new home even in her wearied state.

Somerton was as beautiful inside as it was against the night sky, all elegance and grace. The upper landing was tastefully decorated with marble statues lit by a jeweled chandelier, while flickering sconces illuminated hallways headed in either direction. Fresh swags of winter greenery scented the air. She couldn't wait to see Somerton's charms in full daylight—if she survived the reckoning with her husband.

"This way, my lady."

Matilda guided her to the right, past silent footmen and a line of polished doors. When they arrived at her suite, she found her rooms, too, were elegant and beautiful. The furniture was decorated in a floral motif, and real blooms nestled in vases upon every table, giving the room a homey feel. A gauzy set of curtains concealed the moon and the night's darkness. A fire warmed the soaring space, its occasional crackling a reminder of her childhood bedroom.

The bed was larger than her childhood bed and embellished with a canopy matching the curtains. The carved headboard was tall and imposing, while the footboard was lower and cushioned across the top. A thoughtful artisan had added a stepping stool in the center, sure to come in handy since it was such a high bed. As she kicked off her slippers, a soft wool rug cushioned her feet.

Matilda led her through the dressing room to a private bathing chamber with its own fireplace and a steaming tub of scented water. Jane sank into the bath with a relieved sigh and washed herself with rose scented soap as her maid rinsed bits of hay from her hair. The faithful servant promised to do her best at brushing clean her soiled traveling gown and cloak before she sent them to the laundress.

After her bath, Jane put on a diaphanous white nightgown and robe in the softest embroidered lawn, a gift from her husband. If he could have, he probably would have taken it back after the evening's events. As she toweled dry her hair before the fire, a note arrived at the door.

Please present yourself in my chambers when you have completed your evening toilette.

It wasn't signed—it didn't need to be. The note's tone was unpleasantly terse. *Present yourself?* How dire that sounded.

"I suppose I must go to him," she said to Matilda. "Or...shall I wait for my hair to dry a bit more?"

The older woman's expression softened with sympathy. "My lady, if he wishes you to attend him, it might be best to go right away."

Jane wished she could hide in the cozy curtained bed and wait for her husband's mood to improve, but it was their wedding night, more or less. Matilda showed her to the proper door across the hall and Jane steeled herself for whatever lay on the other side. She knocked quietly, then straightened as the door swung open.

Her husband looked out at her, but she didn't meet his gaze right away. Instead, she stared forward at his chest, barely covered by his night robe. She'd never seen a man in such a state of undress.

"Come in, Jane," he said, his voice level enough after his earlier shouting. "How do you like your rooms?"

"They're lovely." She finally met his eyes. "Somerton is a beautiful manor."

"A bit chilly in winter."

She realized she was clutching her robe tightly about her, but it was not from cold. She felt hot and embarrassed to be so close to him, this veritable stranger she'd married. They were alone together in his bedroom, while he wore only a robe and perhaps...nothing else?

"Thank you for the night clothes," she said, trying not to betray her unease. "They make me feel like a princess."

He ran his eyes over her. "I see you haven't managed to drag them through any mud puddles yet."

Her cheeks flamed at his laconic remark. He was handsome, yes, but frightening as well. He was so dark, so very *masculine* without his starched coats and shirts and cravats to make him civilized. She could see hair on his chest, and his pulse beating at his neck.

He is just a man, she told herself. *This is how men look in their bedrooms, half-undressed.*

She cast a glance about, trying to calm her unfettered thoughts. His room seemed suitably grand and imposing for the lord of the manor, with dark furnishings, a pair of sturdy chairs upholstered in dark blue velvet, and a massive, canopied bed. In fact, his bed was a match to hers, down to the cushioned footboard with the handily placed step stool, although he surely wouldn't need one with his height. Oh, staring at his bed did *not* calm her nerves. Nor did the pressure of his disapproving gaze...

"I can't apologize enough for what happened earlier," she said, facing him in the center of his high-ceilinged chamber. "I suppose I didn't make the best first impression before your household staff."

He sighed. "It's not about first impressions. It's what almost happened to you. I nearly had to write to your family with news of your demise."

"That would have been awful so soon in our marriage, wouldn't it? We both would have seemed rather careless."

He sighed again, even harder. This discussion was not going well.

"You're right to be angry," she said. "I wasn't thinking properly when I barged into that stall."

"You didn't tell me you had a pet snake. I thought you had a dog or something."

He was not as angry as she feared. Rather, he seemed unhappy. Brooding.

"I do enjoy dogs," she said. "We could get one or two if you liked. Well, as long as we kept them away from my other animals."

"Jane."

He was *extremely* unhappy. He cut off her attempt at cheerful banter with a frown and walked to stand before her with his arms crossed upon his chest.

"I wish I could let this pass without some reckoning," he began. "I tried to dress for bed, indeed, to go to bed and conduct this discussion in the morning, but I cannot do it. You have exhibited behavior I cannot abide in a wife."

Her whole body tensed in shock, and her heart pounded. "You will leave me already?"

"Leave you? No, we're married now, for better or worse. At the same time, I find you bring flaws to this marriage which must be corrected. You did not tell me, for instance, that you kept wild animals for pets, to include an exotic snake that looks like a devil's novelty."

"It is an albino snake," she murmured. "A natural, if rare, mutation in pythons."

His dire look silenced her. "You hid it from me because you knew I would object."

"Perhaps, my lord, but only because I love my pets and I was afraid you'd tell me not to bring them, or decide not to marry me because I had them at all."

"Such honesty would have been appreciated before now."

She winced inwardly. "Would you have decided not to marry me?"

He thought a minute, then shook his head. "No, I still would have married you. I was forewarned about your intense attraction to nature. Your misstep was being secretive, hiding things from me that I had a right to know. Furthermore, in the stable just now, you ignored my warnings, ignored me. Did you not hear me shouting at you to come out of Gallant's stall?"

"But Mr. Cuddles was in there—"

"Did you hear me? I shouted very loudly."

He was close to shouting now.

"I did hear you," she said in her softest remorseful tone. "However—"

"There are no howevers. You cannot put your life in danger for the sake of a reptile, albino or no. Your behavior was reckless and unladylike, and witnessed by a dozen of my stable staff, who are surely wondering why..."

Why I married someone like you.

He didn't say it, perhaps because he saw the tears welling in her eyes. Even so, she knew what he *meant* to say, so those tears spilled over onto her cheeks. "I'm sorry things have started so badly. I wish…" *I wish I were more like my mother, or my sister, or any proper lady.* "I wish I had not displeased you so."

"I believe I must punish you, Jane, if we're to move past this unfortunate beginning. I must know you won't behave so rashly again."

She wiped away a tear. "Oh, no. Of course I won't. I feel very badly."

"Come here to me, now."

She quailed at his stern manner. How awful, to be punished the second day of their marriage.

"Please, my lord, I'm so sorry."

He took her hand and drew her resisting form closer. "I'm sure you are. A sound spanking will provide the needed correction for your actions, and allow me to work through some of this…"

She stared at him. "This what?"

"Agitation," he said, his gaze holding hers. "Perhaps it's a good thing for you to learn early on what will happen when your behavior falls short of my expectations."

Before she could fully process his intention, he drew her toward one of the blue velvet chairs. Oh no. He meant to spank her over his knee, and though she wasn't experienced in corporal chastisement, she was sure his giant hands would hurt like anything.

"Please, my lord," she said, dragging her feet. "I will try to do better. I'll be more honest. I'll be more careful around your horses, and not do anything else to endanger my life."

"I will teach you to do better. I'd be shirking my husbandly duties if I did not."

She glanced wildly about, trying to think of a way to avoid what was to come.

"I don't want you to spank me," she said, tears flowing anew. "I am embarrassed. Ashamed."

He appeared sympathetic, but unmoved. "As this is your first punishment within our marriage, I will not be heavy handed. You'll be spanked hard enough to pay penance for your misbehavior, no more." His eyes held hers, deeply amber, and so sincere. "That's the point of marital discipline, obviously. A spanking for any infraction will, over time, change your behavior."

"Marital discipline?" she echoed, her voice cracking. "But I can try to change it now! I will try. I will be more thoughtful. Less reckless."

"I believe you will once you have experienced the resultant penalty."

His tone was so immovable, so firm. His gaze was patient, but his stance brooked no resistance. Of course, husbands had the right to discipline their wives as needed, but to do so on the second day of their marriage? Here she was, dressed in his lovely gift of a gown...

"Come, you must lie over my lap now." He sat and patted his thigh.

Her voice had left her. She could not move. Well, she might have moved if he didn't have a hold of her hand. She might have run away, but then, surely, he would have chased her.

"I don't want a spanking. Please, my lord. I'm so sorry to have angered you."

He disregarded her apologies, pulling her resisting figure down across his legs. She had never been in such close contact with any man, had never felt the hardness of a man's thighs and the strength of his grip. She reached to brace her hands on the floor as he arranged her position to his liking. She cried harder, in fear and dread.

"There now, I'm not going to kill you," he said. "Fussing won't work with me when it comes to discipline. You'll see, in time, that these checks upon your behavior will make our marriage better."

"I'm not so badly behaved," she sobbed. "Not to deserve this."

He made a dismissive sound, and she too knew her words for a lie. She *had* hidden the nature of her "pets" from him on purpose and caused a ruckus in his stables because of it. She'd embarrassed her new husband in front of his servants and made a very poor first impression. They'd surely gossip about her belowstairs.

Yes, she had behaved badly, so she would accept this spanking, but she was still unhappy about it. She couldn't stop trembling as he pushed up her robe and nightgown to expose her backside.

"Oh, please," she whispered, reaching back. "Please let me stay covered."

"No, Jane." He caught her hand. "You must be spanked upon your bare bottom. It may be embarrassing, but it's the most effective way." He pushed her gown all the way up as she cringed in humiliation. "Were you spanked as a child?"

"Never." Her face burned as he exposed her bottom completely. "My parents did not believe in corporal punishment."

His "hmm" sounded like criticism. She could not dwell on that as he rubbed his hand across her exposed cheeks. His fingers felt huge and threatening as he seemed to take her measure.

"You must resign yourself to occasional spankings," he told her as she cried quietly. "Remember, I'm doing this to teach you a lesson, not to be needlessly cruel."

Her only answer was renewed tears. Cool air blew across her bottom, reminding her how naked and exposed she was. He placed a hand upon the small of her back to still her fidgeting.

"You're not to move about or try to evade this punishment," he warned. "You're to be still and docile with your fingertips and toes remaining on the floor. Do you understand?"

She cried louder.

"Answer me, if you please."

"Yes, my lord," she said, sniffling.

"Although, this first time, it might be easier if I held your hands behind you so you aren't tempted to interfere."

He drew her hands to the small of her back and gripped them there, so she was forced to balance over his thighs, hiding her face against the fabric of his robe. If this was marriage, she hated it. She ought to have stayed a spinster after all.

Once he had her arranged, he drew back his other hand and landed the first volley of blows. She surged up and tried to turn toward him. "Oh, you must stop, my lord! Ow, ow, ow!" The words tumbled over each other, out of her control. It hurt so badly, stung so hotly she could barely catch her breath.

"Be still," he reminded her.

"I can't. It hurts too much."

"I know it hurts." He smoothed a hand over her burning bottom. "But we've barely begun."

He began to spank her again, and she realized now why he held her hands so firmly out of the way. If they were loose, she would have fought him, would have done anything to protect her backside. His blows hurt more than anything she'd yet encountered in life, more than falling on the stairs, or baby hedgehog bites.

"Oww," she said, "Ow, ow, please." How long would he smack her bottom? She barely cried anymore. It was all she could do to breathe.

"Are you thinking about why you're being punished?" he asked, as her legs kicked up.

"I'm thinking about that, yes. And also thinking that maybe I've been punished enough already."

"My darling," he said in his cool, authoritative way. "We are only halfway through."

* * * * *

Townsend released her hands and gave her a moment to rest and rub her bottom. How outraged she was, to be bent over his lap. She had not been punished enough yet, because she was still complaining and resisting, but she was new to spanking, clearly, so he didn't want to push her too far.

Once she'd had a bit of time to snivel, he retrieved her hands and landed another set of measured spanks. He would not flail at her in anger. No, he'd waited for his anger to subside to a certain point before he'd summoned her to his room, for this wasn't about bullying. This was about consequences and setting expectations for future lapses of judgment. She wasn't happy at the moment, but she'd come to understand the wholesome balance of discipline soon enough.

He took another break when her cries deepened, stroking the backs of her legs to calm her. Her bottom had turned a nice, even pink. Why, he could have walloped her until she was scarlet. He was hardly hurting her on a scale of true punishment.

"Give me your hands once more," he told her. "Take this last bit of spanking, then we'll be through."

She complied with sniffling, offended sobs, but no talking back. Her arse cheeks were unused to spanking and would probably stay sore at least a day or two, he warranted. Yes, it was nearly enough.

He gave her ten more spanks, five upon each cheek. They were the hardest by tradition, and she struggled and fought against him, but she didn't protest.

"Well done," he said. "That's all for now."

He almost hated to draw her nightgown back down. Her bottom was lovely, pert and round and firm, and gorgeously tender from punishment, but this was not about his sexual response to spanking. It was about setting the groundwork for a marriage of balance and trust.

So he pulled her gown and night robe down and helped her to her feet, and held her when she tottered. "Sit with me a moment," he said, pulling her into his lap even though she resisted.

She pointedly looked away from him, toward the window. He could still see tears on her cheeks in the candlelight as she settled unhappily into his arms. He wiped them away with his fingers, then rearranged her on his thighs so she wouldn't feel his erect cock pressing against her. He did enjoy spanking women, and spanking his own wife had carried an affecting frisson of excitement.

He could not bed her tonight, though. It would confuse the punishment, to follow it with lovemaking, especially since it would be her first sexual experience. She was so achingly innocent, so virtuous for all her secret snakes and rabbits. He supposed he ought to be grateful that was all she'd brought to their marriage. She might have brought a damned badger, or a wolf.

"This looks very pretty on you," he said, as the silence between them grew onerous. He brushed his hand over her gauzy nightgown. "I hope it is comfortable."

"It's very soft," she said, with forced politeness. "I think I would like to go to bed."

"Let's talk together a moment first. It can be difficult to weather your first spanking, I know. But I hope you've learned something."

After a moment, she sighed. "I learned that I hate being spanked."

"Indeed. Going forward, you must consider your behavior's consequences, especially now that you're married." He put a finger beneath her chin and made her look up at him. She looked awfully tired. "The nice thing about being punished is that you're absolved afterward. I forgive you for bringing your snake to Somerton and sending my horses into a panic."

"And you into a panic."

"And me. I have barely come to know you. I wouldn't wish to lose you already. I was afraid you'd be hurt, Jane."

"I was hurt just now," she said. "By you."

Those amber-gold eyes of hers, part sullen, part apologetic...

"You know what I mean," he said, resisting the urge to kiss her. "You're my wife and I wish to protect you from any harms, now and always. I care for you, no matter what you think of me at the moment." He felt her tense spine relax the smallest bit, and drew her closer, now that his erection was not so obvious.

With a faint, tired sniffle, she laid her head upon his shoulder. Her hair was down, so he felt its velvet softness against his chest.

"I suppose it would have been awful if your horse had injured me...or killed me," she said, as if she were just now contemplating what might have happened. "It probably would have hurt terribly, to be trampled. Even more than the spanking."

"It would have hurt far more, and it would have been tragic."

He ran a hand up and down her arm, soothing away the last of her sniffles. "Are you feeling any better now?"

"A little."

She turned her face into his neck, even as she shifted uncomfortably on his lap. She was not like any woman he'd known, not graceful and polished as he would have liked, but holding her now felt strangely pleasant. She was not the wife he'd wanted, but she *did* need him to teach her discipline. She was not perfect, but they had something upon which to build a marriage, even though it was not the marriage he'd envisioned for himself.

"It's been a very long day," he said, when he felt her growing heavier against his chest. "A very long pair of days to travel from London. I think we both ought to rest tonight."

"Mm. Yes, my lord."

He stood, lifting her in his arms, and carried her across the hall to her bedroom. The blankets were turned down and the fire banked for the night. He laid his wife down gently, setting her head upon her pillow. She was nearly asleep, worn out by the spanking, he supposed. Her eyes blinked open as he released her, gazing at him with intensity, with some question. She held his hand a moment, then let it go.

He paused, looking down at her tousled, long hair. The candle at her bedside reflected upon the strands, made the orange-red tone more vibrant. He was tempted to lie down beside her and take her virginity when she was in this sleepy, pliant state, but he wouldn't. He wanted her first time to be pleasant, to be meaningful to her, even though he'd probably have to fantasize about Ophelia to perform with appropriate passion. Jane wouldn't have to know.

"Good night," he said.

"Good night, my lord."

"You must call me Townsend now that we're married. Or Edward, if you wish."

"Edward." She drew it out in a sleepy whisper as he tucked the blankets around her and blew out the candle.

No, he would not stay tonight, but tomorrow he would bed her. It would solidify their marriage far better than a disciplinary spanking, and she would likely enjoy it a great deal more.

Chapter Six:
Customary Intimacies

Jane opened her eyes and stared at the vase of white carnations on her side table. Somerton must have a hothouse for forcing flowers in the cold winter months. The thought of such an enterprise raised her spirits.

Then she turned onto her back and winced, her spirits plummeting again. It hurt just to move, because her sore, sensitive buttocks would brush across her nightgown's fabric or the smooth scented sheets and bring to mind her spanking from the evening before. It seemed a cold, gray winter day indeed, knowing she had to face him after he'd disciplined her in that manner. She'd been so embarrassed, her feelings so injured, to be spanked over his lap like a child.

But then, afterward, when he'd held her in his arms and comforted her...

Well, that had been an entirely different feeling. In that moment, she'd felt warm and safe sheltering against his chest, even as her bottom throbbed in pain. His daunting size for once felt like a desirable thing in a husband. She'd felt so cozy resting against him, once she calmed down from the spanking he'd given her.

She sat up in bed, gingerly shifting on her hindquarters, then lay back down again. How could she still feel so sore the morning after? She did not want to experience husbandly discipline again. She resolved to walk a narrow line. She would be so honest, obedient, and ladylike he'd never have another opportunity to fault her. Surely, she could manage it.

She stretched and rose and performed her morning ablutions in her bathing room. The high windows admitted morning light, so the room felt warmer in the winter's chill. Screwing up her courage, she turned her backside to the mirror and looked over her shoulder to survey the damage. There were two neat sets of bruises upon her buttocks, right in the center where his hand had assailed her.

She pulled on a fresh chemise but did not have the energy to struggle into her stays properly without Matilda's help, so she rang the bell. The maid appeared, curtsying with uncharacteristic shyness. She'd probably heard gossip about what had occurred last night. How many servants had overheard her crying and those loud, rhythmic smacks?

Jane's face flushed with embarrassment as her maid helped her select an outfit and dress for the day. The maid insisted on a new gown, a brightly embroidered floral ensemble, then sat her down for an intricate hairstyle, curling her hair atop her head and smoothing every strand.

"We must have you looking your best," she said, as Jane watched her deft hands in the mirror.

In the subtle language of mistress and servant, Jane understood her maid was in sympathy with her, and meant to show Lord Townsend that his new lady was no one to be trifled with. It soothed Jane's feelings a bit. As alone as she felt this morning in Lord Townsend's great house, she had one ally in Matilda, and would hopefully find more as she explored this place where her husband ruled.

She would start at the stables because she had to attend to her pets.

She put on a warm wool spencer and matching bonnet to insulate her from the crisp winter weather, and somehow managed to find her way to the front door. The house looked different in the daytime, a bit more welcoming and less imposing.

Once outside, it was a short walk to the stables. A few horses grazed in adjacent paddocks, beautiful beasts who appeared to receive excellent grooming and care, which reassured her. A house that took care of its animals was a healthy, good place to live.

She peeked in at the stable door then stepped inside, pausing to allow her eyes to accustom to the dimmer interior. It was pleasantly warm and smelled of straw and horses. She proceeded to the area where her pets' enclosures stood, trying not to get in anyone's way. As she leaned down to check on them her eyes were drawn to a tall figure just at her periphery. She knew those legs, those arms, that broad chest by now. She turned and met her husband's gaze.

He was in riding clothes, leading his stallion toward its stall. The first thing her father always did when he came to the country was ride about the property and environs, making sure everything was well. Lord Townsend must have done the same. He wore a smartly tailored wool jacket but no overcoat. His cheeks were red from the winter air.

"Aren't you cold, my lord?"

Her concern overcame her shyness as he walked toward her. He shook his head.

"Not cold. It was warm when the sun broke through the clouds, and riding Gallant takes a strong arm."

She'd felt that strong arm last night. No doubt her cheeks were flushing red as his, but not from cold. Some regard passed between them, the shared memory of last evening along with the accompanying tension. He did not ask if she'd slept well.

"I suppose you must show me these pets of yours," he said instead, gesturing toward their enclosures. "If they're going to live here, I'd like to know about them."

He did not say this in an unfriendly way, and she felt heartened by his interest. Perhaps he was only asking to ease some of the tension between them, but she was always happy to talk about her animals.

"Well, my lord—"

"Townsend," he said. "Or Edward, please."

"All right. Edward." It seemed strange to call him by his Christian name, as little as she knew him, but she would try her best since she ached for closeness between them. She did not want a cold, sterile marriage. That was not in her nature, so she smiled past her nerves and led him over to her pets.

She opened the first enclosure, a spacious wire cage for her mud-brown rabbit. "This is sweet little Bouncer. One of my father's staghounds caught him and brought him to me, thinking him a fun toy. I saw his back leg was damaged, leaving him vulnerable to all sorts of predators, and I wept over him so much my father said I might keep him, even though cook wanted to have him for dinner." She frowned. "She said she would put him out of his misery, but I don't think he's been miserable with my help, and he was too little to eat then, at any rate. He loves to be snuggled and petted. He practically preens."

She picked him up and cradled him against her chest. "Would you like to pet him? I promise he's very clean."

He stroked the rabbit gently, as an Edward might do, instead of a Lord Townsend. While Bouncer leaned into his touch and twitched his ears, Jane stared at his long, manly fingers, wondering when her intense fascination with her husband's body would end.

"He's very calm when you hold him," he noted. "Not like a wild animal at all."

"Yes, I've tried to help him feel secure. There's always been a question—was he abandoned by his mother for his damaged foot, and therefore caught more easily by my father's hound? Or did the hound damage his foot in catching him? I tried not to blame Pagan too much."

"Pagan, the naughty bunny snatcher."

Jane smiled at him. "Yes, it was naughty, but I suppose it worked out in the end." She held Bouncer up, watching his nose wiggle and his eyes take in the stranger beside her with curiosity. "Some people think of rabbits as little more than rodents, but they are not at all like rodents. For one, they have two extra incisors that rodents don't have."

"How interesting."

"They also have larger ears than most rodents, so they're able to hear from much farther distances. Their long ears also disperse heat to keep them cool on warmer days. When it's cooler, as now in winter, they wear them closer to their bodies."

"Hmm." He gazed down into the enclosure. "Do you think they're cold out here, your animals?"

"With additional warmth from the stove, they can survive English weather. Back in you go," she said, placing her rabbit in his pile of cotton scraps and straw. "I'll feed you more hay tonight."

The snake's enclosure was next, longer and low, with a glass front.

"Do you want to meet Mr. Cuddles?" she asked uncertainly. "I'll understand if you don't, after what happened yesterday."

"I would like to meet Mr. Cuddles on the condition that he not be released from his cage."

"It wasn't meant to happen yesterday," she said. "He was in a traveling box, you see, and the boy dropped it from surprise. Anyhow, we needn't open the enclosure. You can look through the window and see him if you prefer."

"That does sound safer. How did you come to own this reptile, Jane? Did you buy him at the Exeter Exchange?"

"Oh, no. I did not have to buy him. He was so ill; they'd pretty much left him to die. They don't care properly for their animals, it's very sad. A man who worked there told me he was in peril, and I demanded the manager surrender him to me."

"You are an enterprising advocate for animals. I suppose they knew you from your protests outside."

She detected the disapproval in his voice. It *had* been outrageous to stand outside the Exchange and entreat patrons not to support the zoo. She'd been raised well enough to know that, and in the end, her efforts had not worked, and her father had ordered her home. It had also been outrageous to adopt an exotic python, but in this her papa had allowed her to prevail. She pointed to the snake, now curled up in a cozy bunch of moss. "I think he was grateful for my help. He has never been aggressive toward me."

"Do you handle him often?"

"Not excessively, but enough to ensure he is healthy and happy. He loves to wrap about my hands and arms and stare up at me. He can be quite affectionate in his own way."

Her husband made a soft sound, something between a laugh and a groan. The poor man, just now realizing how bizarre a woman he'd married. Well, he'd probably realized that last night, but here he was, listening to her. He hadn't ordered her pets to the devil yet, although it was within his rights to do so.

"England isn't the best place for a python," she admitted. Around them, the groomsmen half listened, watching the enclosure as they attended their duties. "Perhaps I should have left him where he was and let nature take its course, but he would have died so young. I try to keep him as content as possible in captivity."

"He's doubtless grateful," he said with a smile. "If snakes can feel gratitude."

"A professor at Cambridge University told me that, if he stays healthy, Mr. Cuddles might live twenty or twenty-five years."

Edward's smile faded. "Twenty-five years, you say? My God. What do you feed it?"

"Mice or rats. He has a rodent meal once a week, usually a half-dead critter the kitchen cats bring to the doorstep. At my father's house, my pets lived in the kitchen, you see. It was warmer and busier, and the staff enjoyed feeding them scraps. Well, Bouncer anyway. Mr. Cuddles doesn't eat scraps, and none of them liked to feed the snake."

"Imagine that."

She straightened and smoothed her skirts. It had been nice of him to express interest in her animals, but she mustn't "go on too long," as her mother used to say. "Thank you for listening to me." She drew a deep breath. "And for forgiving me for...for yesterday. I was afraid you'd be all frowns next time we encountered one another."

"All frowns? I try not to hold grudges once the price is paid." His dark brows rose as his amber gaze held hers. "You kept the pets in the kitchen, you say? You believe it works better for them?"

Hope warmed her, tentative excitement. "I do believe so. It's a sanitary arrangement if they're kept in their cages."

"Would you prefer to do that here?"

"Oh yes, my lord! I mean, Edward. It would be warmer for them in the kitchens, and easier for me to see to their care. But you said you didn't wish to have pets in the house."

He waved a hand. "I meant dogs and cats roaming the hallways. If your pets are confined to these cages, I don't see the harm." He leaned down, studying the latches. "As long as these enclosures are secure."

"They are very secure. Your man did a wonderful job with them." Still, she checked each latch one more time. "I have kept you too long," she said when she finished. "You'll be growing cold now for sure."

"You're so eager to be rid of me." He gave a light laugh to tell her he was teasing. "What are your plans for today, Jane?"

"I suppose I'll look around my new home. It's such an expansive place."

"There's a great deal to see. You're welcome to explore the gardens, but if you wish to ride out to the creeks, ponds, and woods, you must take someone with you. No wandering about on your own."

"Are the woods dangerous here?" she asked.

"Not especially, but for you, they'll be unfamiliar. It's best to be safe, and Somerton has plenty of staff at your assistance. Ask Mrs. Loring and an escort will be arranged."

He was being so kind. She felt grateful, scared, and untethered all at once. "How about you?" she asked. "What will you do today?"

"I have to consult on certain things with my staff now that the house has opened up again. I'll see you at dinner, Jane. We eat promptly at eight in the country. I hope you won't be late."

She unconsciously reached behind her. Late? Never. She'd give her new husband no excuse to punish her again. She imagined his notion of "marital discipline" would apply even to small, petty crimes.

"Then after dinner..." His voice trailed off a moment, as he looked around to be sure they were alone. "After dinner, I think we ought to retire together. It's time we shared the customary intimacies of a married couple, don't you think?"

The *customary intimacies*? Jane nodded, trying to seem confident. "I think we'd definitely better. I'm not at all nervous about that. I understand a great deal about...biology."

She sputtered out the last word, wishing she'd never begun the sentence. How crass he must think her. Oh, well.

"I'll see you at dinner, Edward." She barely stopped herself from dropping a curtsy to him, as if he were some king she might have offended. He flustered her, that was certain, and it was hard not to look over her shoulder as she left.

Customary intimacies...

She'd be thinking about that for a while.

* * * * *

Townsend stared after his wife as she exited the stables. What an odd, prim little woman. She knew about biology, did she? He doubted she knew enough to survive more than a minute or two with him in bed. He wondered if she'd lose her nerve tonight and be coy, and ask him to let her alone, or if she would be brash as she sometimes was, comparing his erect cock to some exotic snake or garden vegetable.

Whatever she threw at him, he'd handle it. They'd been married nearly three days now, and the greatest intimacy they'd had so far was the spanking she'd received over his lap. Tonight, he'd show her a different sort of control and make sure she enjoyed it. He would not be hot-blooded or intense with her. Not yet. When she understood more about biology, perhaps.

He grinned as he headed to the house, thinking of the way she'd said *biology*, with all the bravado of an utter, innocent virgin. Did she realize she blushed three shades of red as soon as he broached the topic of marital intimacy?

He went to his rooms before dinner to clean up and put on his evening clothes. His valet took extra care shaving away the day's stubble and making an ornate knot in his starched neckcloth. It looked fancy and formal, perfect for their first real dinner at home together, but within a short while, he'd be struggling to unknot it so he could bed his wife.

At the eight o'clock hour, Jane walked into the dining room looking sweet and graceful in a pale pink gown. If she'd gone gallivanting about the woods, her maid had done an excellent job straightening her up. Her light copper hair was smoothed into a crown of curls, her gloves were pristine, and no hint of mud sullied her hem. He seated her to his right side instead of all the way at the end of the table. Formalities need not stretch that far.

She smiled at him. She did not hold grudges either, apparently. That was a good thing for their marriage—and their disciplinary life.

"How beautiful it is here," she said, as the servants bustled in with the first appetizing dishes. "It's a glittering old place." She caught herself, not wishing to offend him. "It is old, isn't it? It seems to be."

"It's middling old, for these parts. My great-grandfather built it, to have a country home not terribly far from London. Much of my family is in Oxfordshire, you see, but my father took a liking to this place and put down roots here with my mother, modernizing many of the rooms and expanding the stables. I was born in your bedroom, which used to be my mother's room, if you can believe it."

Jane shook her head. "I can't. I mean, I believe it could have been your mother's room, for it's very nice, but I can't believe..." She smothered a smile. "I can't believe you were ever small enough to be a baby."

He laughed aloud at her droll expression. "We all begin as babies. A naturalist must know that. No creature springs to life full grown."

"Well, there is a type of gnu in the African wilds called *Connochaetes taurinus* which can stand and walk mere minutes after birth, and run fast enough to escape a hyena by the end of its first day of life. The young of these herds have an eighty percent survival rate, compared to the more usual fifty percent survival rate for other African grazing species. Which, honestly, one would expect."

He saw one of the servants nearly fumble a platter of sauced potatoes at this recitation. His wife noticed too and bit her lip.

"I suppose this is not the most ladylike sort of dinner conversation."

"I only wonder where you've learned all these fascinating facts. Have you been to Africa, Jane?"

"Oh no, my lord. It's such a wild place; I think I would be afraid to go. But I learn things in books I borrow from the Zoological Society's library, and from my uncle, who has traveled throughout Europe, India, and the Far East. He has dozens of books on exotic animals, and as I read them, certain facts get stuck in my head. I've read extensively on African wildlife since adopting Mr. Cuddles." She took a bite of roast wearing a dreamy look of recollection. "I love to imagine the newborn baby gnu outrunning a hyena, then curling up with his mother to have a nap. Wouldn't it be so sweet?"

The one thing he knew about nature was that it was rarely sweet. She said *gnu* with a very hard g, the silly thing. Townsend turned his attention to the food on his plate, as once again, his wife had left him at a loss for follow-up conversation. After a moment, she turned the subject back to the house.

"My father's country home is not as old as this one. It's a solid, cozy pile of stones, but not very big. It doesn't have a name either, like Somerton does."

"My great-grandmother named the house Somerton because she thought it sounded elegant," he said with a laugh. "You ought to see my parents' mansion, the Lockridge estate. You will, eventually, because my oldest sister and her husband are planning to visit in the spring."

Her eyes went wide. "The prince, you mean?"

"Her husband is a prince of Italy, yes. Although I have it on good authority he won't ever be king, for his father is full of energy for his age, and he has three older brothers besides."

"I've never met royalty except when I was presented at court, and I was so nervous about embarrassing my parents that I don't remember any of what happened during the audience. It was the most terrifying day of my life."

"Not the day you married me?" He winked at her. "You were afraid of me. I could sense it."

"I am still afraid of you," she said, and it was the second hilarious thing she'd said to him in the space of two dinner courses. They laughed together, and he thought, for all his misgivings, she'd not be a completely intolerable wife. While he might always carry a flame for Ophelia, he and Jane would find their way in this mutual journey, starting tonight when they went to bed together.

"I hope you are not too tired for...later," he said, as they finished dinner. The servants had brought port, but he didn't wish to linger over it.

"No," she said brightly. "I'm not too tired. I wish to be a...a customary wife in all those...customary matters of marriage."

Oh, my awkward dear. So you shall.

"Why don't you go upstairs and dress for bed, then," he said. "I'll join you in, shall we say, half an hour?"

"Yes, of course."

"I'll come to your room, Jane. Leave the door ajar when you're ready for me."

This spate of instructions seemed to leave her breathless, unable to speak. She blushed red again, redder than that morning, and somehow managed to excuse herself.

He stayed and sipped at the excellent port, master of his house, newly wed to a somewhat unconventional wife. He *wanted* to go to her, which surprised him. He wanted to play with her and learn what excited her, and show her what excited him. He was already growing hard, thinking of her upstairs waiting to accommodate him. Yes, he wanted her far more than he'd expected to, and started up the stairs a full five minutes before the half-hour had passed.

Chapter Seven:
Joined as One

Though he arrived early to her rooms, he saw the door was already cracked open. He waited, listening before he entered, but heard nothing. He wondered if she'd already retired, but when he walked through the silent sitting room into her bedroom, he found her seated against her pillows, nearly obscured by the bedcurtain.

"Good evening," he said. "How are you?"

"Very well. How are you?"

He was touched by the exquisite care she took to smile as she answered, even though he could read the nervousness in her gaze. By candlelight, her hair was not so orange, but more of a soft golden color. She had made herself very small in her bed, or maybe she only seemed small. It was a giant bed, wasn't it, for a virginal maiden?

She was not wearing the nightgown he'd gifted her. He supposed he'd ruined it with bad memories.

He would try to make better memories for his wife tonight.

When he moved closer, he saw she was wearing a plain, girlish shift of gratifyingly thin cotton. Only her shoulders showed as she clutched the sheets against her front, but he imagined he'd be able to see her nipples through the material if she lowered them just a little. He was still dressed from dinner, but wouldn't be for long. He unbuttoned his coat and waistcoat and set them over a chair, then walked toward the side of the bed.

"Can you help me, Jane? My valet's the devil with these fancy knots."

"Oh. Yes. Of course."

She left her clutched sheets and crawled to where he stood. It aroused him, and he helped her to her feet facing him. She was taller than him now, her fingers just at the height to loosen his neckcloth.

His eyes were just at the height to ogle her breasts.

Ah, they were lovely breasts. He did not stare at them, not yet. It was enough to see the tips of her nipples pressed against the thin gown, the points hard with anxiety or excitement. Her hair, which was pulled up in a chignon-and-curls by day, now hung loose, wavy and voluminous.

"Don't be gentle," he said, as she plucked ineffectually at his necktie's folds. "You won't hurt me."

A smile smoothed the concentration in her features. "I think I've got it now."

It took her about twenty seconds more to undo the largest knot and unwind the frills behind it. Her fingers brushed his chin, soft and warm, nimble and delicate. Even that touch sparked his blood. Who'd have thought a tentative wife would arouse him so, when he was accustomed to the brazen tarts at Pearl's?

"There, I've done it," she said proudly.

"Unwind it for me, then."

She had to come closer to do that. He held her waist to help her balance as she perched on the mattress. The long silk neckcloth was wrapped twice around his neck and she undid it carefully, as if he were made of glass. He wasn't fragile. In fact, he was a solid mass of inappropriate impulses.

Be calm, Ed. She is just a woman.

She would not meet his gaze, though he stared at her. When she handed him the silk, he tossed it upon his coat then turned back to her.

"My buttons, now."

Why was he making her undress him? Did he enjoy her tentativeness, her fear? A little. At the same time, she must come to feel comfortable with his body. When politeness and basic decency compelled him to stop staring, he turned his eyes to her bedside table, now crowded with three formidable stacks of books.

"I see you've visited Somerton's library," he said.

"Yes, my lord. I mean, Edward." She bit her lip as she shyly corrected herself. "It seemed too cold to go exploring out of doors, so I asked the way to your library and found it quite impressive and quite...quite full of books."

"Not surprising, for a library."

"No." Her blushing smile almost undid him. Was she the world's slowest unbuttoner, or was she dawdling on purpose?

"I suppose you chose books about animals?"

"And gardening, and a few on human anatomy. Goodness, there is so much to know."

Her gaze dropped from his chest to the front of his trousers for a moment. She was taking so long to undress him, it was becoming unbearably titillating foreplay. His erection strained to be free of his clothes. She finished with his buttons and he shrugged off the shirt, then tried to be matter of fact in removing his trousers.

At last he stood before her, casually naked. He let her look at him with her shy, darting glances a moment or two before he moved toward her and bore her back on the bed.

"Oh goodness," she whispered as he took her in his arms. "Are we beginning?"

"More or less."

"All right."

She squirmed from beneath him and turned herself onto her hands and knees. Once arranged, she peered back at him. He stared at the marvel of his bride on all fours, her pert bottom barely obscured by her diaphanous nightgown.

"I'm not sure what to do now," she said, when he made no movement. "Do I need to be naked as well?"

"My dear Jane."

"Am I in the proper position?" She shifted her hips in a manner both tentative and seductive. "If you'll tell me what to do…"

Goodness, what to say to her? "Jane, this is not how things customarily begin."

"Isn't it?" She turned onto her side and regarded him as if he might be lying to her. "That is how animals do it. Horses and dogs and—"

"Even so, people do it differently from animals." He pulled her into his arms again. "Married people, anyway," he added beneath his breath.

She gazed up at him, frowning. "I've already mucked things up, haven't I?"

"Nonsense. Everything will be fine. Why don't we begin with a kiss?"

Before she could answer yes or no, he lowered his lips to hers and played gently over her mouth. He'd never bedded a virgin before. She was not an experienced kisser, but she learned quickly beneath his measured tutoring. A nibble there, a brush of tongue over teeth, and she was opening to him with a small sigh. One of her hands trailed up his arm, coming to rest upon his shoulder. He suspected the other was still twisted in the sheets.

"How was that?" he asked, touching his forehead to hers. "A good enough kiss to begin things?"

"Yes." The word was mere breath. "That felt very different from anything I've experienced before." He drew back and her gaze moved over his chest and shoulders. "My lord…Edward…" she began.

"Yes?"

"So far, everything feels very nice. *Very* nice."

She looked on him with admiration, and it warmed his lusts further that his trembling virgin felt at least a little earthly desire.

He drew a finger along her jaw's delicate contour. "I think you should know, sweet Jane, that marital lovemaking has nothing in common with what you see in the stable yards. It's much more refined, more measured and slow."

"Ah." She studied his lips. "Will there be more kissing?"

"Yes, and other pleasant things too. Lots of touching and exploring one another's bodies."

As he said this, he left off caressing her jaw and slid a hand beneath her now-rumpled nightgown. Not to grope her. No, he traced a line up her outer thigh instead, soft enough to relax her, but meandering enough to tease. He initiated another kiss, tasting her sweet, generous mouth. Yes, a quick learner indeed. She warmed to his advances, gasping against his mouth now and again as if he were working some sort of magic. There was no magic in it, just long, dissolute experience with women of the night.

And fantasies of Ophelia... Of wedding her, worshipping her, bedding her...

It was not fair to Jane to invite Ophelia into their wedding bed, but he'd pictured this wedding night with her, pictured taking her virginity with consummate skill, which was why he felt entirely prepared to bed Jane, even though she was the wrong woman.

No, he mustn't think so. Enough.

He caressed higher beneath her gown, whispering fingers over her hips and waist, and just beneath her breasts. He could feel her breathing quickly, like a frightened animal. No, an inquisitive animal. She shifted her legs beneath him, like a fawn—or a gnu—taking her first steps. He tugged up one of her knees so she was open beneath him, still clothed, but open to his hard shaft. With the women at Pearl's, he would have surged inside them now, to their coos of simpering delight.

Here, with Jane, he was careful and slow, allowing her to first feel his length along her thigh.

And she felt it... Her eyes met his in wary recognition. His naturalist had, after all, seen horses and dogs mate, and God knew what other kind of animals in her zoo-faring crusades.

Well, if she was still wary, she was not primed enough. He put a hand over her breast, letting her accustom to the warmth and weight of his palm before he brushed fingertips over her nipple. Her gaze went wide, and her hips twitched up against him.

"How beautiful you are," he said, moved by her trust, her courage. She didn't shy away from his caress the way he'd imagined a virgin might, but rather moved into it. "How are you feeling, Jane?"

"I... I don't know." She thought a moment, or tried to as he continued teasing her nipple. "I can feel your touch in so many places, all warm and tingling."

"That's an excellent sign."

He lay her back on the bed and fondled her other breast, dropping kisses along her shoulder and neck. Her shuddering breaths urged him on. He paused to stroke her clenched fist where she gripped the bed, and pry open her fingers.

"You can touch me too, sweeting. Our bodies belong to each other now."

Our bodies belong to each other now. That was a line he'd planned to use when he bedded Ophelia, but both of them were in his mind now, one a lost dream, and the other a very real woman reaching to touch his chest. Her fingers played over his own nipples as if to gauge his reciprocal reaction. A scientist at heart, this bride of his. His cock bucked against her as she traced the contours of his shoulders.

"I think you're so very handsome," she said softly. "Like nothing I ever imagined. All of this is...so..."

He didn't know a great deal about his wife yet, but he knew she chattered when she felt anxious. He took her speechlessness to mean she was not anxious. In fact, she seemed dreamily engaged, her wide amber-gold eyes taking him in as if she could not look enough.

He wished to look too. He drew up her nightgown's hem and helped push it over her head, then kissed her shyness away until her hips and legs moved as restlessly as before. Her combination of innocence and building energy was an intoxicating brew. Ophelia barely entered his thoughts now as he leaned to kiss one pebbled nipple and then the other. Jane gasped and clutched at his hair as he used his tongue to draw the pink tips to pointed peaks.

"Oh, that feels incredible." Her voice shook. "But I must make you feel good also, yes? I don't know what to do. What should I be doing?"

"Nothing, love. You're exciting me in your own way." He traced down the curve of her belly to her damp cleft, then stroked gently, caressing her gathering wetness. She gave a surprised moan as he found her hidden, sensitive pearl and swirled around it. "How does that feel?"

"Oh my. Edward. I can hardly say."

She might plead a loss of words, but her body responded in sinuous detail. She squirmed beneath his touch, seeming to ask for more at the same time she balled up her hands and pushed him away. He persisted, slipping a finger inside her tight sheath. She never stopped moving, never stopped squeezing upon the intrusion, and his excitement built alongside her own.

"I want to come inside you now, as a husband should." In truth, he wouldn't last much longer. Her unfettered reaction to his love play had him hard as granite, randy as a bull. "Are you ready for me, darling? You feel ready."

She blinked up at him, breathless. "Do I... Do I turn over now?"

He fought with himself. Was it appropriate to take his wife's virginity with her on all fours? She clearly still believed this was the "right" way. Was it really the wrong way? He adored taking a woman from behind.

"Yes, darling, turn over now. Let me help you."

He put her on her knees, his cock going even more rigid as she positioned herself. The sight of her previously spanked bottom, the very faint bruises, nearly broke his control. He grasped her hips and caressed her curving back, and told himself this was not so lurid. She was interested in natural things, after all. He slipped a hand beneath her to massage, with deft expertise, the hidden apex of her sex. Her hips jerked lustily in response. She was so sensitive! How was he to bear it?

He positioned himself at her entrance and gritted his teeth as he pressed in ever so slightly. He could not thrust himself home, right to the hilt. He was too large and she was too inexperienced. He would go slow, like a proper bridegroom.

Oh, God, she was so tight and slick.

* * * * *

Jane trembled on her knees, her arms weak with the pleasure his fingers wrought upon her. This was not how she'd expected lovemaking to go. She'd thought it would be fast, rough, and businesslike, but her husband had been right: people and animals mated differently.

There was nothing rough about the way he touched her, but it created such an outsized storm of pleasure inside her body that she could hardly control her limbs. She felt exposed but protected; endangered but eager. His thighs brushed the backs of her thighs and then he was pushing his shaft into her, just a little. It was the oddest feeling, to be entered by him that way.

"All right?" he asked. His voice sounded tight.

"Yes. This is... This is marvelous."

He pressed deeper, and the odd feeling of penetration became a stretch. He supported himself with one hand and her waist with the other, and though she wished he could touch her in that one particular spot without ever stopping, it felt good to be held by him too. He pressed in so much deeper than she thought possible, and she breathed and trembled and tried not to move because there seemed some peril in it.

"Is it supposed to feel this way?" she asked.

"What way?"

"It's very tight."

She twitched her hips experimentally and stopped when she heard his gasp. He gasped again when she squeezed upon his length, and she went perfectly still.

"Am I doing everything wrong?" she asked. "Maybe we should stop."

"No, just..." He'd gone out of breath. "Give me a moment without moving. It feels...feels very good to me right now. Too good."

"Oh. It feels very good to me too," she said, to reassure him. "I mean, not bad in any sense. Just very tight."

"That feeling will pass presently."

With those words, he slid his hand down to her sex and grasped her there, in a way that made her blood rush. When she sighed from the sensation, he touched that tingling button between her legs again and it felt, somehow, even better now that they were joined as one. While her body drew up tight with pleasure, he began to move, stroking into her from behind and then retreating.

She knew this as the mechanics of mating, but it was more than that in practice, so much more. As she moaned, he made a deeper, guttural sound and pressed into her harder. His force increased but his hands grew more tender, cradling her and stroking her shoulders and neck. She liked it. Oh, she loved it.

He settled into a delicious rhythm, and with each thrust forward, the blissful sensations grew. Half the time she braced her hands upon the bed, and half the time she reached back to touch him, to ground herself in this momentous act. They were joined together, husband and wife, and it was amazing. No wonder June smiled so giddily whenever she was around her new husband.

Jane moved her hips to meet Edward's thrusts, and he growled approvingly. It felt so good, so lovely as he fell into a rhythm. When she arched her back to feel more of his hard member within her, he grasped her shoulders and made an even harsher growling sound.

Something about that sound's wildness heated the place between her legs until the tingling in her middle grew nearly unbearable. When he teased her nipples, she squeezed on him hard and adored how that felt.

"Oh my goodness, oh my goodness," she whispered.

She felt Edward's cheek beside hers and turned her head. He kissed her, moving his fingers through her hair, and she felt something let go deep inside. As she surrendered her lips—and her body—to him, her middle contracted and then exploded in ecstatic waves. It was such a shock she almost bit him. He was so tightly fit within her that she could feel every inch of him as her body squeezed and quaked.

She wanted to make sense of this exquisite climax even as it peaked and faded too quickly. She wanted to know how, and why, and what for? She wanted to know how to make it happen again, even though she felt too tired and sated to reach for it at this particular moment.

He thrust inside her three or four more times, his arms wrapped about her shoulders to grasp her against him. She could feel his muscles working against her back, and then he, too, seemed to experience an acute paroxysm of pleasure. He gripped her, thrusting hard until his groan turned to a growl and then to a drawn-out sigh. Humans and animals might mate differently, but he sounded like an animal all the same. Perhaps... Oh, perhaps she had sounded like one too, groaning and sighing. She couldn't remember now and rested her head down on the bedclothes in exhausted relief.

It did not matter if she'd made unrefined noises. All of this was natural and good. She felt boneless as he guided her down to rest on her stomach, then he lay beside her, his legs warm and strong against hers. How contented she felt when he put an arm around her, holding her close.

"We are well and truly wed now," he said.

Jane turned her head into his shoulder. "Yes. It feels as if we are. I thought I would be shy when we had these sorts of relations, but there was no reason."

"You were not shy at all. It went exceedingly well for our first time."

"There will be more times, yes?"

He laughed and raised himself on one elbow so he could lean down and kiss her. By the time he finished his kisses, she was grasping his shoulders, not wishing them to end.

"There will certainly be more times, my enthusiastic minx," he said as they parted. "But we mustn't go too hard, too fast. You'll be tender from this first time."

She felt a flush rise in her cheeks. It wasn't polite for a woman to be lusty, was it? It was only that it had felt so good to couple with her husband. She reached out for him in a sudden burst of contentment and happiness.

"I'm so happy we're married. I'm so happy to be married to *you*, Edward. I feel lucky as can be."

She thought he might return the sentiment, and agree he also felt lucky, but instead he chuckled.

"Goodness, Jane, don't you know that ardor within marriage isn't the thing anymore?"

"What? What do you mean?"

"It's considered gauche for husbands and wives to fawn over one another. And love is out of the question, fully out of vogue."

She stared at him, shocked, and was relieved to realize he teased her. Or did he?

"Your parents are in love," she said. "And my sister and Lord Braxton. Even my parents have a loving marriage, for the most part."

"They're all hopelessly out of style, aren't they?" His fingers fluttered in hers. "At the most stylish balls, married couples don't dance together, stand together, or share more than a handful of words. They dance and flirt with others."

"I don't want to do that," she protested, then felt sheepish. Her voice had been too loud in the quiet room. "I mean, I want to dance with you at balls in the spring. I shall be so proud to have you for a husband."

He kissed her forehead, then soothed her with a finger traced along her cheek. "Dear Jane, we shall dance together if you wish. Don't be upset, love."

"I'm not." But she was, a little. She could not read his manner, his expressions. For all the pleasure they'd just shared, there was something he held back from her, some coolness or mystery. "Do you love me?" she asked. "I mean, now that we're married and bedded? You just called me 'love.'"

Again, she wished for an unambiguous answer, an enthusiastic *yes* that he loved her, out of politeness if nothing else, but instead she got hesitation and a lack of eye contact on his part.

"Well, we're still coming to know one another better, aren't we? We can't yet claim a deep, poetic love. But I care for you as my wife, as a proper husband should."

It was not a satisfying answer, especially as he rolled onto his back, away from her.

"You ought to sleep," he said, stretching his arms above him in the manner of a satisfied cat. "I should go to my own room so you can perform your toilette."

"You needn't go." His body was so beautiful, so strong and warm. She hated for him to leave. "Will you come back and sleep beside me?"

"Of course I will, if you wish."

She suspected he was only agreeing to it for her sake, but she was not strong enough to say, "that's all right, never mind." Tonight, at least, she needed him close, for their bodies had been so intimately joined. She wanted him to hold her in his powerful, comforting embrace, and when he returned, he did. She'd put her nightgown back on for modesty's sake, but he doffed his robe before he joined her in bed, so her wispy gown was the only thing between their bodies.

As they drowsed so close together, she wondered at the scent of him and the way his limbs felt against hers, at least until she got too tired to concentrate anymore. She wished to know him so well. How marvelous it felt to be falling in love with the man she'd married.

She finally drifted to sleep listening to his steady breath and thinking how infinitely lucky she was.

Chapter Eight: Lessons

Their winter honeymoon continued through cold and snow flurries, with their bed a warm, welcoming place for both of them. His wife's enthusiasm for coupling was a delightful feature in their accidental union.

Within a fortnight, Townsend had taught her to locate her body's particular sources of pleasure—as well as his. He taught her to lick and caress his cock, and to fellate him as she faced him on all fours. This enticing stance of hers was still the only position they used. He would teach her other positions...someday. For now, coupling with Jane was almost like coupling with the earthy courtesans at Pearl's.

He gave back in kind, of course, mouthing and kissing her eager pussy, and even fingering her bum. She cried so enthusiastically when he demonstrated his oral skills, he feared the servants would break into the room to be sure nothing was amiss. Nothing at all was amiss. If theirs could not be a true love marriage, it could at least be a nightly sharing of pleasures. He'd surely acquired the most sexually adventurous of all London's marriageable crop.

Things progressed in the daytime hours too. His wife requested some small pens be built near the edge of the woodlands, so her disabled rabbit might waddle around and enjoy some fresh country air. Not that Bouncer's life in the kitchens was miserable. The little rabbit was such a favorite his cage had been redesigned with an open top, so the staff might pet and coddle the bit of fluff each time they passed, and drop in tasty snacks.

Well, whatever kept his wife happy. He had been known to visit the kitchens himself to scratch the little fellow on his downy brown head, and to stare into the snake's enclosure. Through the glass side of the cage, one could see Mr. Cuddles draped over a branch, or basking beside his water bowl against the side nearest the fire.

It was not the marriage he'd pictured, but it was not a bad marriage.

And there could be children soon, based on her affinity for carnal activity. To be on the safe side, he'd consulted a friend who studied animals, to be sure her pets wouldn't pose a threat to his wife's health. As it turned out, the gentleman already knew of Lady Jane, the animal defender, because she *had* tried to sneak into a Zoological Society meeting dressed in a coat and trousers. His wife was notorious, and he could only be relieved their betrothal and marriage had happened over the winter months, and not during London's Season, when gossips' tongues wagged without cease.

By next Season, a few months hence, he hoped to have his new marchioness polished to a smoother, more deferent shine. He'd be a duke one day, and she his duchess, so a high, glossy polish would be a necessity.

He walked out from his private library onto the back balcony, only to see his future duchess striding, nay, practically jogging across the back garden toward the west woods. What was that he'd just been brooding over, about polish? Her hood fell down and she lifted it up again, for the wind was blowing cold this day. He was so engrossed in her hurried progress he didn't realize for some moments that she was alone.

She was not allowed into the woods alone. He'd told her so on three occasions now since he'd met with resistance and protests of "what if I don't go very far?" or "what if I only go a short while?" He'd been very explicit in his requirements for her safety if she wished free rein about Somerton's wild places. She was hurrying because she was disobeying.

He went to the stables for his horse and located the head groom.

"Tell me," he said. "Have you noticed the marchioness walking to the woods on her own, without anyone to escort her?"

"Sometimes, my lord," the man answered. "Sometimes she rides Snowbell around the meadows too. She said you didn't mind it if she wasn't planning to muck about too long."

"Did she say that?"

"Yes, my lord. I did tell her she oughtn't to go alone but she said something about quiet and the magic of the forest, and other things. The mistress is a lover of nature for sure."

"Indeed."

"Though it's coming to the cold winter season, and the days so short. If she were to get lost out there without a mount to bring her home again..."

The worry in the man's eyes reflected the very real danger of his wife roving around Somerton's extensive wild lands on her own.

"From now on, she is not to set foot outside the house or stables proper without an escort. Make sure all the stablemen know it." His voice sounded tight, perhaps from irritation, perhaps from fear. If she got lost, she could freeze to death in this weather. It was an unusually bitter winter, for God's sake.

"Yes, my lord," said his head groom. "I'll tell everyone so."

"And if my wife says otherwise, you are to fetch me and let me handle things."

"Yes, my lord."

It was beginning to dawn on the man that Lady Townsend might be in trouble. Another sober-faced groom handed him his stallion's reins, and Townsend swung astride it to go fetch his errant wife. Fortunately, he knew exactly which direction she'd gone.

* * * * *

Jane loved Somerton's woods at midday. It wasn't only because her husband spent midday in his study, making it easy to steal off alone, without clumsy footmen or stable boys trailing her. No, it was because the winter's light was at its zenith then, and a variety of animals could be depended upon to show their faces, to soak up what light and life they could. Even in rain they'd emerge, although one had to listen harder to hear them.

But today, oh, it was a glorious winter day, crisp and clear as anything, without a cloud in the broad, blue sky. She bundled her cloak around her and took a path that eventually meandered to a pond bordered with hedges. She always saw deer when she took this walk, and worried for them in the cold and wind, although they didn't seem touched by it. She wished she could befriend the creatures so the quick-eyed does would let her pet their young ones, but as a principled naturalist she understood she mustn't interfere in nature, only observe it.

Well, except in cases of lame rabbits and dying snakes, she thought ruefully. She could not seem to abandon animals in need.

Still, she would try not to grow her wildlife menagerie, lest she set her husband against her. She wanted to please him, wanted him to love her in truth, and not tease and look away whenever she spoke of loving him. Perhaps all men behaved that way?

She hadn't the experience to know, but her heart wanted a true-love marriage now that she'd been rescued from the bleak abyss of spinsterhood. She wanted affection and kisses, and deep, soulful connection. She wanted what her sister had, a doting husband whose gaze followed her each time she left his side…

She heard a rustling in the underbrush and watched a gray squirrel plunge out, as if caught up in an adventure. The animal noticed her and tore away, and she wished him good nut-hunting. A pair of woodlarks could be heard a bit farther off, their sweet calls drifting among the bare trees. She'd not yet seen a fox; it was likely Lord Townsend's hunting dogs kept them some distance from the house, but she hoped to run across one of the curious creatures one day. Now and again she'd see them at home, or more often hear them as they screamed during mating season for their mates.

She was nearly to the pond when she heard an entirely different sound, something she'd not heard before. Someone was approaching on a horse. She put back her hood to hear from whence they came, her heart beating fast. Who was it? If it was a poacher or trespasser, she was out here alone with nowhere to hide amidst the bare trees and bright winter sun.

She turned in trepidation, then sighed in relief. It was only Lord Townsend atop his stallion. But...shouldn't he have been in his study at this hour? Her relief turned right back into trepidation as he approached her. He did not look happy. His expression was not that of a doting husband.

"Hello," she called, smiling and waving, hoping for the best.

He stopped a few yards away. "Hello, Jane." Then he made a great show of looking about for some other person, though it was quite clear she'd come out alone, against his wishes. "Where is your escort? The person supposed to accompany you in case you become lost or hurt?"

"Well, I... I do not have one today," she said. Out of fear of his dark frowning, she told a lie. "No one was able to come with me, so just this once I thought... I thought I would be very careful and not...stray from the path."

"Just this once, you say?"

Oh no. She should not have lied. He knew she'd lied and now he was even angrier. "I spoke to the head groom and he tells me you've gone exploring the woods alone several times now. That you told him I said it was all right to do so."

"Well, I..." She cast about for excuses, anything to help her case. "I did not want to inconvenience your servants, Edward. They are always so hard at work. And as you can see, I stick to the more established paths." She gestured about. "So it's not like I'm exploring the *woods* alone, as you forbid me to do."

"Are you telling me that as long as you're not off the path, then you're not in the woods?"

"I *am* in the woods, but I am safe. How could one get lost following a path?"

He was getting ready to deliver a sound lecture. She definitely deserved it.

"Do you know how many paths there are in these woods, Jane?" he said, his amber eyes snapping. "Or the vast extent of Somerton's property? You could walk for miles in circles, only to get farther and farther from the house. Why am I explaining this to you again? You already know it."

She hung her head at his scolding. Yes, she knew it.

"You know also that these woods are thick and wild, and full of animals, some of which might be dangerous if provoked. Animals aside, you might twist your ankle on a root or be felled by a plummeting branch, and who would know if you were out here on your own? How would we find you if you were too injured to cry for help?"

"Perhaps the dogs..." she began weakly.

"Curse the dogs."

She fell silent. He faced her with his hands braced on his hips.

"Explain yourself," he demanded. "Explain why you believed you might disregard my very reasonable request that you not explore on your own."

"At home, I was accustomed to exploring alone."

"Your father's gardens in Reading are neither as extensive nor as wild as Somerton's forests."

"That is true, but I..."

She lost her voice at his worsening scowl. It was true that it was not precisely safe to plunge into wild woods without an escort. She might be injured and need help, for all her care to step cautiously.

"I am so sorry," she said, ready to admit defeat. "It's true I have disobeyed your wishes, and I should not have, but I've always preferred to walk about alone. When your men come with me, they're noisy and clumsy without meaning to be. A group of people creates too much disturbance and I've no chance to observe any animals."

"Then tell them to be quieter. You're mistress of this manor, same as I'm the master."

"I could not scold your servants, sir," she said, horrified. "I'm too shy."

"You're hardly shy. If you can protest animal treatment outside the Exeter Exchange, you can tell a footman to step more lightly."

By now all the animals had fled this area, due to her husband's strident voice. She wished she could flee as well. He was very unhappy with her, for good cause.

"I'm sorry," she said again. "I am very, very sorry. I didn't think..."

"You didn't think I'd find out? Does that make it all right?"

She bowed her head. "No, my lord."

He made a frustrated sound at her show of penitence. "Back to 'my lording' me now that you're in trouble. Your apologies are very pretty, but they are not enough."

She watched with her heart in her throat as he stepped to a nearby ash tree and snapped off a slender branch. "If you will not listen to my words," he said, "perhaps this bit of nature applied to your backside will teach you the error of your ways."

Jane opened her mouth to plead, to beg him to reconsider punishing her. To promise that this time, next time, every time after now she would obey and take someone with her on her adventures, but she knew it would do her no good. Instead, she stared at the switch in his hand and thought how awful it was going to feel.

"Come along," he said. "I'll ride you back."

He lifted her onto his horse, and she struggled to arrange her skirt and cloak over her knees as he seated himself behind her. His arms came around her to hold her safe. She would have enjoyed the protected feeling of his embrace if he didn't also have the switch in one hand, the slender punishment implement rising right before her face.

I don't want this. It's going to hurt. But she deserved it. How foolish she'd been to bend the rules, knowing what a stickler for obedience her husband was. Other husbands might only rail and rant for a moment and let her off with a warning to do better, but Edward was not that type.

She sat very straight in the saddle as they rode back through the woods toward the manor house, right into the stables, where he had her hold the switch while he tended to his stallion. All the stable men saw her, though they pretended not to. She flushed a thousand shades of red and didn't know where to look as he marched her back through the courtyard and into the main door of the house. At the door, he took the switch back from her sweating palm.

"Up to your bedroom," he said, pointing to the stairs.

She climbed with heavy footfalls, fighting tears. He came behind her, and she didn't have to turn around to know he still wore his dark frown.

Why had she been so stupid? Why?

When she opened the door to her rooms, Matilda took one look at them and made herself scarce. Edward led her through to her bedroom and shut the door behind him. She faced him as he removed his riding coat.

"Take off your cloak, Jane," he ordered.

She did so, slowly and disconsolately. Maybe if she looked sorry enough, her husband would relent.

He did not relent. He guided her toward the bed and tapped the top of her footboard with the switch. "These beds, yours and mine, are very meaningful to our marriage. They're the place we lie together, the place we'll make children. They're also the place where you'll pay your toll for poor behavior. Both my footboard and yours are padded on top so you might be punished bending over it when necessary. Do you believe this is one of those times?"

"I... Well..." She stared at the padded, upholstered top. She'd thought it was merely a decorative choice, but no, it was meant for punishment, for spanking or worse. Her very bed—and his—was designed for corporal punishment. "I think I did not behave well."

"You disobeyed me. You were dishonest. This is very like your previous punishment when you did not warn me about the nature of your pets."

It was true. She thought she could get away with things. Her parents had always been lenient with her.

"I'm so sorry. It's a very bad habit of mine, isn't it? I feel terrible."

"Furthermore, you've endangered yourself again, just like last time, by ignoring my directions. I'm afraid you must receive a more severe punishment this time, and each successive time you make the same error. You understand why?"

"Yes, my lord."

She was trying very hard not to cry, but she felt so helpless. So ashamed.

"I'm sorry," she said again. "Please, I will do better. I'll try very hard to be perfect from now on."

"Of course you will, but you must also take your punishment. Come, kneel here."

He helped her onto the small platform, which was not meant as a step stool at all. Once she knelt upon it, she was the perfect height to bend forward over the padded footboard. But oh, she couldn't do it. She couldn't bear to be spanked with the fresh switch. She turned about, pleading one last time. "Please, I'm still learning. I wish to be a good wife."

"I know you do." He turned her around, even though she resisted with all her power. He was so much stronger than her. He put a hand upon her back and pressed her forward until her chest rested upon the bed. She reached back with her hands, but they were promptly captured and set on the bed as well.

"Keep them there," he said. "If you'll take your switching without a fuss, it will be quickly over. If you fight it, it will take considerably longer."

She bunched her fingers into fists. This was not the way she wished to spend time with her husband in the bedroom. He had made love to her attentively, skillfully, so many times in this very bed, teaching her the depths of pleasure she might achieve. It made this awful punishment seem that much worse.

He drew up her skirts and petticoats to bare her bottom, and the first sob caught in her throat. The padded footboard was comfortable on her hips, but she was not to feel *comfortable* for very long. She heard the switch whistling through the air before she felt the connection. *Oww.* Dear God. The slender piece of wood delivered a burn across her backside. She shrieked and tensed, kicking up her legs.

"No fidgeting," he ordered. "Kneel properly and take your punishment. Remember, this is your own fault."

Before she'd recovered from the first blow, the second landed and her hands flew back to shield herself. She couldn't help it. She lifted her head to gaze back at him in entreaty, but he was in strict-discipline mode and was not moved. He only collected her hands and held them at the small of her back, just as when he'd spanked her the first time. With his force thus engaged, she could move nowhere, and had to endure a volley of sizzling hot blows to her bottom and the backs of her thighs with hardly a break in between them.

She wailed. She cried. It was all she could do now that he practically held her down. Her bottom grew so hot and throbby it felt like a raging fire. After twenty or so good licks, he finally left off. The only sound in the resulting silence was her uncontrolled sobbing. He did not release her hands.

"You will receive five more," he said. "I want you to count them aloud, and between each one, I want you to remember the reasons you're being punished, and what you will do differently from here on out. Do you understand?"

"Yes, my lord."

The following stroke was hard and terrible, but she'd assumed these last five were to be the worst ones. She barely remembered to count. "One!"

She obediently thought about what she'd done and what she must do differently. She must listen to his directions. She must not follow her own whims.

"Oww! Two!"

Oh, she was so sorry she'd snuck around and disobeyed him.

"Three!"

It hurt so badly. She tried to pull her hands from his, if only to rub away some of the stinging. He would not let her go.

"Four!"

She hated this side of her husband. She hated that he could hurt her so, even in the name of discipline. It was not loving at all.

"Five! Ow, *ow...*"

She dissolved into hopeless tears as the last stroke landed, harder than any of the others. She felt chastised indeed at this point. Her bottom ached, throbbing with the sensation of being on fire. As soon as he released her hands, she reached back to cover her hot cheeks. At once, her hands were drawn away and deposited back on the bed with a tsk.

"Stay just as you are," he said. "No rubbing away the pain this time. Now, I'm going to get a warm cloth to wash you, since I used a 'wild' switch. Don't move until I return."

She wanted to rub away the sting so badly, but she knew she must obey him or get in more trouble. The only movement she did was to press her face into the bed so some of her tears could be dried in the bedsheets. Cool air blew against her exposed bottom, reminding her of her nakedness and making each stinging welt hurt even more.

When he came back, he did too thorough a job sponging her with the cloth, going over each welt on her cheeks and thighs. Now she wasn't only hurt; she was embarrassed. Once finished, he replaced her skirts and assisted her down from his rack of torture, the very rack she'd been sleeping on all this time.

"Come sit with me now," he said.

She wiped her face with her hands and brushed back the wisps of hair that had escaped her day's coiffure. "I'm not sure I'll be able to sit," she said sullenly.

He returned a look that told her he would certainly repeat the spanking she'd just received if she spoke to him in a poor tone. Then he went to the window. "Stand with me then."

She joined him, feeling her petticoat brush her sensitive backside with every step. They both looked out at the surrounding woods she'd been punished for exploring. Well, not exploring. Exploring *alone*.

"Repeat after me," he said. "*Mrs. Loring, I would like to go out to the woods.*"

She stifled a pout. "Mrs. Loring, I would like to go out to the woods."

"There, you see." He turned to her so his stern, amber-gold gaze bore into hers. "That is all you need to do. She will arrange for the rest, and whomever she sends to accompany you, you may tell them to walk as soundlessly as possible so as not to scare the animals. Do we need to practice that, too?"

"No." She sighed. "I have learned my lesson."

"I'm glad to hear that. I'm sorry it was such a painful one."

Jane suspected he was not sorry at all. He was too adept at punishment to dislike it. As she stood beside him, he brushed his hand over the back of her skirts, right across her tender arse cheeks, as if basking in his craft. Oh yes, he enjoyed discipline. She must work harder to ensure he had less opportunities to mete it out.

"Come closer, Jane," he said. "Let me hold you and make things better."

He would not let her pull away, and in truth, she didn't want to pull away when he offered his embrace. He held her close, stroking a hand up her arm as she rested her cheek upon his chest. She wished she could go to bed and let the day end, and even as she thought it, she knew she wanted to go to bed the way she had the past few weeks now...with him. How was that possible, after what he'd just done to her? She supposed it was the smell of him, the feel of his body...she'd come to know them so well.

"There now."

He drew a handkerchief from his pocket and dabbed at her cheeks, which was when she realized she was crying again. She looked up from her place against his chest and received a sympathetic smile in return. "There, sweet girl," he murmured, drying her tears as even more flowed. "Everything will be all right."

He stroked her hair while she cried into his shirt. It was not from the pain. Her bottom still throbbed, but that was not it. She cried because even now, even after what he'd done to her, she was in love with her husband and addicted to his touch. She'd grown dependent on his strength and his companionship, and the encompassing way he held her even when she was in disgrace.

When her deep sobbing lessened to milder crying, he drew back and tilted up her chin. "Would you like to come to my study until dinner, Jane? Curl up on the divan and read a book while I finish my correspondence?"

"Yes," she said with a sniffle. "I would like that."

"Then we'll know you're keeping out of trouble, won't we?"

"Perhaps," she said, still a little sullen.

He smiled and leaned to kiss her, teasing her lips until she couldn't help but respond.

"Choose a book from that pile upon your nightstand," he said when they parted, "and I'll tell Mrs. Loring to bring us some tea."

Chapter Nine: Loving and Wanting

They spent the rest of that afternoon in his study, but Townsend wasn't able to get his usual amount of work done. His concentration wavered every time Jane shifted or sighed, or stole a look at him when she didn't think he was watching.

He stole glances at her too. What a puzzle his wife was. She could be such an agreeable, sweet woman, and then behave stubbornly to her detriment. He'd barely held his temper as he cut a switch, but once he had it, he calmed and set his face to teaching her a necessary lesson. He'd been hard on her, but a second offense warranted stricter punishment. With her safety at stake...

In time he finished his letters but continued to scribble aimlessly on a discarded sheet of paper. He was enjoying this domestic afternoon together as the cold winds blew outside and didn't wish it to end. When his wife forgot her sore bottom and lost herself in concentration, he discovered that her lips pursed and her forehead wrinkled in a charming way. Now and again she bit her lip, that sweet, uncertain mannerism. He found himself sketching her expressions in clumsy lines, but they changed so quickly it was impossible to catch them before they were gone. He gave up and smudged out the drawings, and tossed the scribbled page in the bin.

"What are you reading, Jane?" he asked, setting aside his pen.

"A book of poetry." She showed him the cover.

"Poetry about nature?"

"No, poetry about love."

He could see the blush rise in her cheeks all the way across the room. Jane and her affinity for love.

He stood and crossed to her, and sat next to her on the divan. "It's a bit late to walk out to the woods, but perhaps we can stop by the kitchen before dinner to visit your pets."

"Would you like to?" she asked in surprise.

"Yes, I would. I've been missing the charming Mr. Cuddles."

This jest made her smile. All through dinner, in fact, he tried hard to improve her mood so she'd be willing to warm his bed that night. She might find it perverse, but when he punished her, he found himself wanting her even more than usual. If she allowed him, he'd show her there were much more exciting things in life than love poetry.

When dinner ended, they retired to their separate bedrooms as usual to undress, bathe, and prepare for bed. After an adequate amount of time had passed, and he heard Matilda leave for the servants' quarters, he stepped across the hall to see how his presence might be received. Her sitting room was dark and empty, so he tapped at her bedroom door. The slight pressure nudged it open, revealing his wife at the window with her profile bathed in moonlight. When she turned, the light bathed her whole face and washed her pale orange hair to silver. Her expression was neither welcoming nor damning, but something in between.

"May I come in?" he asked. "You can refuse me if you'd rather."

"But you're my husband."

"Still. May I come in?"

She nodded, crossing toward the turned-down bed. He'd developed a love for tumbling his enthusiastic wife onto the sheets and she seemed prepared for him to do it, but tonight he decided he would move more slowly. He still wasn't entirely sure she wanted him here—just hours ago, he'd striped her bottom with a switch. Now, he wanted to teach her a different sort of lesson, but not if she was ambivalent to his presence, his touch. He stood near her beside the bed and leaned down to meet her gaze.

"You look pretty by moonlight," he said. "What were you looking at?"

"The trees against the sky. Would you like to see?"

They moved back to the window together and she pointed out the line of bare, twisted trees silhouetted in black against the moonlit clouds. It was a trick of perspective and Somerton's rolling landscape; all of nature appeared spookily needful, as if the bare branches groped for the sky.

"I didn't know if you would come," she said, turning to him in the silence. "I didn't know if you were still angry with me."

"I was never angry." He took her face between his fingers, tracing along her chin. "I was concerned for your wellbeing and safety."

"I'm still feeling sorry." She reached back to furtively rub her bottom.

"And sore, I warrant." He brushed aside her loose, soft locks and tilted her head up, and kissed her with a questing gentleness. *You see, I can be as tender as I am strict.* She responded with a sigh of pleasure, or perhaps relief. Did she imagine any breach of behavior would keep him from her bed more than a few hours? When she was such a delectable, enthusiastic partner?

Tonight, he would teach his delectable partner that couples could make love while gazing into each other's eyes.

He pulled away to gaze at her now. "Before we know it, the trees will be sprouting leaves, and the air will grow warmer." *And we'll return to London, and everyone will see us together, and I'll have to see Ophelia on Wescott's arm.* He must have frowned because she looked at him questioningly.

"Don't you like spring?" she asked.

"I adore spring, just as I adore kissing you."

He leaned to do it again, nibbling her lower lip when she hesitated. His fingers strayed from her hair to her delicate shoulders, to the curving outline of her breasts. She drew in a breath as he caressed her nipples through her nightgown. So many lovely nightgowns she had, each more finely woven than the last, so all of them were see-through. Well, at least by moonlight.

"Shall we have candles?" she asked.

"Yes, lots of them tonight."

They lit them together, a platterful atop her chest of drawers and a four-armed candelabra beside the bed. That finished, she turned to him with the usual intoxicating combination of shyness and lust. He was torn between placing her on her knees to suck his cock and turning her over his lap to inspect the marks from her switching. Well, he was already too strongly aroused so he opted for the latter. She whined softly when he pulled her across his lap and drew her nightgown up, but he silenced her with a quiet, "Let me look."

She obeyed and lay still, and let him trace his fingers across her shapely, striped arse. Such elegant stripes. She probably didn't think so, but he'd done a good job with her. Lots of soreness, but no blood or broken skin. She might complain at his discipline, but he knew what he was about.

"That's a good girl," he said when he'd looked his fill. He righted her and saw relief in her features. "Did you think I'd spank you again? For what cause?"

She gave him a dire look. "For the pleasure of it."

"Hmm." He pretended to consider this. "I have not spanked you for merely pleasurable reasons yet, but I suppose I might some time in our future. Would you enjoy that?"

She shook her head so fast it made him laugh.

"What if I could make you enjoy it?" He shrugged off his robe and helped her shimmy from her nightgown. "It seems a missed opportunity not to, with your bottom so often in the air."

From habit, she turned onto her knees, but he stopped her—after a moment's admiration—and rearranged her so she lay beneath him, her head upon her pillows. She reached for him trustingly as he dipped to kiss her. While he feasted on her lips, she caressed his shoulders and upper back and slid her fingers into his hair, so goosebumps rose along his skin. His mouth pushed against hers, forcing it open. Their tongues warred for a moment; his cock throbbed against her front as her hips bucked against him.

"Do you want me?" he whispered.

"Yes. Please. Very much."

She started again to take to her knees, but he stopped her. "Let's try a different way tonight, darling," he said. "Facing one another."

"Oh." She looked surprised, then considering. "How interesting. I suppose that is possible."

He hid a smile. "Yes, it's possible. I'll show you."

She stared at him as he caressed her thighs and drew them apart. His well-trained coquette showed no bashfulness as he teased his fingers through her moisture, finding her favorite button. In fact, she opened her legs wider, moving her hips to accommodate his touch. He stroked, pressed, petted until she clutched the sheets in anticipation, but he wouldn't let her turn from him onto all fours. He'd let her go on that way long enough. Let her see that mating like animals in rut was not the only option, as much as they both enjoyed it.

When he'd driven her to an appropriate frenzy, he slid his hands beneath her to grasp her bottom. She let out a little hiss as his fingers slid over her welts, but he hushed her and pulled her hips flush against his, teaching her a new way of connection. She was so hot, always so ready. He palmed his cock and began to push inside her, half atop her, half showing her how they were to join. *You see how I'll take you now, little Jane. I'll fit perfectly inside you this way as well.*

Her nervousness transformed to a croon of delight. He was still large inside her, but he fancied that she liked it. He began to move, holding her close as she clutched at his chest, his neck and shoulders. It felt different to take her this way, felt much more intimate.

"Do you like that?" he asked, stopping deep inside her.

"I love it. Please, more…"

She moved her hips to urge him to action again, but he enjoyed her squirming. She had no compunction about asking for pleasure which made her a very satisfying bedmate.

"Move with me," he said, his voice soothing though his cock felt in a frenzy. "Let me lead you."

She acquiesced and he rewarded her by grinding against her hips in a swirling motion that stimulated her hidden pearl. She surged toward him, gasping. He held her as she clung to him, and whispered enticements encouraging her to take him deep, to take him all the way. Soon he had her caught up in a steady rhythm punctuated by her sweet panting.

"Yes, yes, yes," she said as he filled her with his throbbing cock.

"Yes, move your hips for me, take all of me."

"This feels different. It feels so different and wonderful."

He silenced her chattering with a kiss and covered her with his body, bearing her down into the covers. He trapped her beneath him with her head between his elbows and fucked her with abandon. As she neared her crisis, she writhed back and forth making such satisfied noises, it was all he could do to hold back his own climax. Her hair tumbled over her face as she lost herself in pleasure. Her lips parted for his kisses then opened wide to feed him her passions, and still he drove in, drove deeper, drove faster. When she found her release, she nearly bit him but he didn't mind it, and only kissed her harder. Her walls clamped upon him as she let out a long and shuddering groan. No matter how tenderly and politely he began, he always ended with wild, abandoned thrusts, but when she made such noises, how could it be helped?

He emptied himself inside her, arching over her to watch her watching him. She found him handsome, he knew. She found him sexy. He used this leverage to woo her, and she used her enthusiasm to delight him.

And then...

Then afterward she became shy and coy, and avoided his gaze as if she was the world's most innocent wife. Silly thing. When she avoided his gaze, he turned her face back and kissed her, a soft, lingering kiss as they both drifted in satisfaction. She squeezed around his cock, the aftershocks of a passionate joining. Finally, when he broke the kiss, she smiled at him.

"That *was* an entirely different way to couple," she said. "I could watch you the whole time."

"And did you?"

She shook her head. "Not the whole time. Some of the time it felt too good for me to look at anything."

He sighed and sank to the bed beside her. "My dear, you say the best things." For a while, he watched her thinking, then she turned to him, eyes narrowed in question. "How many ways are there to do this? Are there more than the two we've tried?"

"Yes," he said, amused. "There are all sorts of positions."

"*Positions.* Hmm."

She thought some more, doubtless trying to picture them. What a naughty mind.

"What is your favorite position?" she asked after a moment.

"Once we've tried them all, I'll let you hazard a guess."

Why couldn't he stop touching her hair? It was so soft. Her eyes were soft too, and growing sleepy in the candlelight. What was his favorite position? He'd enjoyed making love to her tonight in the more traditional position. To his shame, he sometimes thought about Ophelia when he took Jane from behind, but the temptation wasn't there when they were face to face. He ought to have made love to her this way before now.

"Are you tired, darling?" he asked. "Should I let you be?"

"I am a bit tired. It's been a long day." A hint of recrimination shadowed her features, quickly gone. She was too contented now to hold a grudge.

"Go prepare for bed, then," he said. "I'll put out the candles so both of us can get some sleep."

* * * * *

Jane rose in the morning feeling replete with satisfaction, and sore and disgruntled at the same time. Her husband had left her bed early to ride the boundaries of his property, as was his habit. She was the one left with the memories of his consummate kisses. He'd held her so close the night before, and practically made her cry with pleasure. When she thought she must know everything about lovemaking, he always managed to teach her something new that astonished and delighted her. She could not despise him even though her bottom still ached from his switching. She could only melt for him again and again.

Why was this emotional disparity so difficult for her? Perhaps because she still questioned whether he loved her. Sometimes she imagined he saw her as a toy in the bedroom and a project out of it, a project to mold and develop into his image of a proper lady, an improved lady. She glanced over at the padded portion of her footboard and shuddered, then threw down the counterpane so it would be covered. Even hidden from view, she knew it was there, a constant reminder of the perils of misbehavior.

When she finally rose and washed, she saw that her courses had come upon her in the night, and she was glad, for it would give her an excuse to fend him off for a handful of days. She needed time to sort out her feelings without Edward continually seducing her and making her crave him. She dreamed of him with regularity, of his large, beautiful amber eyes and the deep black hair framing his face. She loved the feel of his hair beneath her fingers. And when he kissed her...

She turned in her dressing room and regarded her striped backside in the mirror. She did not like switches. Still, his punishments were effective, for she knew she would never, ever venture out without an escort again. She hated that his despised techniques worked on her. Perhaps he *would* mold her into a perfect lady and wife.

Perhaps then he'd profess the abiding love she craved.

If anyone knew about marital love, it would be June. Lord Braxton had been so happy standing at the altar with her, he'd practically cried. After she ate her breakfast, Jane returned to her sitting room and took up pen and paper to write to her older sister.

Dearest June,

How are you? I'm doing well here at Somerton. To answer your question, I have found a great many interesting places to observe nature.

Here she paused and cringed inwardly, remembering how this had so recently earned her a punishment.

Townsend is very encouraging that I should do what I like during our days in the country, as long as I am careful and take someone along with me whenever I go exploring. When I stay inside, there is a great deal to do. He has a beautiful, grand library and also a vast greenhouse I'm allowed to poke about in.

Bouncer and Mr. Cuddles are both well. They stay in the kitchens where the air is warmer and less dry than the stables. I take them both outside on mild days. Bouncer enjoys nibbling grass in his enclosure and Mr. Cuddles is content to curl up on my arm or shoulder beneath my cloak. He sticks his head out to see the sun and darts his tongue out to sniff the air! When I walk about with him and the servants see me, they stare and goggle and pretend to swoon, but in truth I think they like him as much as I do. Even Townsend has visited the kitchens to reach into his box and stroke his head, which makes Bouncer jealous.

To answer your other question, yes, Townsend has been a kind husband on the whole. He is rather picky about rules being followed, but they are fair rules, so I try not to mind. He is not like your Lord Braxton, hanging upon my every word and bowing at my feet. (I know I'm exaggerating, don't scold me for it.) But really, June, I don't know if Townsend loves me just yet. That is the only thing.

She stopped a moment as tears blurred her eyes. She blinked them away, for she'd meant to be businesslike, like her husband at his letters.

I wonder if it is natural for new husbands to be a bit stand-offish, she continued. *Especially considering we barely knew one another before we wed. Do you have any sisterly advice on winning a husband's heart? I do promise I am happy and well, just a little uncertain if Townsend is as happy as me, but maybe that is normal.*

I hope you will reply soon, and that you and Braxton are enjoying your first winter together.

All my love,

Jane

Within a week's time, she received June's reply, delivered on paper that still held the scent of her sister's favorite perfume.

Dearest Jane,

I'm glad to hear all is (mostly) well at Somerton. Braxton and I are weathering this first winter with plenty of cloaks and blankets and fond embraces. Does Townsend embrace you often? If not, you must entreat him to do so. A wife needs her warmth.

I think you mustn't worry about him loving you, darling. No one could know you and not love you. He may be slow to express it, as men in general are doltish in the area of feelings, but his regard can only grow with each day he spends in your company. If he will pet your snake, then he will come to love you! One step at a time.

My advice is to smile often, enjoy the freedom he grants you, and for goodness sake, brush your hair when you come in from the windy outdoors. Jests aside, if he is kind to you, that is an excellent basis for a marriage. Try not to compare yourself to Braxie and me, for we'd known one another a long time before we wed, and a great deal of affection already existed between us. In time you and Townsend will feel this same affection within your hearts, I am sure of it.

I wish the very best for your marriage and if you need any more sisterly advice, you need only write me the specifics. Keep me posted as well on the adventures of Bouncer and Mr. Cuddles, the oddest pet duo in all of history. Hugs and love to you and your dashing Townsend.

Your loving sister,
June

Alas, Jane's mind was no clearer by the time her flux passed and her husband resumed his nightly visits. In fact, the pause necessitated by her courses made their passions flame even higher, so she felt even more caught up in a cycle of need and desire. She told herself not to worry, that Edward would not leave her or reject her at this point, but with her history of rejection the fear managed to crop up at the most inopportune times. There were occasions he was very affectionate, but other occasions where he withdrew from her company and stared off into the distance, as if reconsidering every decision in his life.

It was early in their marriage, she reminded herself. *You must give him time to know you.* But she'd feel much more at ease when, some blessed day, she saw her own love reflected back in his eyes.

Chapter Ten: Waltzing

Their first official callers were her husband's parents, the Duke and Duchess of Lockridge. After announcing their intention to visit, they arrived on the sixth of March amid a spate of pleasant weather and warmer days.

Jane had been nervous about hosting such an august couple, but they put her at ease at once, insisting she call them "Mother" and "Father" rather than "Your Grace." They were wonderfully gracious, offering newlywed gifts to her and Edward: a set of gold platters engraved with their initials, a handsomely embossed Bible, and two sets of bed linens embroidered by the duchess herself.

She'd barely retained a memory of Townsend's parents from the wedding, she'd been so nervous that day. Now that they were guests in their home, she had an opportunity to know them better and found them very amiable.

The duke was as tall as Townsend and looked very much like him, with the same dark hair, although the duke's was peppered with a bit of gray. The two men moved in the same assured way and, to Jane's amusement, had the same ability to look utterly, haughtily lofty with the arch of a mere brow. Even so, he was a kind man who seemed to go out of his way to put her at ease.

The duchess was a very sweet, soft-spoken woman with pale coloring and thick golden hair. Edward had told her his mother's given name, Aurelia, came from the Latin word for gold, and Jane thought it very appropriate, for the woman glowed with contented happiness.

Her burgeoning friendship with her in-laws was cemented when His Grace rubbed his hands together and asked if they might meet Mr. Cuddles. "Oh yes, my son has written about your unusual pets," he said, laughing as Edward feigned exasperation.

"I believe my wife will be famous for her snake handling. Or infamous."

"Come now. Apparently, the snake in question would have been dead without her interference. May we see it?"

The head cook nearly panicked to see the four of them crowding into the bustling kitchen, but soon was extolling the virtues of "cute little Bouncer" and the royal python that disposed of a mouse or rat with regularity every other week.

"Will he try to dispose of my hand if I put it in the cage?" asked the duke.

"Oh no," she said. "In fact, he enjoys being handled, if you would like to pet him?"

The duke said he would very much like to, so she lifted Mr. Cuddles from his enclosure and showed the duke and duchess how he liked to be petted and stroked along his back. The duke asked many questions, while the duchess looked on, keeping a certain distance. She apologized that she did not feel comfortable handling the snake, though Jane took pains to tell her she didn't mind. She did finally agree, at her husband's urging, to give Mr. Cuddles a soft pat upon his light-colored scales.

"Do you remember when you bought me that grasshopper, Hunter?" she asked the duke. "It had a special cage and everything."

"A *habitat*," the duke specified. "A fancy enclosure of mesh and wood."

"Yes, a habitat." The duchess smiled in the affectionate way of long married couples. Jane was so jealous of that smile between them, she forgot to ask the obvious follow-up question. Edward asked it instead.

"Father bought you a *grasshopper*?" Edward laughed. "Why on earth would he do that?"

"It was the first real gift he got me. I thought he'd lost his mind."

"It was because I used to call you grasshopper. You didn't like it much, either." He grinned at his wife. "How irritated you used to get."

The duchess fluttered her lashes, as if too proper to launch a retort, but her quick glance at Jane communicated the vexation of wives everywhere: *what are we to do with these husbands?*

"What did you name your pet grasshopper?" Jane asked.

His parents looked at each other and laughed. "It didn't last long enough for a name, did it?" said the duke.

Jane's face clouded. "Oh no. It died?"

"Nothing like that," said the duchess, taking her hand to console her. "In fact, he promptly escaped his habitat and hopped about our bedroom, chirping now and again to taunt us. We decided it would be better to set him free."

"That would have been better for a grasshopper," said Jane.

"We set him free there in the gardens," said the duke, gesturing out the kitchen's open door. "Near the forest behind the house. I imagine his or her descendants are still hopping about Somerton's glades."

Jane put her hands to her face in wonder, while Edward rolled his eyes.

"If you see a grasshopper on your explorations, dear wife," he told her, "please pass along my mother and father's regards."

"I will." She giggled, returning Mr. Cuddles to his cage.

Next the Lockridges lavished affection upon little Bouncer, who preened beneath their attention. She was glad they were the sort of in-laws who appreciated animals. That explained why her husband was relatively tolerant of her kitchen menagerie and her forays into nature.

In fact, by the time they retired to the parlor after dinner, Jane felt so comfortable with them they might have been her own parents. How she envied their relaxed harmony with one another, their obvious loving bond. That would be her life's work, to form such a bond with Edward. She would put her love and trust into her husband, and have faith that over the years, he would come to treasure her as the Duke of Lockridge so clearly treasured his wife.

"Edward," his mother said, when they were seated by the fire and the men settled with their port. "Your sister and her husband will be coming to visit soon. I'm going to have a grand ball in London to celebrate their tenth anniversary, and you and Jane must attend."

"Of course we'll attend. Felicity and Carlo have been married ten years already?" he asked in wonder.

"It seems impossible, doesn't it? But your sister wed at nineteen"—he shot his son a teasing look—"rather than waiting to drag her feet to the altar in her late twenties."

"Hunter!" the duchess protested. "Townsend didn't drag his feet. You'll insult dear Jane to suggest it."

"No, I was an eager bridegroom," said Edward, taking Jane's hand upon the sofa and winking at her. "How dare my father accuse me of dragging my feet?"

"Especially when he was near thirty himself before he deigned to honor our longstanding engagement," said the duchess.

"If I'm to be bullied, I'll take my port up to my room." The duke put on a scowl, then brightened. "It will be your first chance to meet Felicity and Carlo, and the children," he said to Jane. "They were sad they couldn't come in time for your wedding."

"You'll love the children," said Edward. "They'll call you *zia* and speak so quickly in Italian that you won't catch a word."

"I'll begin studying at once." Jane had always wanted to learn Italian.

"They're charming, sweet loves, like all my grandchildren," said the duchess. "Your future little ones won't lack for cousins."

Jane felt a blush rise in her cheeks at the thought of their "little ones."

"Don't worry, Jane," said Edward. "That is not pressure. Between Felicity, Will, and Belinda, my mother has plenty of grandchildren to tide her over for a while."

"And Rosalind wishes to marry soon," said his father with a touch of wistfulness. "My youngest babe."

"She wishes to marry our dear Lord Marlow." The duchess politely suppressed a sigh, while Edward laughed aloud.

"Besides the fact he thinks of her as a sister, I doubt they'd make a match. They're so different in temperament."

"We've all said so, as much as we esteem him. Young hearts like your sister's can be impetuous."

Jane listened to this family talk, absorbing everything. She had not seen Edward's sister Rosalind as the impetuous sort, but she didn't know her very well yet. And Marlow...all she knew of him, besides his striking blond hair, was that his smiles suggested a mischievous heart.

In time, talk returned to the ball and the duchess's grand plans to honor her oldest daughter's anniversary. The duke was an animated contributor to the planning, requesting peacock and lobster on the menu, and a full orchestra to play for the night.

"Oh, will there be dancing?" asked Jane. "I can't wait to dance at my first ball with my husband."

"I've told her it is not the thing for husbands and wives to fill each other's dance cards," said Edward, spreading his hands. "None of them dance with each other."

"Oh, a husband and wife may dance together if they wish," said his mother. "Especially at my ball. Your father and I will dance."

"Will there be waltzing?" asked Jane shyly.

"Do you want there to be waltzing?" The duke stood and bowed to her, offering his hand. "I love a good waltz."

"Here?" said Edward. "This is a parlor, not a ballroom."

"One can waltz anywhere."

"I've never learned how," Jane admitted. "My dance master wouldn't teach it, and at balls... I was never asked."

She blushed a second time, thinking how pathetic she must sound, but the duke's fond regard didn't waver.

"My dear, if you've not learned the waltz yet, it's high time you did. A little music, Edward?"

"Shall I hum or whistle, Your Grace?"

The duke waved him off. "Never mind, I'll do it." He led Jane to an open spot of floor and showed her the proper stance, with her head up and shoulders level, though she could barely stop laughing at his imitation of a young lady preparing to dance. Edward and the duchess looked on in amusement while the duke paused to move a small end table out of the way.

"Is this enough room for us, do you think? You need lots of room to waltz." He hummed a jaunty tune in a rich baritone, speaking words interspersed between the notes. "And we're off. Start with your left foot forward, dear, proceeding in a one-two-three rhythm."

"One-two-three rhythm?" she echoed, gripping his shoulder.

"That's right, Jane. Just follow me."

* * * * *

Townsend watched with a half-smile as his father patiently explained the steps to Jane again. And again. He would not be so mean as to say she had two left feet...but she was not a talented dancer. However, what she lacked in natural grace she made up for with plain determination.

"Show me again," she said whenever she muddled things. "I know I'll get it. I want to dance well at Felicity's ball."

His mother joined Townsend on the divan, taking the place vacated by his wife.

"Jane is simply a treasure," she said. "Thank goodness you married her."

He studied her features for any hint of sarcasm or dissemblance, but that was not his mother's way. Of course she liked Jane. Despite the fact she was not his first choice of wife, she was a warm, excellent hostess, and a steady enough woman to carry on the family line. Even if her waltzing was...oh, quite terrible.

"Don't give up, dear girl," his mother called. "It's not as difficult as it seems."

Jane smiled at them, gripping his father's hand as he demonstrated the one-two-three footwork very slowly for her.

"I never realized Father had talent as a dance instructor," he said quietly.

"Nor did I." His mother turned back to him, patting his hand. "She does seem happy, Edward. I trust the marriage is going well?"

"Yes. I enjoy her. Everything has sorted out, I suppose."

"You suppose?"

Jane gave a small cry of delight as she managed a set of steps without barging into his father.

"Goodness, she is a quick learner," the duke called out to them.

"Indeed she is," Townsend answered, trying not to think about sex in front of his parents. "Very quick indeed."

When he turned back to his mother, she was gazing at him searchingly.

"What is it?" he said. "Out with it. What is it you want to ask me?"

She shook her head and forced a smile. "Oh, nothing to ask. I'm only a bit worried about Felicity's ball."

"Why should you worry? You've never had a ball or party that was remotely unsuccessful, not that I can remember."

"I'm worried about you, Edward." Her gaze fluttered from his. "You know we've been close friends to the Arlingtons since before Felicity was born. I cannot hold this grand ball and not invite them and their children. *All* their children, including Lord Wescott and his wife."

He took in a breath, guarding his expression. "In that case, don't invite Jane's family, especially his sister. They won't wish to see him after the way he jilted June."

"Jane's family will be invited, of course, and will have the option to decline. You will not. You must be there for your older sister and her husband...and accept that Wescott and Ophelia might be there too."

Townsend despised Wescott, and he didn't much wish to see Ophelia, not when his heart was still conflicted. He thought of her too often for a married man, and seeing her after all this time would rip open that wound again. Seeing her on Wescott's arm would flay it raw.

"In fact, it is probable they will attend," his mother went on. "The Arlingtons believe this rift between you has gone on long enough, and your father and I agree."

"You talk about us?"

"Parents always talk about their children, particularly when they've been friends since boyhood and then abruptly stop speaking because one disapproved of the other's marriage."

"I didn't merely *disapprove*." He sputtered at the inaccuracy of the word. "Wescott behaved abominably. He ruined her."

"He married her. She was not ruined." His mother made a motion for him to calm down. His father continued waltzing with Jane, humming as they swirled around the cleared space. "Wescott has owned up to what he did and made it right with his wife and her family. When will you forgive him?"

"Never."

His mother's lips grew tight. "Have you owned up to what you did to Jane?"

"Owned up to...what?"

"You proposed to her only to get back at Wescott. You're not blameless in your conduct."

"That was nothing compared to what Wescott did, and Jane does not need to know."

"Doesn't she?"

They fell silent, forcing smiles as his father and Jane danced within earshot of their testy conversation. Jane grinned over at him with a saucy toss of her head.

"Look, Edward! It's not that difficult now I've got the hang of it."

"You're doing wonderfully, sweeting."

He and his mother waited until they waltzed out of earshot, and he summoned the courage to turn to her again.

"I've been a good husband to her," he said. "I don't need her to know why our betrothal happened. I only need to fulfill my husbandly duties to the best of my abilities going forward, and I have been. We're getting on very well."

"Ah, *very well*. You have moved on, then? It will not bother you to see Ophelia this spring?"

"Can't we drop this topic of discussion?"

"At the very least, you must mend fences with Wescott, preferably prior to the ball. You may not cause a scene at Felicity and Carlo's celebration."

His mother was a sweet, soft-spoken woman who could also be unsparing. He had to force his jaw muscles to relax.

"I would never have caused a scene," he said.

"Indeed, you're not the type. I have only known you to cause a scene once, and that was when Wescott proposed to Ophelia."

He let out a long, slow sigh. His father and Jane weren't waltzing anymore. He was twirling her then lifting her in the air with a flourish. She looked in his direction, her face aglow with pleasure.

"She is so in love with you," his mother said. "Look how she smiles at you."

"She's smiling because of father. It has nothing to do with me."

"Townsend."

He rubbed the back of his neck. "Mama. Please. I am trying to fall in love with her. I just need time. Can't I have more time?"

"Of course you can." She looked down at her hands and touched her fingers a moment, as if adjusting invisible gloves. "I only want you to realize, despite your lingering *tendre* for Ophelia, that there is so very much to love in Jane."

He watched his wife, feeling like a scolded schoolboy. Of course he wanted to love her above all others. Of course he wished her to never doubt his affection and fidelity, but everything after Ophelia had happened so quickly, before he had an opportunity to sort things out. He was married while he was still in the mindset of revenge. If he must put away that desire for revenge, what would replace it?

Love for Jane? It had been two months, and he was afraid he still barely knew her. Was it his fault?

"Your father is such an excellent dancer," she said, collapsing back in one of the armed chairs. "Edward, it was so fun. Can you waltz like that?"

"Better."

He offered a hand to his wife. Meanwhile, his father bowed low before his mother and soon he and Jane were dodging the other couple in a parlor that was not designed for dancing, but had become a ballroom nonetheless.

Jane grinned at him, her eyes shining. "I love dancing. I've never thought myself very talented at it, but now that I can waltz..."

"You're doing beautifully, my love." She looked beautiful too, joyous and out of breath.

"I can't wait to meet your sister and her husband, and your friends, and all your family at the ball. Won't we be busy in London, having them over to your house and paying calls ourselves?"

"Yes, although it will be your house too, you know. Well, if you intend to live there with me."

It took a moment for her to register his joke, a moment when she looked worried. Did she think he'd leave her behind in the country? His mother seemed to believe he didn't love her enough, perhaps his wife felt the same? Why? He was smiling at her, dancing with her. God knew they connected with passionate pleasure just about every night.

He glanced over at his parents. Surely he was doing better than the early days of their marriage, when his father had given his mother a grasshopper as a gift.

"They are lovely, your parents," said Jane. "I can see why you're such a good husband now."

"Am I?"

"Aren't you? I think so."

It wasn't until later that night, as he lay beside her in bed, that he realized he should have reciprocated and told her she was a good wife. He looked over at her in sleep, at her light, fluttering lashes and pouting lips which had given him so much pleasure. He couldn't leave her after he bedded her, for she made sure there was always some part of her touching him. A fingertip, a toe, or her whole hand wrapped about his hand or forearm. They slept together so often at her request that he felt strange now when he woke up alone.

His mother had said "She is so in love with you."

What she'd really meant in her tone and expression was "Take care."

Chapter Eleven: Starting to Understand

Each week grew a little warmer. By the end of March, the trees had budded and the forest was shaking itself to life. Jane seemed delighted with Somerton in spring, and Townsend was glad to see her busy and happy.

He rarely had cause to punish her, for she went out of her way to please him and follow the household rules. She always took attendants with her into the forests, and in fact, put them to work carrying and storing the botanical specimens she collected, as well as small insect corpses and dried animal bones. The servants had grown as fond of their mistress as they'd grown of the much-petted Bouncer in his open cage. Townsend began to fear he might never have another chance to indulge his love of discipline.

Perhaps when they moved back to town...

When they returned to London for the Season, there'd be an entirely new set of rules for Jane to follow, beginning at his mother's grand ball. Any gathering of the *ton*'s best and brightest was sure to harbor a great many gossips, and Jane's conversation still needed some work. Hmm, a spanking each time she brought up the many varieties of wood beetles, a strapping each time she expanded upon the colors of Midland squirrels, and a sound caning when she described the ins and outs of various animals' mating habits...

She still did that far too often, and it wasn't the thing to talk about at balls or during a dinner with acquaintances. Ladies really ought not to talk about animals at all, not at great length, but he let her go on while they were at Somerton, with nature all around. In London they'd only have the gardens and the small greenhouse he was having erected especially for her.

Well, she would adapt. His previous love, Ophelia, had been perfectly suited to city life, being a renowned opera singer. He tried not to think about Ophelia when he overheard Jane warbling some silly tune to her rabbit as she took him on walks about the woods, or humming off key as she yanked weeds from one of her winter gardens. They were not the same person, and that was that. Conversely, he imagined Ophelia knew nothing at all about animals' mating habits...

Ophelia is married to Wescott now, his conscience chided. *It's time to let it all go.*

It was past time, really, and he'd mostly let her go, but he still wasn't sure he could forgive Wescott. When they returned to London, Marlow and August would wish for all of them to socialize together as they had done for so many years. They didn't understand how difficult it would be to look at Wescott after his betrayal, much less accept him again as a friend.

These thoughts weighed on his mind until the last of March when they began to pack for London. Many servants would remain at Somerton, but many more would come to the city with them, for he'd not be keeping a bare-bones, bachelor household anymore. There were many decisions to make: what to bring, what to buy, what to leave in the country. Jane ordered new gowns, bonnets, gloves, and slippers and retired others which had suffered hard use in Somerton's gardens and forests. She conferred with him on a special satin gown for Felicity and Carlo's ball, and he looked over the fashion drawings because she wanted so badly to please him.

She is so in love with you...

Parcels arrived daily, and when he was able, he delivered them to his wife in person because her excited exclamations about his generosity made him feel appreciated. When the ball gown showed up, she modeled it for him with unmitigated glee. The pink and silver confection had a pearl neckline, an embroidered bodice, and stylish cascades of ruffles that suited her sweet personality perfectly. The day before they were to leave, the last two anticipated items were delivered—the ball gown's matching embroidered slippers, and a delicate pearl and diamond tiara he'd ordered her as a surprise.

He went in search of her at once, starting in her rooms, since she often read in the mornings. When he arrived, however, he found both their sets of doors standing open, with the servants bustling about.

"Where is Lady Townsend?" he asked one of the footmen.

The servant indicated that his wife was in his rooms, and that was where he found her, kneeling to look under his bed. When she saw him she jumped to her feet.

"Goodness," she said. "Why aren't you out for your morning ride?"

"Why aren't you in your bedroom?" He placed her parcels on his chest of drawers. "Why are you poking about under my bed?"

She blew out a breath. "It's quite the story really."

The servants stood poker-faced, their gazes darting about the floor. "I think you'd better begin telling it," he said. "Does this have to do with an escaped pet?"

There she went, biting her lip again. "This was not meant to happen. The truth is, I've been bringing Mr. Cuddles upstairs the last few days as I'm reading, because they've been so busy in the kitchens preparing for the move. He usually wraps about my arm or shoulders and we look at books together, but today—"

"You've been reading books with your snake?" The question came out a little too loud.

She wrung her hands and took a step back. "I've always kept perfect control of him, until today."

"It only takes one day, doesn't it? I told you at the start, no pets in the house. That was our agreement. How did he end up in my room?"

"That's the thing. I was reading the best mystery novel, and I suppose I forgot to give him as much handling and attention as he likes, and before I knew it, he was down the bed and on the floor, and heading for the doorway. Oh, why should he go into your room? I'll never know. It's as if he wants to get me in trouble." She brushed a hand through her disarranged orange locks. "The servants are helping me find him. Don't worry. He can't have gone far."

The fact that he couldn't have gone far was of little comfort to Townsend. A snake was slithering over his floors and carpets. It could be setting up a dandy new home among his boots or linens or shirts. Not only that, the cursed thing had apparently been making itself easy in Jane's bed, where he himself rolled about with her almost every night. That had been his one rule about her bizarre pets—that they remain outside the living areas.

"We'll find him shortly," she said. "You're not to worry. If everyone is quiet, perhaps I can hear him rustling about."

"Is he even still in here? He could be anywhere in the house by now."

When she put her finger to her lips and shushed him, he reached the limits of his patience. "Find the snake at once," he thundered. "I want it out of here. It belongs in the kitchens."

The servants burst into motion, but his wife frowned at him with tears in her eyes. "Mr. Cuddles belongs in the African grasslands, but he can't be there because some horrible person trapped him and brought him to the Exeter zoo. It's not his fault."

"Perhaps, but he is in my room at this moment, and that is your fault."

"If everyone would just be quiet. He's probably afraid with all this activity, and your yelling—"

"Lady Townsend?" One of the servants called from his dressing room. He and Jane hurried in and found the man standing in the area beyond, the washroom. He and the snake were going in circles, the creature slithering along the floorboards while his man ran after it as if to corral the thing.

"Gently," Jane warned, kneeling in the snake's way. "Stop running, please. You're making him frantic."

"Is he going to hurt you?" Townsend was caught between a healthy fear of snakes and the desire to protect his wife from the reptile. It had gotten bigger, hadn't it, over the winter? With Jane on one side of it and his footman on the other, the snake coiled in a corner and stared at them.

"Poor thing," Jane crooned to it. "I know you're frightened. Have you gotten yourself into a strange, cold place? These floors aren't cozy and woody like your enclosure, sweet baby. Let me fetch you and I'll take you back where you belong."

Damn him if the snake didn't seem to be listening to her. She took a small step forward, then another. "Please, nobody move. Just be quiet."

Townsend looked over his shoulder and waved off the servants beyond the door. Then he stood, helpless, as Jane approached the snake.

"Is he going to bite you?" He couldn't govern his agitation, but he hadn't the knowledge or experience to assist her. "He looks angry."

"He is upset, but he won't bite me. Royal pythons are docile. Even if he bites me, it won't hurt, for he hasn't any fangs, nor the jaw strength of a badger or dog."

Oh God, a badger or dog. How had he ended up marrying this naturalist? Curse Ophelia, and Wescott, and his misguided quest for revenge. He watched with his heart in his throat as Jane gathered up her skirts and crouched before the animal. Its head moved back and forth but its beady eyes never left her as she reached for it.

"There now," she said quietly. "Come here, sweet, and I'll hold you to my breast and soothe you until your heart stops beating so hard. What do you say to that? I'll hug you close until you feel safe again."

She spoke to it as if the snake might answer her, and then, in a way, it did answer. Its coils grew less tense. It moved its head forward as she held out a hand, and let her pet and stroke him. A moment later it slithered onto her offered palm.

"Oh, good boy." Within moments, the snake was coiled about her hand and forearm, content to lie against her body. "Let's get you back to your enclosure. How tired you must be. I should have let you try to sleep safe in your cage, I know, but it's so hard with the hustle and bustle, isn't it? Don't worry, we'll be settled in London soon enough."

She brushed past him, this outrageous, snake-charming wife, leaving him to stew in lingering trauma. He followed her from the washroom, through his dressing room and bedroom, all the way to the hall door. "As soon as you put him away, return to me," he told her. "We are going to have some words."

* * * * *

Jane stayed with Mr. Cuddles in the kitchen until she was reassured he felt safe and calm again. After that, she spent a few minutes stroking Bouncer's silky ears in an attempt to reassure and calm herself.

She was not looking forward to having "words" with her husband. They'd been rubbing along so well the past few weeks, even with the looming pressure of the Season to worry about.

When she left the kitchen, she walked very slowly to his bedroom so he'd have extra time to gather his temper. She could not lay the blame for this incident at Mr. Cuddles' feet—or belly rather. She was the one who'd been taking him upstairs, thinking Edward would never catch her at it. He usually went riding in the mornings, for goodness sake.

Not that it excused her. No, she was deservedly in trouble. She knocked on his door and tried not to shudder when he said "Enter!" in his disciplinarian voice. She brushed a hand through her hair—which was as frazzled as she was—and tried to smooth it down. Oh, what was the use of any of it?

She found him standing near the window. He held a shining tiara, turning it between his fingers. For a moment, she forgot about Mr. Cuddles and her husband's anger, and crossed to look at the splendid piece more closely.

"It's gorgeous," she exclaimed. The sun's rays illuminated the intricate, gem-encrusted headpiece. "Whose is it?"

"Yours, silly. It's not my style. I ordered it to go with your dress for Felicity's ball."

She could hardly speak, it was so elegant, so perfectly what she would have wanted in a first tiara. For it was the first tiara she'd ever owned or been given.

"Let me see," he said. He brushed back her hair with one hand and settled it on her head with the other. She reached to arrange the combs meant to hold it in place, heading to his dressing room so she could look in his mirror. He stood behind her as she gazed at her reflection.

"It must have cost so dear," she said. "Even my mother hasn't one this grand."

"You are related to European royalty now, through my sister. You'll need a tiara for events like the upcoming ball." He studied her, then the tiara. "It suits you well. The jeweler said it would."

It was a wonder of sparkling diamonds and shining pearls, with a gold setting that complemented her normally uncomplementary hair. She felt so pretty, she wished she could wear it all day, every day. The most touching thing was that Edward had picked it out for her himself.

"I was bringing it upstairs to show you earlier, when the presentation turned to a snake hunt."

That wiped the giddy smile from her face. "I'm so sorry about that."

Suddenly he was standing far too close to her. He plucked the tiara gently from her hair and carried it back to its velvet box as she tagged along beside him. Perhaps he would forgive her for the whole escaped pet drama? After all, he'd just given her such a precious gift.

He closed the box's lid and turned back to her. "I did tell you very specifically that your pets were not to be brought into the house." His expression was stern beneath his dark hair. Not forgiven then. Not yet. "What have you to say for yourself, Jane?"

What could she say? She'd disobeyed him with absolute intention to do so. It wasn't an accident or impulse. No, she'd timed her trespasses with his morning rides about the property, thinking he'd never find out.

"I have nothing to say in my defense," she admitted. "You've been so kind and accommodating with me and my little zoo, with only one rule to follow, and I broke it. I did it intentionally, hoping you'd never find out."

He studied her, his amber-gold eyes calculating in the morning's light. Was he pleased with her contrition, so perhaps he'd be more lenient in her punishment? Or was he furious she'd so brazenly disobeyed him?

"I'm terribly sorry," she said. "I know that doesn't take away my error."

He rubbed his forehead with a tired sigh. "Of all the things, Jane. We're going to leave for London tomorrow. What if he'd become lost in the house and we were unable to go?"

"It's true. Of course you're right, Edward."

"The rules are there for a reason. You must think things through."

As he delivered his lecture, he picked up another box from a side table and opened it, showing her the embroidered slippers within. "These arrived along with the tiara. Won't you be beautiful at the ball?

When we're in society, darling, you can't be impulsive and unthinking. You're a grown woman now, representing two eminent families."

She stared at the fine dancing slippers, wishing she might go back in time and undo her mischief with Mr. Cuddles. Her husband's patient, disappointed tone was worse than the scolding he'd done earlier.

"What shall we do with you, Jane?"

Oh, she couldn't bear it. For the first time, she *wanted* to be punished to assuage her guilt, but she couldn't say that to him. She couldn't ask to be bent over his padded footboard that matched her own, and spanked for her transgressions, because she didn't want to be spanked. But some part of her did, a little.

"You must do what you believe is necessary," she said, tears pricking at her eyes. "I'm sorry I've disappointed you."

"And you're sorry you've misbehaved. I can see it in your face, love. Imagine how awful you would have felt if Mr. Cuddles had come to some harm."

That was too awful to think about, and very true. If he couldn't be in the wild African grasslands where he belonged, his next safest place was in his enclosure where he could stay secure and warm.

Edward still held the box with the slippers. Now he took one out and turned it over, and ran a finger over the supple leather sole. Then he tested it against his palm, bringing it down with a *whap*. Her stomach turned over as a shudder coursed through her.

"Perhaps a slipper spanking with these dancing shoes is the proper answer, for what they represent. Honor, sublimity, the dignity of your station as my marchioness. I only want you to be your very best, Jane. That's the purpose of discipline, of course."

As she stood, trembling, he used the leather-soled slipper to point to the bed. "You know by now how to position yourself."

Unfortunately, that was true. She walked to the bed and knelt upon the shelf provided for that purpose, and draped herself over the footboard. Each time she had to do this, she berated herself—*why are you in this situation again?* But each time, it was her own fault, for disobedience or impulsive behavior. Someday she'd learn.

She buried her face within her arms as Edward drew up the back of her gown to bare her bottom. She still went hot with embarrassment every time, and probably always would. If he only tossed her skirts up and went about his business spanking her, it would be easier to bear, but he was slow about it, arranging her skirt and petticoat just so. It gave her that much more time to think and dread, and regret her behavior.

Next she felt the slipper rubbed upon her bottom, a warning her spanking's commencement was imminent. "Since you readily admitted your error in judgment, and submitted yourself for correction without resistance, I believe an abbreviated spanking will do well enough. But I shall not be soft, Janie. It's going to hurt."

"I know," she said softly. Her tears were already flowing. *Janie*, he had called her, with something almost like affection. She worried so often that he didn't seem to love her. How strange to feel close to him now.

The first blow fell with a crisp *thwack*. She cried out, her knees kicking up in agony, for the slipper felt even worse than a strap. The leather soles were solid and slightly textured for gripping, and imparted an awful sting. The second blow fell upon one cheek, the third upon the other. *Ow, owww*. Three licks in, and her arse already felt like it was combusting, like there were literal flames upon her skin.

"It hurts," she said, in case he didn't realize it. "It hurts a great deal."

"I imagine it feels very unpleasant. I also imagine you'll be finding it uncomfortable to sit during the ride to London tomorrow."

She gave a soft cry, imagining hours on a carriage seat with a tender, sore backside as they bumped over country roads. The next blow came with the same awful *thwack* and unbearable sting. Though she wished to twist away, the footboard kept her bottom elevated and positioned for continued punishment. No matter how she squirmed and kicked her legs, her arse cheeks remained exposed and vulnerable.

No matter how great the pain, the stinging, throbbing agony, she could only clutch at the bedsheets and wait for her price to be paid.

There was an awful comfort to it, being unable to escape. As she grew more experienced with her husband's discipline, the early days of hysterics and fear gave way to resignation. It hurt awfully when he punished her, but between the blows, as her cheeks ached and throbbed, she was getting better at thinking about the whys of her punishments, and how she might do better.

"Oww," she cried, as heat layered upon heat. Even though she understood the process of punishment better, it was still terrible to bear. "Oh, please, I am so sorry."

"I know you are. We're nearly there."

She'd come to learn that being "there" meant she was spanked enough to feel the effects of the spanking at least another day, and sometimes two. She gritted her teeth, because getting "there" required successively harder blows, with the worst always coming at the end. She whined and kicked as the blows came faster, building pain over more pain. When she couldn't bear it, she moved her hand to cover herself, but he caught it, as always, before she could be harmed.

Now there would be a few extra blows while he held her hand behind her back, but she couldn't help that. It was instinct, to try to protect herself. At least now she was truly powerless to escape, and Edward's tight grasp upon her wrist reminded her there was nothing to do but survive the ending of this.

At last he stopped, and the ball of dread in her middle unwound a little bit. Her body went limp with relief. Switches, paddles, straps, even his hand, whatever he chose to punish her with had its own noticeable evils. With the slipper, she would remember the stinging impact of a thick leather sole. The night she dressed for the ball and put on these slippers, she would remember it.

That was probably his intention in using it in the first place.

She knew she was expected to lie still and wait to be dismissed from the punishment, to have her skirts rearranged by him, to be helped up by those same hands that punished her. As she lay with her spanked arse in the air, she could count her heartbeat in the throbs of pain, and nearly feel where each blow had landed, from the crest of her bottom down to the tops of her thighs.

Today, he made her wait longer than usual. He ran his hands over her cheeks, an action that soothed at the same time it recalled the depth of painful heat still radiating outward.

"You're starting to understand," he said. "I can see it."

She swallowed hard, her face still hidden. "Yes, my lord."

"It pleases me so."

She did not know if *she* was pleased. She wasn't sure how she felt, exposed as she was, in pain. Yet somehow feeling satisfied too, for enduring the punishment she'd earned.

"I would like to have you now, Jane, just like this, with your bottom red and hot."

Even as he said it, he placed the slipper next to her on the bed and undid his clothes. She could hear the rustling, the unbuttoning as he opened the front of his trousers. His desirous words had the effect of readying her, making her wet. When he grasped her hips and slid into her, it was an odd melding of two separate activities, lovemaking and punishment.

Yet it felt so appropriate in the moment to combine them, she wondered why they hadn't melded together before now.

Oh goodness, he drove hard in her, so her knees slid forward upon their platform. His hips hurt her tender arse cheeks as he thrust forward, so she felt the pleasure of his thickness and the lingering pain of her spanking at once. Was she allowed to enjoy this? Or was she still in disgrace? It did not seem the time to ask, and soon enough the choice was taken from her as she began to feel so warm and aroused in her middle she could hardly be still.

She began to arch back to him, to swivel her hips so he might thrust deeper. Each time he did, he drove her mons against the footboard and her arousal flared higher. His fingers stroked up her spine; it seemed silent permission to seek the same relief he was. The whines and "ows" of her spanking were replaced by breathless moans, and then she was clenching around him in trembling release. She tried to muffle her sounds of bliss in the bedsheets, caught between punishment and ecstasy. Edward rode her so hard then, she was glad the footboard was padded for cushioning. He pinned her against the bed as he finished, gasping and clutching her hips.

Afterward she could not have proceeded without his assistance, she was so drained. She was still sore from the slippering, but oh, weak from satisfaction too. Once he collected himself, he helped her wash up and rearrange her gown, and then had her sit on his lap, as he always did after punishments.

She shifted, trying to find a comfortable position upon his hard, strong thighs—as she always did after punishments.

He was generally quick to launch into a post-spanking lecture, just to be sure the point had been driven home, but no such lecture came today. Well, she had shown him that she understood things better now. She had taken a very hard, very painful spanking with relative grace, and he had recognized this progress, and told her *It pleases me so.*

As she nestled against his chest, he stroked her arm and back and played lazily with her hair. *Janie,* he had called her with clear affection. She wished he would say it again like that.

"We are not such a bad match," he said after a long silence. "We aren't, are we? It's true I punish you sometimes, but it's only to keep things properly in order. Are you happy enough?"

The wistfulness in his question unsettled her. "I have been happy here," she answered. "You've been very kind."

"I appreciate you saying that after I've just spanked you." He sighed. "Now we will go to London and live in the greater world again."

"I'll miss Somerton."

"It will always be here, as our escape. This is where we've grown to know one another."

But not fallen in love.

He didn't say that. He never said anything about love, and she knew he didn't love her because of those sighs, and the wistfulness that often crept into his expressions. She adored him so much, even after he spanked her, but he still seemed to wonder if they were a good match. Perhaps it was because she owned a snake...

She didn't want to cry. Oh, her emotions were all over the place. She was probably just worried about the move to London. She rested her head on his shoulder and tried to enjoy this moment of closeness, however imperfect. It was the worst feeling, trying to figure out when you might win your husband's heart. Perhaps in London, if she was perfect and elegant enough, he would grow to love her. Hopefully it was just a matter of time.

Chapter Twelve: Business to Address

For Townsend, the trip to London was far easier to manage than the journey to Somerton after their wedding. Now, his wife was no longer a stranger, and his anxiety over his marriage had mellowed to a comfortable resignation.

No, it wasn't kind to think of it as resignation. He enjoyed Jane very much. He no longer thought of her as plain or unrefined, as he had at their initial introduction, and this time, fortunately, their arrival wasn't marred by the escape of Mr. Cuddles.

Progress, if not perfection.

Jane seemed very happy with the house in town, as it was a light, airy domicile just a short walk to Hyde Park. The servants had done an excellent job setting up the house for marriage as opposed to bachelorhood. All lingering traces of ladies' stockings and accessories left behind at various parties had been expunged, likely donated to the poor. In this house, Jane's rooms adjoined his rather than being situated across a corridor. And, as he had bought it already furnished, the footboards were not ideal for punishment like the ones at

Somerton, but he had no doubt he'd manage if the need for a spanking arose.

As they settled into their city routines, he could see Jane was doing all she could to be right and proper in society. She'd ordered new stationary and even practiced refining her handwriting so she could send flawless invitations and calling cards. She studied fashion circulars and read the newspapers to know what was happening around town. Every other day or so, she paid a call to June, or received her sister in the parlor, so she might learn from June's extensive knowledge of London's social circles.

Despite these occupations, she still made time for her pets, and the London kitchen staff grew used to them and made sure to give Bouncer his allowance of ear pats. The only deficiency he could see in his wife's day-to-day happiness was that she missed Somerton's wild places, its forests and streams, mightily. His town house boasted designer gardens, but they were heavily landscaped and more lawn than forest.

So he took her to the park, which had trees and grass and hundreds of animals; unfortunately, the animals were mostly of the human variety, but Jane made do. As the scions of society strolled about exchanging gossip and catching up on family happenings, his wife studied the most popular ladies' mannerisms, trying to make herself into one of them. She did not wade into the ponds to study spring's new duckling broods, nor crash into clusters of trees in search of rabbits and squirrels. Lord knew the effort of self-control. He rewarded her with smiles, with his full attention.

Even when Ophelia was in the park.

Sometimes she came with Wescott, other times with ladies of her acquaintance. Jane watched them along with all the others as Townsend tried very hard not to. For almost two weeks, they were able to avoid the Wescotts through timing and circuitous routes along the busy walkways, until Marlow and Augustine materialized one day and steered them together before Townsend could draw Jane in another direction.

"Look at us all, together again," said August, too loudly. "It's been so long."

"I saw you both yesterday," Townsend muttered.

"But not Wes." Marlow's light words had a note of steel beneath them. "You've not seen one another in so long."

He and Wescott exchanged quick, uncomfortable glares. This man had been his closest friend once, a defender and confidant, a keeper of secrets and a fellow rake in their bachelor conquests. But the last time he'd seen him they'd argued to the point of blows, until they had to be dragged apart from each other. He'd wanted to kill him for stealing Ophelia, not to mention disrespecting and dishonoring her. Even if he'd married her to repair the damage, even if they were in love now...

By God, it had not been well done, and his fury still lingered like a brick wall between them.

"You ought to introduce your new wife to the Wescotts," prompted August, as Townsend stood with his fists clenched.

Jane looked at him, knowing the tension in this meeting if not the true reason, and he realized for her sake he must not cause a scene. He forced a tepid smile and the words of introduction.

"Lord and Lady Wescott, I'm pleased to introduce my wife, Lady Townsend."

Jane offered her hand and Wescott bowed over it, as if he didn't already know her from jilting her sister. Jane was equally gracious, but her smile was not her usual, natural one. Good. She turned to Ophelia next, her smile more genuine. "I'm pleased to finally meet you."

Because you weren't at our wedding, because your blighted husband daren't show his face there...

Townsend burned with anger and emotion. He knew people were watching this meeting, had been waiting for it. It had been his mistake to air the business about his vengeful—and mistaken—betrothal in the middle of White's dining hall, and now the *ton*, hungry for gossip after their winters in the country, was untangling the story and having good private laughs about it.

Let them laugh, as long as Jane never heard the wretched story, that their marriage was born of bungled revenge. He tried to keep his face bland, his expression pleasant as he faced Wescott, and was careful not to stare at Ophelia. He dared not address her beyond the barest niceties, if only to spare her the embarrassment of recalling his passionate declarations of love. By God, he'd been so gone with obsession he'd tried to break up their betrothal. If he hadn't been dragged away by burly footmen, he probably would have tried to abduct Ophelia. Such had been his madness. Now there was only awkwardness and pain.

"I trust you had a pleasant winter season at Somerton," said Wescott, cautiously. "I never had the chance to congratulate you both on your nuptials."

"Oh yes," added Ophelia, her blue eyes bright. "We are so glad for your happiness."

Jane smiled and thanked them. "It is wonderful being married." She winked at Augustine and Marlow. "You two ought to try it."

"In time, dear lady," said Marlow, bowing. "But for a little while longer, I'll let the debutantes of London believe they still have a chance."

"A chance at what?" muttered August, with his usual impeccable timing. "Misery?"

"Someone will be happy to have me," Marlow shot back.

"Of course. Someone...eventually..."

Wescott's droll response had them all laughing again, everyone but Townsend. He only managed a tight smile. Curse it, why must everyone around them pretend not to watch, when they obviously were? He couldn't bear their scrutiny, which was why he'd tried to avoid this meeting. He hated providing fodder for society's vicious tongues.

"Say, Wescott, weren't you just telling us you had some business to address privately with Townsend?" August said.

Marlow nodded at his friend. "He did just say that to us, didn't he? We'll be happy to take your wives for a jaunt about the park while you two discuss things."

"Indeed, we'd be honored," August agreed. "No trouble at all."

Townsend didn't know who irritated him more—August and Marlow with their clumsy meddling, or Ophelia and Jane, who so readily accepted the men's invitation. Before he could protest, August had offered an arm to Jane, and Marlow to Ophelia.

He and Wescott watched the couples walk off, leaving them stranded with each other. Wescott adjusted his hat; he fidgeted with his gloves. Who would say the first words? Would they be antagonistic or dismissive? Heated or blasé?

"It's been a long time," Wescott began, which wasn't saying much at all. "How were your travels in Europe?"

"Unsatisfying." He saw Jane look back at them, worry in her expression. "Let's walk as well. I fear we've gathered an audience, standing here."

"If you like."

"I do like."

They set off in the opposite direction from the ladies. Townsend tried to keep his expression neutral, but imagined he failed at it. Wescott was better at hiding his feelings, or perhaps he hadn't any in his cold, dead soul.

"I suppose there is no use in small talk," Wescott said. "We must settle these differences between us, or Marlow and August will never let it rest."

"Were you in on the plans for this 'accidental' meeting?"

"They did tell me you and Lady Townsend had a habit of walking in the park this time of day." He sighed. "I've wished to meet with you in any case to express my sincere apologies for the way things happened with Ophelia. I wrote to you..."

"I burned your letters without reading them."

"Townsend, for God's sake. You're the one who attacked me. I had a bloody shiner at my wedding."

"You deserved worse." He took a slow breath, keeping rein on his temper even as the old outrage flooded back. "You disrespected Ophelia. You took advantage of her."

"There was a fire, remember? I tried to do the right thing by saving her."

"And then you did the wrong thing and seduced her."

"I didn't realize who she was, or that you idolized her so. None of us knew you loved her! You didn't tell anyone, least of all the lady in question. Ophelia had no idea who you were."

He knew he'd conducted himself like a lovesick madman, and it stung to be reminded of it. "I would have told her eventually, when the time was right. I might have married her if I'd had time to be introduced, to get to know her. You destroyed those opportunities."

"Not intentionally." Wescott pursed his lips and looked away. "You must try to be happy for me now. Happy for us. I've fallen deeply in love with her. She's such a wonderful woman, as you know, and while we haven't told many people yet...she is soon to be the mother of my child."

"Is she?" Townsend took this felicitous news like a dull blow. "Congratulations."

"In fact, everything is going so well, and so happily. The only dark spot in all of this is our lost friendship." He looked back at him. "It was hard for Ophelia and me in the beginning. I could have used your steady head and your support with all of it."

"Forgive me if I didn't feel up to helping with your godforsaken marriage."

"Don't call it that."

His raised voice doubtless carried to the eavesdroppers around them. Both of them fell silent and walked faster, as if they could outpace this uncomfortable discussion they must have.

"All I can do now is ask you to forgive me for impeding your way with Ophelia. I never meant to. It was my ignorance and weakness, and yes, poor behavior that disrupted your dreams. But Towns, honestly, what love did she ever show you? She didn't know you from any of the dozen men who mooned at her during concerts and balls. Now you have Jane, your Lady Townsend, who gazes at you like a God who walks among us. Can't you be content?"

"Content?" He stopped and turned on his friend. "I proposed to Jane to get back at you, because I thought June was Jane, or Jane was June." He waved a hand and narrowed his eyes. "I proposed to her as revenge."

"So I understand. It was awful of you, at least as awful as what I did."

They scowled at one another, then Wescott cut his eyes away, to look at Jane in the distance. "The gossips say what a lark it is, that your wife gazes at you with such adulation. It disgusts me, how they mock her when you're to blame. She's paying the price for our disagreement, for our misbehavior and your insincere offer for her hand."

"She does not know they talk about her."

"If you keep taking her out in society, she'll realize they're discussing her business."

He shook his head. "No, I mean she doesn't *know*. She doesn't understand that I proposed to her by accident, in a fit of anger. She doesn't know about Ophelia's part in all of it, either."

Now Wescott was the one narrowing his eyes. "You never told her the truth?"

"What? That I was so in love with Ophelia I entirely lost my scruples and proposed to her as retribution? No, I haven't told her. I don't want her to know. It belittles her."

"But she ought to know, don't you think? It will break her heart if she discovers it by mistake."

"Her heart was already broken by damned Hobart, who scuttled their betrothal just before I came along. I let her believe his perfidy was my reason for proposing."

"You lying pair of bollocks."

"Shut up, Wescott. You've no moral high ground to lecture from."

"It seems neither of us have."

It was true. They'd both behaved so badly. Wescott had endangered Ophelia's reputation to the point he had to marry her. Townsend had let a vulnerable woman believe he'd married her for caring reasons, when really he'd been out to get back at a friend. Worse, he'd bragged about the attempt in a public dining room, so everyone knew why their unsuited marriage had taken place.

"I'm not happy with any of it," said Townsend miserably. "I hate how all of this turned out."

"Is your marriage so bad?" Wescott sounded genuinely concerned. "Are you too different for things to work?"

"We're very different. I suppose things work well enough day to day, but she is so..." He did not know how to describe how she addled him. She was just so *open* to him, so pure, so needful, so deserving of love, and he was so conflicted and ashamed.

"I had a vision of who I would marry," he continued, "and Jane is so outside that vision. Sometimes I look at her and think, how can this be? She is sweet and endearing, and tries hard to be what she imagines I want, and I think I ought to consider myself the most fortunate of husbands, but there is this lingering feeling that... Forgive me. That I'd rather have married Ophelia."

"What a horrid person you are, then."

Townsend couldn't deny it, even though Wescott's words were rude.

"You were never like that before," Wescott said. "You were the steadiest of all of us, except maybe August. You believed in honor and wisdom and doing the right thing."

"I still do."

"No, you don't, because you have a charming, loving wife who idolizes you, and instead of returning that love, you're pining over my wife."

It was the plain truth, even though Townsend hated it. Wescott followed up his scathing lecture with a tight laugh.

"And for the record, my friend, Ophelia is not the idyll of perfect femininity you've built in your mind. She can be moody and headstrong, and sometimes has terrible taste in the colors of her gowns. She likes boiled Brussels sprouts, which I detest, and she's constantly begging to visit my crazy relatives in Wales." He shrugged, more fondness in his expression than irritation. "Ophelia's imperfect, just like your naturalist Jane, but I still love her because she loves me, and we are there for each other every hour of every day. It's a wonderful feeling to love someone when that love is returned."

Townsend knew the wisdom of these words. Ophelia, imperfect? Of course she was, like any woman. He still wished he'd had a chance to explore his feelings for her. He said so to Wescott, who replied, simply, "My friend, that is water under the bridge."

They stopped walking. Wescott faced him and offered a handshake of reconciliation.

"Look, Towns, I can only tell you how sorry I am that things worked out the way they did. I miss your friendship and I want you to forgive me. It's time for all of us to move on."

Townsend hesitated only a moment before extending his hand in kind. "I'm sorry as well. I had no more right to Ophelia's love than you did. I suppose it's time to put all this behind us, for our wives' sakes as well."

The men shook firmly, their gazes holding without rancor for the first time in a while.

"And our friendship's sake," said Wescott wryly. "August and Marlow have been at me to the point of distraction, wishing for us to fix our differences."

"Me too. They meddle like old women."

Having shaken on things, Townsend felt an ease he hadn't enjoyed in many months. They turned back toward their wives, who were strolling from the opposite direction on their friends' arms.

"Are we at peace again?" Marlow asked as they joined them.

"I can see it in your faces." August nodded in approval. "You don't look like you want to kill one another anymore."

"For the moment, we're at peace," said Wescott.

"For the moment," Townsend echoed. As close as they were from earliest childhood, they'd had their share of petty disagreements and probably always would. He took Jane back from August and they bid goodbye to their friends.

"Did you enjoy your stroll with Lord Augustine?" he asked as they walked back toward their home.

She laughed. "Both your friends are charming as can be. Lady Wescott and I could barely catch our breath from laughing."

"Indeed, they're both buffoons."

"It was good, wasn't it, for you and Lord Wescott to mend fences before Felicity and her husband arrive?"

"Of course it was. We could not stay enemies forever."

"Sometimes you have to forgive. And now that June's so happily married to Lord Braxton, much of the sting of Wescott's disloyalty is gone." She studied him with a regrettable level of instinct. "Or was there more between you than June's jilting?"

He shrugged, playing off his deeper feelings. "There was some question whether he behaved honorably toward Lady Wescott amidst the whole debacle. I'd rather not discuss it, for her privacy."

"I see. I don't know anything about that."

Nor do I wish to tell you more about it, he thought. As Wescott said, it was all water under the bridge, and the most honorable thing to do—in both their cases—was to move on and make the most of their marriages as they were.

"Shall we play cards tonight after dinner?" he asked.

"Yes. I want to get better at my gambling before your sister and her prince arrive."

"Your gambling? My dear, bezique is hardly gambling, and at my parents' parties they always play whist."

She waved a hand. "Oh, I'm very good at whist already. Do you think my nieces and nephews will like me? I haven't any yet, except for the ones in your family."

"They'll adore you," he assured her. "Once they've settled in, you'll have to invite them over to meet Mr. Cuddles and Bouncer. They'll consider you the best, most interesting aunt of all time."

This idea seemed to please her greatly. Sweet Jane, whose dearest hope was to please others...and become good at gambling.

"We'll play for bonbons rather than points," he suggested. "I fear if we play for money, you'll bankrupt me."

"If I did, I'd share the money back with you," she said brightly.

Yes, she would. She was the sort of wife one should be grateful for, and he was going to be more grateful from this moment on. No more speculating about might-have-beens with Ophelia. From now on, he resolved to leave that madness behind.

Chapter Thirteen: Princess Felicity

Prince Carlo and Princess Felicity, Royal Highnesses of the Duchy of Tuscany, arrived on a breezy, sunny day, sailing up the Thames to the center of London on a beautifully festooned state ship. Jane stood at the landing with Edward and his family at the appointed hour to see them arrive, along with many other friends and well-wishers. The duchess seemed nearly beside herself, she was so excited to see her oldest daughter and her beloved grandchildren.

When the travelers appeared, waving and hurrying down the gangplank, the crowd burst into excited applause. Felicity was a Townsend through and through, with long, dark, wavy hair and gorgeous features. Her husband was shorter and less imposing than Jane had imagined a prince might be. He seemed very kind in temperament as he guided his wife and children, making sure they didn't trip. They didn't wear crowns or display any outward signs of royalty, but they held themselves in that manner, at least until they reached the land and Felicity threw herself into her parents' arms with joy. It was a lovely welcome, full of laughter, exclamations, and some tears.

So important were Jane's new sister-in-law and Prince Carlo that His Majesty the King sent a retinue to the dock to welcome them as well. The Italian royal couple were invited to the Palace for a reception with King George that very afternoon, and while Townsend's parents, the Duke and Duchess of Lockridge, were included on the guest list, she and Edward were not. Which was just as well, for Jane was sure to embarrass herself and everyone around her in a royal audience. Instead, they were asked to look after the couple's three children, Flavio, Graziella, and Sofia, who were too wound up to endure a royal gathering after the excitement of their arrival.

"This is your chance to become their favorite aunt," Edward teased, though so many family and friends traveled with them to the Lockridge mansion, she couldn't believe the children would remember her at all. There was also the language barrier, somewhat mitigated by bilingual Italian nannies, bodyguards, and servants. The older two children had very good English and a memory of their relatives from earlier visits, so *"Zio Edoardo"* was already ahead of her in their affection.

But they would be in England for nearly a month, so there was time to build a relationship. Young Prince Flavio told her very politely he was happy for their recent marriage. With his dark, handsome features and formal manner, he was sure to be an object of much admiration when he came of age to marry. Princess Graziella was amiable and mischievous in nature, and the baby Princess Sofia too adorable for words.

Lady Wescott asked to hold the baby and took over her care, while people smiled and murmured that she must *practice*. Wescott's sister Elizabeth whispered to Jane that Lady Wescott was early with child. It explained the beatific way she cradled the child. Jane noticed her husband stealing glances at them and wondered if he was thinking of fatherhood. Goodness, would she fall pregnant soon? Would motherhood come as naturally to her as it came to the women around her, who corralled nieces and nephews and cousins with laughter and affection?

The happy gathering continued even after the royal children were put to bed alongside their sleepy cousins. When Carlo and Felicity returned from their audience, they shared news of the palace and the king, praising his spirits and good health.

As the night wore on, Jane began to put together the names and faces around the room. There were the Lockridges, with Townsend and Felicity and their other five siblings; the Arlingtons, who claimed Lord Wescott, his younger sister Elizabeth, and their four siblings. There were also the Marquess and Marchioness of Barrymore, Lord Augustine's parents; and the Earl and Countess of Warren, Lord Marlow's parents, along with more handfuls of siblings, all of whom had grown up together through the years.

What a jolly crowd they made now that they'd all come together to celebrate Felicity's anniversary visit, with a ball still to come. Jane had lost track of her husband entirely when Felicity approached her sometime after midnight.

"Dear sister-in-law," she said, holding out her hands. "How pleased I am to finally meet you in person. Mother has written and told me what a lovely woman you are, and how happy you've made Edward. I'm sure he would have written too if brothers were good at that sort of thing."

Jane laughed. "I haven't any brothers. Perhaps that's a blessing. At any rate, I'm pleased to meet you too."

"We shall call each other sisters from now on, not sisters-in-law, don't you think? Nothing would make me happier."

Felicity was a beautiful, dazzling woman. She possessed the stately manner required by her position, but a warm persona as well. She gave Jane's clasped hands a squeeze, holding her gaze, and her friendliness put Jane at ease.

"I would love to be sisters," she answered. "I've truly enjoyed becoming part of your family. Your parents have been everything kind, and your children are simply…" Jane cast about for a flattering enough word. "Delightful. Scrumptious. Honestly, I'd love to eat them up. But not in a cannibalistic way, of course." *Hush, Jane, you babbler. For goodness sake.*

But Felicity only laughed, and agreed the children were delightful most of the time. "Not always, though. Sometimes they're a great handful of trouble, like all children. I'm happy if you've enjoyed their company so far. I hope they will grow close to your own children one day."

"Oh yes, won't that be wonderful?"

"And we'll have none of this prince and princess while we're here in England," she said. "Call me Felicity or sister, and I shall call you Jane rather than Lady Townsend while we are among family."

"Of course, if it pleases you."

Edward finally appeared beside her. Being closest in age to Felicity, there was an obvious bond between them.

"You are too late," Felicity told him. "I have already introduced myself to your wife, before you could come and tell her falsehoods about me."

"She picks her nose when no one's watching," he told Jane in a loud whisper. "And she has a pet snake. Oh no, that's you who has a pet snake."

Felicity's gaze brightened. "Honestly? You have a pet snake? How wonderful! What sort of snake is it?"

"A *python regius* from Africa. An albino royal python. It's very light in color."

"I can hardly believe it. What a lark, to have a pet that's so exotic. A royal, no less. Please tell me the creature has a stellar name, like Caesar August-hiss, or Queen Sss-harlotte of Snake-sony."

Edward chuckled beside her. Jane was forced to confess her exotic pet's name was the very not-exotic Mr. Cuddles. Felicity's laugh was not the mean sort, but one that loved to share a joke.

"Well, I hope we can meet this Mr. Cuddles at some point during our visit, as he sounds very charming indeed." She glanced at Edward.

"My brother must adore you, Jane, to be willing to share you with a snake. He has no love for the things, as I recall."

"The choice was out of my hands, Felicity. She showed up with it on our wedding day."

"Did she?" His sister probably pictured her carrying it up to the altar.

"It was the day after our wedding, actually," she explained. "It wasn't until we arrived at Somerton that he learned of my snake's existence."

Now Jane and her husband shared a look, and she had to try hard not to squirm at the memory that had resulted in her first spanking.

"Mr. Cuddles lives in the kitchens," Edward told his sister, "in a very secure enclosure. You're welcome to visit him at any time. He's never too spoiled for attention."

"Well, I must say, Eddie, I'm happy you've married an adventurous lady." She turned to Jane. "In my opinion, my brother has never been adventurous enough. I think you'll be good for him."

"We are very happy together." Jane felt a little shy to say it in front of her husband. What if he didn't agree? What if it wasn't true? But he only smiled and kissed her hand.

Later that night when they finally arrived home, Edward took her to bed in a heightened sort of state. At bedtime, anyway, he loved her company. He undid her clothing with fewer words than usual, and left his own clothing strewn upon the floor so they could be naked together as soon as they got to her room.

"So much family. So much politeness all day. I've ached to be alone with you," he whispered.

"And I you."

"I don't wish to be polite tonight, sweet Jane. I hope you'll forgive me." His caresses ended with a nipple pinch that made her squeak.

"You needn't be polite if you don't wish to."

His hand crept up to her neck, squeezing a little, which excited both of them. There was some need in him, she could tell. He turned her onto her hands and knees and pushed inside before she could even brace herself.

"I want you. I want you," he murmured repeatedly, like some meditation.

"You have me. I'm here."

She pushed her hips against him and gave herself to his frenzied lovemaking, arching her back to meet his hard thrusts. He surged into her, kissing, stroking, grasping at her waist and shoulders until they rushed together toward the height of their bliss.

"Jane, oh Jane," he cried as he reached that apex.

His hard lovemaking, his dark passion stoked her own fires so much she followed right after. Her whole body had been possessed by his energy, and she trembled to feel his hard, thick member pulsing within her as she squeezed in release. Afterward they collapsed to the bed together, exhausted, still connected, for neither made a move to pull away. *I am yours, don't you see, dear Edward? I love you so much. Tell me you love me...*

"Oh Jane," he said again, burying his face in her nape, clutching her wrist as if she might steal away even though he lay on top of her, pinning her to the bed. "I've come to enjoy you so much. I pleased you, didn't I? I wasn't too rough?"

"No, it was fine."

This was always fine between them, whether he was rough or sweet, or some mysterious mood in between. But...

"Do you love me?" she asked, hating the pitiable treble in her voice. But she had to know. "Have you come to love me, Edward?"

He drew back and turned her about to meet his gaze. "Oh, darling, of course I love you. Don't you know it?"

He petted her as if to reassure her and kissed her forehead. She searched his eyes in the dim light, but too soon he moved away, urging her to perform her night's toilette so they could get some sleep.

He loved her, of course he did. He had said so. He treated her kindly, with respect in all things, so of course he must love her. When he returned to bed, he took her in his arms and held her close as he drifted to sleep, but she didn't sleep.

He loves me, she thought, drowsing on his scent. *He loves me. He loves me, even though I'm not as perfect as he is. That has to be enough.*

* * * * *

Townsend avoided his gentlemen's club for a while, but now that he was back in town his friends expected at least occasional attendance. He entered in a wary mood, making his way toward the dining room. Last time he'd visited these august, wood-paneled walls, he'd been full of smug glee for proposing to Jane, who he thought was June.

He was not that man any longer. For one thing, he was no longer obsessed with Ophelia. That's what it had been, an obsession. He'd taken a few of her qualities—her beauty, her talent, her delicate manner—and conjured her into a woman of goddess-like perfection, when the truth was, she was as human as any other woman in his life. Why had he done it? Perhaps he'd needed some lofty ideal to pine over. He'd been a dissolute bachelor for so long, frequenting Pearl's erotic house with his friends on far too regular a basis...

Well, that embarrassing obsession was over. Wescott had been kind enough not to mock him for it when they finally made up their differences. A man was permitted an occasional lapse in sanity, wasn't he? If he'd been asked a couple weeks ago, he'd have said his marriage to Jane was the lapse in sanity, but now he saw things differently. Now he realized Jane had come along at just the right moment to save him from himself.

She'd saved him from being too pretentious, too unbending, too apt to expect perfection of himself and those in his life. The last few days, especially, he was coming to see the blessings she'd brought to him, blessings he hadn't perceived until he realized he had idolized the wrong woman.

And so he entered White's dining room a very different man, and greeted his friends with a refreshed realization of their importance as well as their foibles. He took care to greet Wescott as warmly as he greeted Marlow and August, and as he took his seat at their luncheon table, the world felt in balance again.

"What are we eating?" he asked.

"Pheasant pie and some sort of healthy soup," said Marlow. "It tastes good nonetheless."

"More importantly, what are we drinking?" August held up a mug of ale and signaled the waiter to bring one for Townsend.

"How are things at your parents' house?" asked Wescott when they were all set up with food and drink. "The ball's tomorrow, yes?"

"It is, therefore I've stayed away. Jane's gone to help my mother, though, or perhaps just keep her calm. She's still on her quest to become the children's favorite aunt before they return to Italy."

"How do Belinda and Rosalind feel about that?"

Townsend shrugged. "Belinda's preoccupied with her newborn and Rosalind's caught up in preparations for her coming-out this season, so neither of them is putting up much of a fight."

"I believe in Jane," said Marlow. "She's delightful, Townsey. I'm sure your mother is grateful for her assistance."

"Jane's delighted to help. It's to be her first ball as a married woman, and my father taught her to waltz like an ace, so there's that."

"I shall be sure to request a place on her dance card, then," said August. "If I make it to your parents' house."

"I hope you'll screw up the courage to come. Mother will want to see you." He poured a bit more ale into his glass. "I know it's difficult seeing Felicity."

"It shouldn't be, should it? God's sake, she's been married for years."

"Ten years," said Marlow. "It's a ten-years anniversary ball."

Poor August. Unlike his quicksilver obsession with Ophelia, August's love for Felicity had been a lifetime in the making. Perhaps it would take an entire lifetime to undo it, although Townsend hoped not. He himself was proof that one could find happiness where least expected.

"I am intensely happy," he pronounced to the group, without any forethought.

They stared back at him.

"That's good, I suppose," said Marlow. "Jolly chap."

"No, I mean, I thought I would love Ophelia forever. Apologies," he muttered in an aside to Wescott, who waved a hand.

"No apologies necessary, Towns. We've made our peace."

"And I wish for you to make peace too," he said, turning back to August. "It may seem Felicity was the only one in the world for you, but you may find another when you least expect her to appear."

"Perhaps she will enjoy owning exotic snakes," said Marlow, taking up the spirit of the conversation.

"And communing with nature?" August smiled. "I wouldn't mind such a wife."

Wescott made a quelling sound. "Don't go developing a *tendre* for Jane, you two. We've already been through this. It causes tensions like you wouldn't believe." He rolled his eyes toward Townsend. "Speaking of tensions...the tales about your accidental proposal to Jane aren't going away. I overheard some ninnies at Lord Hargrove's garden party gossiping about it last week, and another conversation at Covent Garden on Saturday."

"I heard Lady Arabelle Wilton's catty group discussing it in the park," said Marlow, serious for once. "It was all I could do not to barge into the group and dress them down, but it only adds legs to the whole thing."

Townsend appreciated his friends warning him about this, irritating as it was. When would these blighted busybodies find something new to gossip about? Aside from walks in the park, he and Jane had stayed close to home since they returned to London. Maybe, without realizing it, he'd been trying to protect her from society's barbs.

"She can never know I proposed to get revenge against Wescott. I wish it hadn't happened that way, for I'm thrilled to be married to her now. I suppose I ought to come clean about all of it, but I'm afraid it might devastate her."

"Is she the sensitive sort?" asked August.

"Unfortunately, yes, very sensitive. Exquisitely sensitive. It's one of the things I've come to love about her, how open and emotional she is."

"Goodness." Marlow gave an appreciative whistle. "You used to run the other direction from sensitive women. I suppose it really is love, gentlemen."

They made approving noises and raised their glasses in a toast. Townsend drank, and worried, and drank again.

"It will die down soon, won't it?" he asked. "The amusement? The gossip?"

"It will die down when people see you out and about with your new marchioness, in love and everything." Wescott cocked a brow. "It takes the zing out of the whole story, doesn't it, that you fell in love no matter how the betrothal happened?"

"Hopefully, it will die down after Felicity's anniversary ball tomorrow," Marlow said. "So much of society will be there."

"You're right." Townsend took a deep, steadying breath. "After tomorrow, it won't even be a topic of discussion. With any luck, the ball will spawn some fresher, more exciting gossip. Maybe you can engineer something, Marlow," he said, poking his friend. "Set some tongues wagging?"

"Sure. Rosalind will be there, won't she? It's her big coming-out? Maybe I'll dance with her far too many times."

"Capital idea," said August, taking up the joke. "I will too. Every dance a scandalous waltz."

Townsend threatened both of them with a fist. "If either of you miscreants touches my sister, you'll limp out of that ballroom with a black eye or worse."

"He'll do it too," Wescott teased, ruefully rubbing his cheek. "Anyway, I've got a better plan: we overwhelm the dance cards of Arabelle Wilton and her group. Let's keep those clucking hens too busy waltzing to spread anymore godforsaken gossip." He grinned. "While we're at it, we can step repeatedly on their toes."

"Genius," exclaimed August.

"Hear, hear!" said Marlow.

They drank another round. By God, it felt great having the four of them together again, sharing jokes, schemes, food, and drink without any tension between them. As Jane said, sometimes you had to forgive. Now that he'd let go of his drama with Wescott and Ophelia, it freed up more room in his heart to love his kind, sensitive wife. Why, he was even growing fond of Mr. Cuddles.

He'd deny that fact if Jane asked him, but it was unfortunately true.

Chapter Fourteen: Honor, Honesty, and Truth

Jane woke the morning of the ball in a great state of excitement. Before she went to breakfast, she paused in her dressing room to look over her outfit for the hundredth time: the soft, flowing, pink embroidered gown, the gloves, the slippers—which were still pretty even after her spanking—and the exquisite pearl and diamond tiara Edward had bought her as a gift.

After that, she went downstairs in search of her husband, who was always an earlier riser than her. She found him in the dining room having eggs, toast, and tea. Last night, again, he had taken her with unusual fervor, with a grasping, possessive intensity she enjoyed even if it unsettled her. Funny how he could sit at breakfast proper as anything the next morning. She could not be as proper. She was too excited.

"It's the day of the ball," she said.

"Indeed it is. Come kiss me good morning."

She obeyed, laughing when he tried to pull her into his lap. "Don't. You'll wrinkle my nicest morning dress. I'm going to wear my favorite clothes all day, and then tonight—"

"Tonight, you'll be a marvel. But how dare you scold me for wrinkling your dress when you routinely ruin your morning gowns mucking around in the gardens?"

"Morning is my favorite time to work with plants. They're so fresh and sleepy at that time."

She took her customary place at the table and then jumped right back up as Rosalind entered the dining room.

"Jane, dear," she said. "I'm sorry to call so early but I'm restless with anticipation for Felicity's ball tonight."

"I know, I can't stop thinking about it. Come eat with us," Jane said.

"Yes, join us," said Edward. "How's Mother this morning?"

"She's calm as anything, just as you'd expect. She's so good at planning these things. She sent me over to ask if Jane needed anything for tonight. Jewelry, gloves, stockings?"

"As it happens, I actually provide clothing and necessities for my wife."

"Oh, hush, you." Rosalind stuck out her tongue at him. "Read your boring paper. Jane, would you like to come back with me to Mama and Papa's house for a while? Elizabeth and Hazel are meeting us there to go over last minute things with Felicity, and you're invited too."

"Of course, I would love to come, if Edward doesn't mind."

"I don't mind at all," her husband assured her. "Mother will enjoy having all of you around."

"Yes," said Rosalind. "Hazel has invited Mira, Lord August's sister, and I think Marlow's sister Amelia will be there too, and Charlotte Mary, she's Hazel and Elizabeth's sister who usually lives in Yorkshire…"

Jane's mind boggled at all the names Rosalind rattled off, but she was nonetheless delighted to meet these additional family friends and relations. She'd worried the day would drag, but in the company of so many cheerful women, the hours went quickly. They made a nuisance of themselves testing foods in the Lockridge's expansive kitchen and exclaiming over the endless flower deliveries until the duchess shooed them away and told them the servants must get at it.

Before Jane knew it, it was time for her to return home and get ready. In the past, she'd always awaited social events with a sense of dread, but now that she was with Edward there was so much less to worry about. She only had to be elegant and amiable, and not do anything gauche like babbling about native English ivy species or tripping over her own feet.

And that wouldn't happen, for the Duke of Lockridge had taught her how to waltz.

Matilda did her hair with special care, and then it was time to don her crisp, new stays, petticoats, and of course her flowing, high waisted confection of a gown. She put on the intricately embroidered slippers, and only then did she sit back at the mirror so Matilda could position the tiara atop her head. It was so lovely, it almost made her orange hair bearable. How it sparkled when it caught the light!

"Edward," she exclaimed, coming to the top of the stairs. "Look at me. I feel like a princess."

"You look like a princess."

He gazed up at her, looking a bit stiff in his formal black breeches and stockings, but oh, so handsome.

"Do I look like a prince?" he teased.

"Indeed, you do."

"Come down, then, so I can escort you to our royal carriage."

"You could use a crown for the full effect," she told him as she descended.

"That would be taking things a bit far." He lifted her hand and guided her into a turn. "Jane, look at you."

His intent gaze made her feel shy, but also joyous. He must love her, surely, to look at her that way.

When they got to the ball, there were so many people already there, one could hardly navigate the room. The women were in a riot of colors and jewels, trying to impress the royal contingent. The men wore traditional, formal black coats and knee breeches, and they all looked dashing, but none as dashing as her own husband.

"All right, darling?" he asked as they stood at the top of the stairs.

"Oh, yes. What a sight this is, and how happy Felicity and her husband seem." She pointed to a cluster of guests in the center, surrounding the smiling guests of honor.

"Lady Townsend, you're practically shining," said a husky voice to her right. It was Edward's friend Marlow. He bowed over her hand, his long, pale blond hair the neatest and most composed she'd ever seen it. "May I add my name to your dance card? Please say yes."

"Of course, Lord Marlow." How things had changed since she'd married. The old Jane had dreaded having no attention from gentlemen. Now she'd been here barely five minutes, and someone already wanted to dance with her.

"Just make sure you behave yourself, George," warned Edward.

Jane's eyes widened. "Oh, is your given name George? I never knew that."

Lord Marlow grinned and winked at her. "Like St. George and the Dragon, my lady."

"Are you a paragon of chivalry then, like your namesake?"

"Hmm." His light blue eyes glinted with mischief. "Well, I try to be."

"Don't believe him, Jane." He took her hand back from his friend. "He doesn't try very hard."

Marlow laughed and told her he would seek her out later. They moved down the stairs to greet Felicity and Carlo, who were no longer the "royal couple" to Jane, but beloved family. Music played, people laughed and talked. After a couple hours they took a break for a lavish celebratory dinner with official state speeches and toasts to Prince Carlo and Princess Felicity. Then the dancing began in earnest.

Lord Marlow claimed his dance for the opening, then Lord Wescott asked for a dance as well. By the time they finished, another gentleman requested a dance, and Jane was glad she'd had waltzing lessons, for the merriment was endless. After several dances in a row, she needed a moment to rest, and some space to recover from the ball's great crush. She followed a group of guests onto the large rear balcony and walked along the columned balustrade until she found a quiet corner overlooking the gardens. The clearings below were lit with flaming torches and the trees illuminated with fairylike hanging lanterns, but the balcony was dark, a perfect place to catch one's breath.

How happy she was for Felicity and Carlo, and for her dear mama-in-law, whose ball would surely go down as the greatest success of the year no matter how early in the Season it was. A group of nearby ladies chatted excitedly and Jane didn't make herself known to them, content instead to listen to their impressions of the evening so far.

"What a grand spectacle," said one of them, a tall girl with rich auburn hair, a color so much more elegant than her copper-orange tresses. "And such eager gentlemen wishing to dance. Is there any one of us who hasn't been hounded by Lord Marlow?"

"He danced with me twice, not that I minded," said the lady to her left.

"Well, I minded," said another lady, practically fluttering. "He trod upon my toes three times."

"It was Lord Wescott who trod my toes," said a fourth woman. "But only once. He didn't even apologize."

"I suppose they've had too much to drink. That lot are not usually clumsy when it comes to women, if you know what I mean."

Jane blinked as the gossiping women giggled. She did not know what she meant by her comment.

"Well, we shall hide out here for a while," the first woman continued, smoothing a hand through her auburn hair. "It truly is such a success, our toes notwithstanding. I wouldn't be surprised if the king himself shows up after midnight."

"Perhaps he's arriving right now," said her fluttery friend.

"Good luck to His Majesty, finding space to dance among all these couples. There's barely room to waltz," said another friend.

"The crowd would give way for him," said the auburn woman, with a jaded air of knowing. "Speaking of waltzing, did you see Lord Augustine dance with the princess?"

"All of us saw." The fluttery girl waved her fan. "No lady shall have a chance to win his heart while he pines so pitifully for the former Lady Felicity. When will he get over her? He'll find himself thrown in an Italian prison if he does not take care."

"Prince Carlo watched them dance, did you see? He scowled like a hawk," said another woman.

Jane frowned, for none of that was true. She'd seen Lord August and Felicity waltz together when the dancing first started, and they'd been perfectly genial to one another. The prince, far from scowling, had been dancing with Edward's mother at that time. She thought she ought to speak up and correct the gossiping ladies, but she'd promised herself she would not make a cake of herself at this ball and draw undue attention, so she leaned back into the shadows and bit her lip to still her tongue.

"On the topic of unrequited love," said the auburn woman, in a malicious tone, "isn't it fun to watch Lord Townsend and Lady Wescott pretend the other doesn't exist?"

"His *beloved Ophelia!*" The high-strung fan-flutterer cried it so loudly her friends hushed her, and all of them giggled again.

"I'm astonished any of them are here dancing with one another after everything that went on. They had a drag out fight, you know, Townsend and Wescott. I heard Lord Townsend practically took his head off."

"I heard the other way around, that Lord Wescott injured Lord Townsend so badly he had to go to a hospital in Switzerland to mend."

"Oh, he wasn't in Switzerland *mending*, my dear. From what I understand, he was in Paris drinking and seducing aristocrats' wives."

Jane could barely keep track of who was speaking, much less understand their catty jibes. What a load of nonsense. Gossips ought not to be allowed at balls. If the one lady didn't stop fluttering her fan in that hysterical manner, Jane would grab it from her and throw it down onto the lawn.

"I don't see what makes Lady Wescott so special," said the first woman, who seemed to be the ringleader of their gossip circle. "Just because she can sing, he turns his world upside down for her."

"Who, Lord Wescott?"

"No, silly, Lord Townsend. He ran off to Europe to nurse his broken heart—and a black eye or two, I suppose—then came back to propose to Lady June out of spite and jealousy, because she'd been meant for Wescott before."

A third woman tittered. "And then botched it all and proposed to her bizarre sister by mistake."

All of them laughed now as the blood drained from Jane's face. They were speaking of *her*. She was that bizarre sister. But it couldn't be true. No one made a mistake like that, not in the matter of marriage.

"I'll never understand why he went through with it once he realized his error," said the first woman. "It's obvious to anyone they don't suit. Why, he's avoided her all night. When they take walks in the park, you can see he wants to be anywhere else."

"Wouldn't you?" the flutterer said meanly. "I hear she keeps a menagerie of badgers, skunks, and snakes."

They made disgusted noises that stabbed at Jane's heart.

"His parents probably made him go through with the marriage," said the tall one. "The Lockridges are such sticklers for honor and propriety and all that. And with Ophelia married to Wescott, he can't ever have her now, no matter how hard he stares at her with that longing in his gaze."

Jane could bear it no longer. She turned to leave, but heard her name spoken in cutting vitriol. "And that Jane, swanning about on his arm like the cat that got the cream. I can only imagine the awkwardness in that marriage. He calls her a stunning creature..." She paused, her voice going sour. "And she takes it as a compliment."

They all laughed as the third woman leaned in. "She's a creature all right. She should have released him from his proposal. She wasn't the sister he wanted."

"She was never meant to have him," agreed the auburn-haired gossip. "She should have kept to her weasels and snakes."

"I would rather have had him," said the third woman. "And his *snake*, if you know what I mean."

They all tittered. "Does she pet his snake just right, I wonder?" said the auburn-haired woman. "Is that why he hasn't left her yet, his stunning creature? His mistake?"

Jane was not a creature. She was not a mistake. These were only mean ladies making up outrageous stories. She crept from her shadowed place before they noticed her and made her way back toward the ballroom. She would find Edward, or his parents, and tell them these ladies had to be turned out of the ball for being so completely bereft of respect and manners...

"Jane, dear!" Rosalind caught her hand as they passed one another. "How are you enjoying yourself?"

Jane tried to govern her expression, but she was so close to tears. Rosalind's smile faded as Jane gazed at her, wordless, wounded. Elizabeth stood a few feet away, and she, too, noticed something was terribly wrong.

"What is it?" she asked. "Jane, what's wrong?"

"There is a group of women here," she began, so overcome she could barely get out the words. "They're saying the meanest, most awful things. Why, they ought to be thrown out before someone else overhears the silly...horrible...things they're gossiping about. They're saying things about me and Edward that can't possibly be true."

"Come with me," said Rosalind. "Come, let's find a private place to sit for a moment. Elizabeth, come too."

Her friends helped her away from the whirling ballroom when she could barely see from anger. Or was it sadness? Rosalind led her down a corridor to a dim, unused parlor and took her over to the window, near the fire. Elizabeth appeared a moment later with a glass of cool, clear water.

"Drink this," she urged her. "Breathe deep and try to calm down."

"Yes, be calm," said Rosalind. "I'll have my father find those ladies and toss them out. How dare they insult you?"

"They didn't speak to me directly, I overheard them," said Jane. "And don't tell your father, please. I could never repeat to him the things they said." She gazed at her friends, with too many questions and too much fear of the answers. "Is it true that... Oh goodness, I am so upset. You must tell me, honestly." She held their gazes, tears spilling onto her cheeks. "Did your brother propose to me by...by mistake?"

"What?" Rosalind shook her head. "No. Who said such a thing?"

"A group of women were talking about it and laughing. They said..." She took a shuddering breath. "It's so outrageous. They said Edward meant to propose to June to get back at Wescott because...because he loves Ophelia..."

She burst into fresh tears, shaken, remembering the times he'd seemed to look through her, as if thinking of someone else. Remembering the times he couldn't quite tell her he loved her. It was because he loved another. He loved Ophelia, the woman she'd considered a friend!

"It's true, isn't it?" She gazed at Rosalind and Elizabeth through a blur of grief. "Because it never made sense for him to propose to me."

"Who is telling these tales?" Rosalind asked.

"It was a tall woman with auburn hair, and her friends."

"Arabelle and her lot," said Elizabeth.

Rosalind nodded, eyes blazing. "I know exactly of whom you speak, Jane. Lady Arabelle is the worst sort of person, a vile gossip. I tell you right now, I'll never acknowledge her existence again."

Her friends' outrage was all well and good, but it didn't take away what the women had said. *A stunning creature. A mistake. Does she pet his snake just right?* Jane wished to believe it was all made-up gossip, but Elizabeth and Rosalind's expressions unsettled her.

"Is it true?" she asked, with a plea in her voice. "Does Edward love Ophelia? Of course, that's why he and Wescott turned against one another," she cried, answering her own question. "How stupid I've been. It wasn't because Wescott jilted June. It was much more than that."

"You must calm down, dear love." Rosalind put an arm around her as Elizabeth tried to dry her tears. "My brother does not love Ophelia. He loves you. You are his wife, Jane."

"By accident, it seems." She sobbed harder. "By mistake."

Rosalind was staring hard at Elizabeth. Elizabeth stared back.

"We must tell her," said Elizabeth.

"No." Rosalind's lips grew tight. "This is not the time or place. We'll throw out Arabelle and her mean little cabal and..." She turned to Jane. "You must let Edward address the rumors. It's a more complicated story than they make it seem."

"It's true though, isn't it? He never meant to marry me. It was a mistake. *I* was a mistake."

Elizabeth led her to the divan, sat beside her and put her arms around her. Rosalind sat on the other side, more stiffly, her features dark with misery.

"You are *not* a mistake." Rosalind was crying now, too. "You are a treasured member of our family. You are Edward's beloved wife. I know my brother, Jane, and he loves you."

"But there is truth in the gossip you heard," said Elizabeth gently. "Edward ought to have explained what happened before now, so you would have been prepared for their rude whispers."

"That's all they are, rudeness," Rosalind said. "Vile gossip signifying nothing."

"Jane deserves to know the truth for her own understanding." Elizabeth stood fast in the face of Rosalind's rising agitation. "What's more, until she knows the truth, their union cannot be whole and good. That's my opinion on it."

"Despite what you believe, Elizabeth, your opinion is not always right."

"Please," Jane said. "Please stop arguing and tell me the truth of our betrothal, all of it."

Her strained voice sounded harsh in the silent parlor. Elizabeth sighed and took her hand, squeezing it gently.

"To understand all of it, you should know that, not very long ago, Townsend fell in love with Lady Wescott. She was Lady Ophelia Lovett then, for she was not married yet. He was obsessively in love with her, to be truthful about it."

"Elizabeth!" Rosalind warned.

She gave her a cross look. "She must know the whole of it, or she might as well know nothing at all." She turned back to Jane. "It will make you feel better to know this obsessive love was not returned in kind. Anyway, one night last fall there was a fire in the theater district, and when my brother rescued Ophelia from the spreading flames, they became trapped together and forced to spend the night in East London. To prevent undue gossip and to protect her character, Wescott proposed to Ophelia shortly afterward. You see, this is why he had to break things off with your sister so abruptly."

Jane had not heard any of this before now. "So...it was not a selfish, capricious thing, when he jilted June for Ophelia?"

"Some might say my brother was wrong to remain with Ophelia the entire night, or even to carry her off from the fire in the first place, but she might have died and..." Elizabeth shrugged. "Well, it is neither here nor there. But you may believe Townsend was heartbroken, for he had wished to court and marry Ophelia. He and Wescott fought—

truly fought, until the servants had to separate them—and Townsend went to Europe in a temper."

Jane looked at Rosalind, but her sister-in-law didn't deny any of this. She scowled at Elizabeth, yes, but did not interrupt.

"And then?" prompted Jane, wiping away tears.

"Winter came and Townsend's parents called him home from Europe to spend the holidays and hopefully mend his rift with my brother. Instead, he got a plan in mind to exact revenge on Wescott by proposing to the woman he'd intended to marry. That is...your sister June."

"But June was already married by then."

"Indeed, but Townsend was still in such a fury over Ophelia, and so gleeful in his plan that he mistook you and your sister, with your names so close in nature, and offered for your hand instead."

"You make my brother sound awful," Rosalind said to Elizabeth. "He kept his word with Jane, after all of it. He married her despite his error."

"His error," Jane repeated softly. "So our marriage *was* a mistake." Her voice caught in her throat. "No, it was a revenge."

"You mustn't think of it like that," said Rosalind, before turning on Elizabeth again. "Now, what good has it done to tell her? You'll do nothing but drive a wedge between them, and for what?"

"For her to know the truth," said Elizabeth. "For her to understand."

Oh, Jane understood. At last everything added up—Edward's surprise proposal, the quick wedding, and the worrisome emotional distance between the two of them. He'd married her due to a mistake, a plot gone awry. He'd meant to propose to June to get back at Lord Wescott for marrying his beloved, and ended up with her instead, and married her because he could not get out of it without the loss of his lofty, upstanding reputation.

"How ridiculous," she said. She felt numb. Bereft. Heartbroken. Humiliated in the extreme.

"Dear sister, you mustn't cry anymore." Rosalind embraced her, her eyes deep with sympathy. "My brother behaved badly, yes, but don't cry here and let everyone see your misery. It will only make things worse."

"Indeed, why cry about it now?" Jane said, grief giving way to something else, something rougher and wilder. "It's done, isn't it? All done and done for months now, and he's stuck with me forever, and Wescott with Ophelia, although they seem happy enough."

"Townsend is happy with you too," Rosalind said. "He's become very fond of you."

Fond, as if she were some pet, for his greatest love had been spent upon another woman while gossips laughed behind her back. All through the early weeks of their marriage she'd blamed herself for not being good enough, obedient enough, polished enough to earn his love. Not only that, he'd punished her more than once for the capital crime of dishonesty. Why, she'd been punished for neglecting to tell him she owned an exotic snake, while he'd neglected to tell her the entirety of their marriage was a vengeful, failed plot based on his adoration of another woman.

Worse, he'd told her he'd proposed to her because she'd been jilted by Lord Hobart. He'd framed his proposal as some great act of honor when he wasn't an honorable person at all. If only she'd overheard this gossip about her marriage sooner. If only she hadn't been such a fawning, believing idiot, such a pitiable fool.

With a twist in her stomach, her numb roil of feelings was replaced by searing anger. How dare he be so dishonest? So duplicitous? So selfish and uncaring? He'd kept his misdeeds a secret from her because admitting the truth might paint him in an unflattering light. Meanwhile, gossips giggled at how stupid she was...

"I must speak to him," she said, her voice hard and shaking.

"No," they both said at once.

"Not here," pleaded Rosalind.

"Wait until you've calmed a little." Elizabeth reached for her hand, but Jane was already leaving, propelled by fury.

"Look at what you've done," she heard Rosalind say to Elizabeth as she stalked away, but Jane was grateful to her, for she finally understood what had been standing between the two of them in their marriage—a lack of honor, honesty, and truth.

Chapter Fifteen: Terribly Unfortunate

Townsend looked across the crowded ballroom. It was time to fetch Lady Wescott for the dance she'd promised him, the dance Wescott and his parents had encouraged him to request.

He didn't wish to cause a stir, or draw attention from his sister and her husband on their anniversary, but it was important to show all the gossips that the great Wescott-Townsend feud was over, and that he was no longer enamored of Ophelia.

And all of this was highly important because he didn't want any lingering, pernicious gossip to reach his wife.

He walked to Ophelia and offered his arm. He knew many watched as she accepted his invitation with a smile. There was a time he would have been beside himself with excitement and anguish, to even be this close to her. He'd been caught up in a spell of his own making; how silly and impetuous it seemed now.

He nodded at Wescott as he led Ophelia into the opening steps of the waltz. He immediately spoke before he lost his courage and sense of purpose.

"Thank you for granting me this dance," he said. "I've made things right with your husband, but it occurred to me that I have not made things right with you."

Ophelia met his gaze with friendly ease. "Dear Lord Townsend, there is no need. I'm only grateful my husband's circle of friends is intact again."

"Still, I must apologize for my abominable behavior that day." He did not have to say which day. They both knew. They both remembered. "You must have thought me a madman when I burst into your room and professed to love you."

She laughed, her blue eyes sparkling with humor. "I did, honestly, for I didn't know who you were."

"I'm so sorry, Lady Wescott. I became carried away with emotion. I look back now and think how foolish I was to ruin your private moment together, your betrothal. I'm grateful you're still willing to call me a friend."

"Wescott's friends shall be my friends, now and always. Let's speak of the past no more. The gossips may do so, but I will not."

"Then I shan't either."

"You've made a fine marriage in the former Lady Jane McConall, have you not? I've meant to tell you how much I enjoy her company."

"Indeed, I'm honored to be her husband."

"Everything has worked out for the best," said Ophelia with satisfaction. "Now that Wescott's sister Hazel is situated, we may turn our attention to your youngest sister Rosalind. She's eager to be married."

"I know it." Townsend had to laugh. "Seems like yesterday she was mucking about in short skirts, carrying around her ever-changing collection of dolls."

"Ever-changing?"

"Oh yes. My sister was forever having her dolls die and be reborn whenever her big brothers were home from university. I attended more doll christenings and funerals than I care to admit. Rosalind may seem sweet, but she hides a certain flair for the dramatic."

"Aren't sisters wonderful? I doubtless tormented my brother in the same way."

He felt a tug on his arm. For a moment, he was waltzing with two women instead of one as Jane insinuated herself between them. The dance's graceful sway ground to a halt. The couples around them had to change direction to avoid running into them.

"What's the matter?" Jane did not look pleased. "What's happened?"

"I didn't know." Tears glittered in her eyes, sparkling as brightly as her tiara. "You didn't tell me you were in love with her. Why didn't you tell me?"

"What? I— I'm not, not anymore."

"You're dancing with her. You still love her! I saw you laughing together from all the way over there. Everyone here can see."

Yes, everyone could see, and his wife was shouting private things at him over the music so everyone could hear as well. He turned to apologize to Ophelia, but she'd already melted away as any proper lady would do in the midst of a madcap situation.

"What on earth are you about?" He took her arm to lead her somewhere private, before they created a worse spectacle at his sister's anniversary ball.

"I *know*," she cried, trying to pull away from him. "I know about you and Ophelia, and that you never meant to marry me at all."

"Hush. Let's not talk about this before the entire *ton*."

People moved out of their way as they passed. Already half the couples had stopped dancing in order to crane their necks and see what the Marquess and Marchioness of Townsend were going on about. "How dare you make such a scene," he said through gritted teeth. "Stop fighting and walk with me."

They passed his parents, whose smiles hid a note of sympathy. "Is there anything I can do?" his mother asked quietly.

"No. I'm sorry. I'll take her to the east parlor until she's calmed."

"I'll send tea—"

"Don't bother," he said. Neither of them would be in a mood to sip tea when he was done with her. How dared she attack and embarrass him, here of all places? And Ophelia as well?

"Why didn't you tell me?" she asked, still resisting.

"We'll speak about this when we're alone, in private," he snapped. "Not before."

"Oh, are you *embarrassed*? Imagine how I felt when I overheard gossips on the balcony cackling about our betrothal, about the fact you meant to propose to my sister!"

"Jane, enough."

"They thought it hilarious that your attempt at revenge ended so badly."

He pulled her into the parlor at the end of the hall, checked it was empty of errant couples, and slammed the door.

"How dare you?" he said, dragging her to the sofa. He didn't think, only reacted as he threw her over his lap. "How dare you cause such a scene in front of everyone?" He flipped up her skirts and petticoats, baring her bottom. "In front of Ophelia, my friends, my parents, Felicity and Carlo, and the entire *ton*?" As he scolded her, he spanked her with hard, steady smacks, though she kicked and fought him. "Is that any way for a proper lord's wife to behave?"

"You've behaved worse," she said. "How dare you punish me?"

"Because you're my wife, and you're in dire need of a lesson in ballroom etiquette."

"You loved her, not me," she wailed.

The piteousness of her cry snapped him out of his disciplinary fervor. He was too angry to mete out a punishment, and she too frenzied to benefit from it. He pulled her skirts down to cover the scarlet handprints on her backside and let her up.

"So what if I loved her?" he asked. "You little fool, that was months ago, and now she's married to someone else."

"To Lord Wescott, and how did you exact your revenge?" Her chest heaved, as if her heart wished to escape her bodice. "Tell me!

Never mind, you needn't tell me, because I just heard the whole story from a group of giggling women."

"They exaggerated it, I'm sure."

"Your sister told me the truth afterward, she and Elizabeth, and I'm grateful someone finally did. *You* should have told me, Edward."

"Stop shouting at me." He put his hands on his hips, not sure what to do with them. He wanted to embrace her, to apologize, at the same time he wanted to spank her some more. She'd embarrassed him badly, behaving like a jealous madwoman in front of their entire social circle.

But she was also very upset.

"I'm sorry you had to learn it that way," he said, tempering his tone. "I'm sorry you had to learn it at all. I didn't want you to know the truth, Jane, because it wouldn't have changed anything. It would only have turned you against me, and against our marriage, and while I proposed to you in error, I have been determined from the start to make the most of things."

"The most of things?" She was already tearful, but now she burst into bitter weeping. "I was a mistake. All of this was a mistake. I came to this marriage in love with you, honored to marry you, like the stupidest of idiots."

"Don't say that."

She paused in her tirade to rub her bottom. He should not have spanked her, not at this time, no matter how angry he'd been.

"Whether I say it or not, it's the truth, isn't it?" she cried. "When I think of those early days, how hard I tried to please you, and you were in love with *her*. You were angry about *her*. Do you still love her?"

"No, of course not. Jane, I'm married to you now. Ophelia was a silly infatuation. Now she is only a friend."

"A friend who is so much more beautiful than me. So much more talented and...and refined."

He feared for her, she was so upset. He offered a handkerchief, but she wouldn't take it from him, choosing to wipe her tears aside with her own trembling hands. She kept ten feet of space between them, no matter how he tried to approach her. When he opened his arms to offer her solace, she warded him off with upraised hands.

"I don't trust you anymore," she said. "You might as well be a stranger to me. Our whole marriage was built on a mistake, on vengefulness, dishonesty."

"That doesn't matter now." He tried to sound calm. "Jane, none of it matters now. Wescott and I made our peace at the park the other day. You were there, you saw us settle our differences."

"I didn't realize what those differences were. You said he lost your regard because of how he treated my sister. I thought you were on my side, on our side. I thought you were so proper and honorable."

She spit out the words as if he disgusted her. He wanted to protest, to say that he *was* proper and honorable. "I didn't tell you the whole story, that's true. I wanted to protect you. I wanted to forget the things I couldn't change. I've tried to make the most of our marriage, to be a caring husband to you. It hasn't been bad, has it?"

"I don't know anymore." She was looking at him as if he were some strange man she'd just met. "I don't know anything. I don't know *you*, Edward."

He sighed, looking at the tiara he'd given her, now knocked slightly askew. "It's terribly unfortunate these things had to come out tonight."

"That is your fault, isn't it?" she said, her voice rising again. "They might have come out before tonight if you'd only been honest and admitted our marriage was a mistake. *Your* mistake." She crossed her arms over her chest, glaring at him. "I don't want to be near you. I want to go home."

"I suppose it might be best for you to leave. We can discuss this in greater depth when you're in a calmer frame of mind."

"No, I want to go home to Reading, to my parents' house. They're there yet, for they do not enjoy London, and I don't either."

"You will not go to your parents' house."

"Why not? You don't want to be married to me."

"That is not true, Jane. For God's sake, we'll talk more about things when you're not in a rage. Neither of us was ready to have this conversation tonight." If it had been up to him, he'd never have had this conversation with his wife, but some damned group of gossips had taken the matter out of his hands.

"I just want to go." She sank into a chair by the fire and buried her head in her hands. "I want to go away from you. From everyone."

"You're my wife, so you'll return to my home, where you may keep to your private rooms until you're feeling more yourself."

She looked up at him, her eyes red and tormented. "I have always been myself, Lord Townsend. Always, since the start of our marriage. It's you who's been dishonest and false. You punished me for that more than once, for being dishonest with you. It seems a marvelous hypocrisy now."

"Perhaps you're right," he admitted. "But you do not seem in the mood to accept an apology right now."

"Why should I believe any apology when I no longer trust you?"

Her voice was scathing, her tone cold as ice. He had never seen this Jane, never suspected this angry, scornful, weeping female existed in their marriage, but there she was, regarding him accusingly from her chair. He wished he could have the other Jane back, the cheery, eager-to-please one, but he feared he might have lost her forever. Maybe he deserved to.

"If you wait here, I'll make our excuses to my parents and bid Felicity goodbye." She didn't answer, so he went to the door, then looked back at her. "Stay here, all right?"

"Yes, I'll stay like a proper trained dog," she said. "I won't run after you and make any more scenes. I know you hate that."

Goodness, how small and petty she made him feel. All this time, he'd thought her agreeable as an angel, but she had a bit of the devil when she was wronged. He considered for a moment how things would have gone if he'd been honest from the beginning. He'd have hurt her feelings, yes, but she would have come into their marriage knowing where she stood.

The irony was, he had slowly fallen in love with her over the previous months. And it wasn't the false, obsessive love he'd felt for Ophelia, but a true, deepening, honest love borne of spending days and nights together, learning about each other.

But now...

I'm sorry, so sorry I hurt you, he wanted to say. But she'd told him she didn't want his apologies, and he feared more of her cold, uncaring responses if he attempted it. He'd take her home and give her some space.

He left her in the parlor and went to find his parents, ignoring all the curious stares. Truth be told, he'd earned this embarrassment through his dishonesty. It wasn't a spanking, but it smarted just as much.

Chapter Sixteen: Space to Breathe

The morning after the ball Edward came to her room while she was still asleep, before she had time to wake up and hide from him. She opened her eyes to find him sitting on her bed, staring right at her.

"I'm sorry," he said before she could speak. "I'm sorry I kept my poor behavior from you, the behavior that led to our betrothal. I should have explained."

When he reached to touch her face, she frowned and turned away. "Yes, you should have. It wasn't pleasant to hear about it from gossips."

"I'm also sorry I spanked you last night, when we were both upset."

It had been a hard spanking too, short as it was. He did not go so far as to say she didn't deserve it. Maybe she had, for breaking the most important rule of London society—never making a scene.

"I wish we could return to Somerton," she said, staring at the far wall. "I don't want to be here in London. They'll talk about me even more now."

"It may be that people will always talk about you. Perhaps you must come to terms with it, and me as well. We can't leave as I have duties here, and I want you with me."

"Why?"

"Because I love you, Jane. You must believe me. I've grown to love you so much."

How defeated he sounded, which pleased her. Let him feel as defeated as her for once.

"I doubt you understand how much I loved you from the beginning," she said, turning back to him. She'd spent all her tears the night before, so she was able to sound calm and heartless, the way she wished to. "I loved you from the moment you said you wished to marry me because I'd been abandoned by another man. How kind and honorable you seemed to me."

Seemed. Past tense.

He left her bed without touching her, perhaps realizing she would have drawn away if he'd attempted it. She spent the next few days avoiding him, for she felt dazed, restless, full of uneasy emotion. She needed space to breathe and recollect herself. Everything she thought she knew about her marriage was wrong and she wasn't sure she could ever trust her husband again, which made her afraid.

When she did come across Edward, he seemed a stranger in some sense. Oh, he looked the same. His voice sounded the same, his stature and features were all the same, but also different. Was his smile sincere? Did he love her—as he repeatedly claimed since their argument—or did he not?

Thank goodness she had her pets to lift her spirits. She spent time each day in the kitchens, holding them in turn, stroking their smooth and furry heads, confiding her problems to the only ears that could be trusted not to spread gossip later.

On bright days she took them from the busy kitchens and let them spend time out of doors. Bouncer had his own little corral, just as he'd had at Somerton, and it brought the bunny much joy to hop about and explore new smells and surroundings. She kept sharp watch for hawks who might be attracted to his twitching brown fur.

She took Mr. Cuddles outside in a portable container so he could bask in the sun's rays to his heart's content. Edward had had the container specially made with bars set wide enough to allow sun and air for the reptile, but not the opportunity to escape. The container had a strong lock and secure handle so it would not be dropped or accidentally opened. In fact, he'd put a great deal of thought into it before he set his craftsman to the job. The pen for Bouncer, too, had come from Edward's thoughtfulness. It had been completed already when they arrived in town.

He could be so kind in some things. Was this grounds to forgive him for a marriage tainted by lying and revenge? She wasn't sure yet. Perhaps his kindness had been born of guilt for his dishonesty, which made it tainted kindness.

On dreary afternoons she went downstairs to the library to keep her mind from spinning in circles. She avoided poetry and romance in favor of grisly murder mysteries and wordy scientific tomes. She was glad her husband had accumulated so many books about animals: habitats, husbandry, observational accounts from many areas of the world. Was that typical for an aristocratic gentleman's town library, or was this too a kindness he'd performed on her behalf?

In the course of reading books about reptilian species, she came to suspect Mr. Cuddles must be miserable in his existence as her pet. Like her, he was out of his element in a place he never belonged, a place he was forced to stay. She'd done the best she could since she rescued him, giving him a warm habitat and dead rats, and affection.

Perhaps Edward was doing the best he could as well, giving her a safe home and books, and affection enough for a man who hadn't meant to marry her.

Her mind always turned to such thoughts. One quiet, rainy day, she found herself staring at her book's pages, not even seeing the print.

"Jane?"

She raised her head at Edward's voice. He stood in the door of the library, *his* library, as if he were afraid to approach her in it.

"Hello," she said. "How are you?"

"I'm well. I've just come from Parliament and nothing much is going on, so..." He paused, noting the books piled around her. "Shall I expect you at dinner?"

"No, I would rather not tonight."

She turned back to her book, but he didn't leave. She could feel his eyes on her.

"Rosalind has left another calling card," he said. "She wishes she could come visit, and Elizabeth too."

Jane did miss her friends. She supposed they worried about her, but if they came to call they'd try to smooth everything over between her and her husband, and Jane would go along with their efforts to placate them, and it would just be more dissemblance.

"Maybe next week," she hedged. "In the meantime, I'll write to them."

"I'm sure they'd like that." He leaned back against the doorjamb. Even in her peripheral vision, she could see his lips were tilted in a frown.

"It's been over a week," he said quietly. "How long will you stay angry with me?"

She stared down at her book. "As long as it takes. I do not really know."

"Forever?"

She thought of his nighttime visits, now put on hold. She remembered the way he'd caressed her and made her forget everything but the heft of his body over hers. She remembered his patient lessons, revealing all the exquisite sensations contained in her womanhood. She thought of the children she'd envisioned having with him. She thought of good moments they'd enjoyed before the bad, before the realization that maybe those moments had been faked.

She thought of Bouncer's enclosure and Mr. Cuddles' handsome new container. Forever was a long time. She meant to answer him but couldn't because her throat closed with emotion.

He sighed so softly she almost didn't hear it. "All right, Jane. Have a good dinner."

"You as well," she murmured, studying the page hard. She wasn't learning anything. She was just waiting for him to go away.

* * * * *

If Jane wasn't going to dinner, Townsend wasn't going to dinner. Instead, he told the kitchen staff to take the night off from cooking and went to the club in search of Marlow and August, who might be able to take his mind off his troubles with their talent for spouting nonsense.

Unfortunately, he didn't find them. Perhaps they'd already gone to Pearl's for the evening to play bachelor love games, to spank pretty, willing courtesans in trumped up scenes. To his surprise, the idea of it no longer appealed to him, not when he'd spanked the most exasperating, spirited, wonderful wife in the world.

Curse it, he had to find a way to mend their rift. Without much thought, he started walking toward Wescott's house. His friend had been married several months now. He might have some useful advice.

When he rang the bell, he was admitted to the foyer. Wescott's youngest sister materialized, greeting him as he gave the butler his hat and cane. "Townsend, how lovely to see you."

"Likewise, Elizabeth. Are the Wescotts here?"

"They are. Hazel and I came over to visit Ophelia because she's helping plan Hazel's wedding, but they're being so tedious Wescott and I stole away to have dinner alone."

"I see. Do you think I might join the two of you?"

"Of course." Her steady gaze sharpened. Elizabeth knew more than most about his struggling marriage, for she had been with Jane the night of the ball when his lies of omission had come due.

He could see her searching for the words to pry, to ask after Jane's well-being. He might as well come clean about the fact his marriage still wasn't functioning up to par. "I'm hoping Wescott can give me some advice."

"Advice? Wescott can't give advice to save his life," she said. "But he'll be a good ear for listening. He owes you that." She walked him toward the dining room, then stopped and touched his arm. "Jane loves you very much, you know. *Very* much."

"I'm not sure she does anymore."

"She does. She wouldn't be so angry with you otherwise."

He could see more in her open gaze. Questions, concerns, the desire to reassure. But she did not reassure. Sometimes he wondered if Wescott's youngest sister had powers of divination. She did have the appearance of a wild Welsh fairy, and otherworldly eyes. Did she already know his and Jane's future? He was afraid to ask, so he turned from her and continued toward the dining room.

"When will Hazel marry?" he asked, to change the subject.

"In June, to Lord Fremont, and goodness, they are sickening together. It makes me jealous, how perfect they are."

Just as Elizabeth read others easily, she made an open book herself. She did not find the planning tedious at all; she was jealous her sister would soon marry someone she loved, while she was the youngest, still waiting...

"Wescott, your friend is here," Elizabeth announced as they entered the dining room. "You'd better order another plate. He looks hungry."

"Towns! What a pleasant surprise. Have a seat."

Wescott gestured for the footman to set another place. Townsend had clearly interrupted their meal, but neither seemed to mind. Elizabeth was picking at her plate, nearly finished, and Wes was at least half done, but he took second helpings to keep him company.

"Sorry to barge in," he said. "I went to the club, but August and Marlow weren't there."

"Our unmarried friends have more freedom, don't they?" Wes said with exaggerated wistfulness.

Elizabeth looked over at her brother. "You don't mind the loss of freedom. You were beside yourself that your wife was too busy for dinner."

"Not *beside myself*," he protested. "Who wants to be involved in wedding planning?"

"You do," said Elizabeth, relentless. "You kept making suggestions and vying for Ophelia's attention until she sent you away."

"A breeding woman is a sensitive woman," he told Townsend. "She says I hover too much. I'm beginning to think *you're* hovering too much," he told his sister. "Why don't you go check how the wedding plans are going, so Townsend and I can have some private talk?"

Elizabeth pouted to be dismissed, but Wescott's expression brooked no argument so she excused herself and left them alone.

"When did Elizabeth get so old?" asked Townsend once she'd left. "She's not a little girl anymore."

"No, she's a royal pain in the— Well. She is Elizabeth. Age hasn't tempered her moodiness."

"She admitted some jealousy of Hazel when we spoke in the hallway. I suppose she's found her perfect match."

Wescott shot him a rueful grin. "How lucky Hazel is to marry for love, rather than searching for it after the fact."

"But you found it," Townsend said. "You and Ophelia are happy." He accepted a steaming plate of roast beef, potatoes, and asparagus from a footman and wasted no time digging in. "I never thought much about love before now," he said between bites. "It didn't seem important or interesting. Marriage, relationships, any of that. Now it's grown upon me like an ivy vine, tangling me up. Tripping me up so I've fallen flat on my face."

"You must hang in there, friend. You'll find it worth the trouble. I'd all but written off Ophelia early in our marriage. She despised me, you know. You missed all the drama following our wedding, but I'll tell you, she gave me a run for it in the beginning of things. I'd nearly given up winning her over because, well, I thought love and affection would happen more easily. I was such an idiot."

It surprised Townsend to hear his friend had struggled in marriage. He'd never seemed an idiot with women, not in all the years he'd known him. "What changed?"

"What changed? I changed. I realized I didn't know her at all, hadn't made an effort to know her because I was so caught up in my own head. It's hard to love someone you don't know."

Those words cut straight to his heart. Jane must feel that way, that she didn't really know him. He'd lied to her so blatantly about the reason he'd married her.

"But once I started to know Ophelia, I realized how lovely and fascinating she was. There were parts of her I never expected, and parts that drove me absolutely wild. In a good way," he clarified. "Not to put too fine a point on it."

As his friend's expression turned dreamy thinking about Ophelia, Townsend waited for feelings of anger or envy to develop, but there was none of that, just pleasure on their behalf. Pleasure, and a wish to mend his own marriage.

"What is the real problem between you and Jane?" asked Wescott.

He didn't need to think very long. "She doesn't trust me. I had come to know her, come to love her quite easily over the early days of our marriage, and she felt the same, but now she...she has lost faith in me."

"That's a shame. And you are here for dinner, rather than with her."

"She prefers that I'm not there. I know I wronged her, that I behaved awfully to her, to you, to Ophelia, to everyone for those few ridiculous months... But her coldness now is so unsettling. She is not usually a cold-natured person."

It was hard to explain how bad things had turned between them; he was ashamed to reveal the mess his marriage had turned into. Wasn't a man supposed to be able to control his wife?

"Ever since she learned that I proposed to her in error, she's been avoiding me. I suppose I deserve it."

"Have you apologized?"

"Of course, very sincerely. I have explained. I have apologized. I have told her I love her in no uncertain terms. Unfortunately, she remains unmoved."

"These wives." Wescott shook his head. "They hold you to an impossible standard when you're barely capable of acting civilized."

"I am civilized," said Townsend. "I've come to my senses. I'm perfectly happy to be married to Jane now and I'm no longer enamored of Ophelia. I've told Jane so, but she won't believe me."

"Perhaps you haven't groveled enough yet?"

"I'm not a good groveler."

"You'll grow better at it," said his friend, with the weary jadedness of someone who'd been married years rather than months. "Sadly, it's necessary when you're in the wrong, which I frequently am. It *is* worth it, though, to fight for your relationship." He pushed his plate away and poured himself an after-dinner glass of port. "I never thought I'd enjoy marriage, especially the quieter things. Intimate meals together, secret smiles, fireside chats about what the future may bring. A warm body in your bed, a gentle head rested upon your shoulder. A woman who is happy to be at your side without demanding money for it."

The two men fell silent. Townsend added some more marital qualities in his mind. *A woman who lives and breathes nature and rescues helpless animals. A woman who responds to your boldest caresses without coyness or reproach. A woman who loved you from the start, though you didn't deserve it.*

"I ought to go home. I must go home and see her." He looked down at his ransacked plate. Where were his manners? But he needed to fix things with his wife. "Sorry to eat and run, but I need to go home and mend what I've broken. I don't know how, but I... I've got to make an attempt."

Wescott gave him an understanding smile. "Try not to worry too much, Towns. I can tell you from experience that women possess a great facility for forgiveness, much as we men rarely deserve it. As long as you love her, all will be well."

"I hope you're right." He paused at the door. "Give Ophelia and your sisters my best."

"I will. Now get out of here."

Townsend accepted his hat and cane from the butler and started the short walk home in the crisp night air. He tried to make plans for what to say or do when he arrived, but then realized it would probably be best to let his heart guide him. Wescott's words were true, they had to be. As long as he never stopped loving her...

He arrived home ready to sprint up the stairs to beg his wife's forgiveness, to grovel if he must, but the butler stopped him before he could hand over his hat.

"There has been an *incident*, my lord, in the kitchens. A most unfortunate one."

The butler's voice was steady, for he was eminently versed in decorum, but Townsend could read the anxiety in his tone. "What has happened?" he asked, thrusting his hat at him. "Lady Townsend?"

"She is safe, my lord, but you are needed in the kitchens at once."

The butler handed Townsend's hat and cane to a footman and followed along behind him as he ran toward the servants' wing. He tore through the kitchen door to discover a room in chaos. Maids were chattering in groups. Footmen wrung their hands. The housekeeper accosted him with tears in her eyes.

"There was no one here, my lord," she said. "You gave the kitchen staff the night off. I don't know who left the cage open. The snake escaped and...and..."

"Where is my wife?" he shouted, his voice carrying over the shrieks, screams, and sobs. The servants parted to reveal Jane standing just beyond them, gazing into the corner.

"It is natural," she said, turning to him with tears glistening in her eyes. "It is how snakes naturally act."

"What do you mean? What has happened?"

She tried to hold her composure, but her features collapsed. "He has... He has consumed..."

She could not seem to say what he had consumed, but a glance about the kitchen brought the situation horribly clear. No one had been there, and one of the staff had left the snake's cage open. The maids stood sobbing around Bouncer's enclosure, with its reach-in top.

"Oh, Janie," he said. "Oh no."

"It is natural," she repeated, her raw voice cracking with emotion. "I cannot be angry with him."

The cook berated some scullery boys in the corner, threatening to beat them and turn them out as they sobbed their innocence. Anyone might have peeked in at the snake and left the latch half closed by accident. "Stop yelling," he snapped at the cook. "Let them be."

"It was an *accident*," his wife said, as if these steady explanations might erase the tragedy. "No one is to be punished for this. Pythons eat small prey. They...they squeeze them until they've died and then consume them, and Mr. Cuddles has done this...and..."

Townsend went to his wife, not knowing what to do, how to help. The snake was a long, pale line along the far wall, with the bulging outline of a freshly ingested meal distending its usual sleekness. "I am so sorry," he said, holding out his arms for her.

She threw herself into his embrace, erupting in noisy tears.

Chapter Seventeen: Forgiveness

Jane had told herself she would not do this. She had not wanted to sob in front of everyone, especially not in this uncontrolled way, but when Edward offered his arms, she realized she was not strong enough to maintain her composure. Oh, it was so awful. What had happened to poor little Bouncer was too awful to think about.

She clung to her husband, seeking solace if not healing. He felt as solid as ever. Though she'd regarded him as a stranger for days now, he was not really a stranger, especially now when she needed him. His arms were warm and supportive. His chest rose and fell against hers.

"I cannot be angry with Mr. Cuddles," she said in between crying.

"No, but you can be sad, darling. It's so sad this has happened."

"It's not Mr. Cuddles' fault, though. It's my fault for housing Bouncer in an open-topped cage. I thought he would be happier if people could reach in and pet him."

"He was happier," Edward said, stroking her hair. "You mustn't assign yourself any blame. He was a very happy bunny with a much longer life than he might have had otherwise."

"I bet he was scared, though, when Mr. Cuddles squeezed him." She soaked Edward's shirtfront with a fresh spate of tears. She could not stop crying.

She could not stop picturing the horrifying event.

"He must have been so confused," she sobbed. "He must have wondered why it was happening to him."

"We can only hope it was over quickly." Edward produced a handkerchief to wipe her tears, but his gentle dabs were no match for her grief.

"I cannot seem to compose myself," she said.

"You don't have to. It's been a very sad evening."

He let her cry, cradling her against him. It helped a little, but nothing could take away the pain she felt. She didn't think she'd ever get rid of it. Poor, sweet Bouncer, meeting such a fate.

"Can we help with the snake, my lord?" asked one of the footmen beyond his shoulder.

"No." Jane lifted her head, alarmed. "You mustn't touch him now, after he's had such...such a big meal. You may harm him if you try to move him. He must rest where he is for at least a couple days. He'll be tired and docile from...eating... I'll let you know when he can be moved back into his cage."

"Ask McArry if he can fashion a temporary barrier around the snake," he told the butler. "Would that be all right, Jane?"

"Yes. Yes, I suppose that would be best, so he does not wander when his digestion is complete." She buried her head back in her husband's chest. "Oh, the poor thing."

"The poor thing? Mr. Cuddles?"

"Yes," she sniffled. "I am sorry for him, despite his m-murderous act. He was never meant to live in England, in a noisy, busy kitchen in a cage. We've tried our best to give him a good life, but you see he is still a wild creature. I cannot be upset with him for what he's done.

Well, I am upset, but I must forgive him, for he was only behaving according to his nature."

"I see what you mean. It is unfortunate all around."

The kitchen had quieted. Mr. Cuddles lay still, blinking occasionally and darting out his tongue. Despite the sadness around him, he must have felt very full and content.

"If it's any help, my lady," said the cook in a quavery voice, "Bouncer was a happy little fellow until the end. I scratched his ears just the way he likes, I promise I did, this very afternoon... Near everyone who passes through my kitchens took the time to give the little fluff a tweak upon the ears, and feed him treats too when they thought I wasn't looking."

"It does make me happy to think of that," she said to the kindly woman.

The three of them looked down at Mr. Cuddles' distended body, just about the size of a small rabbit. A sob escaped her, one last sob, but she was nearly out of tears.

"I must go," she said, handing back her husband's handkerchief. "I must... I must rest a while."

"Is there anything I can do, Jane?"

"No, I think..." She felt colder now that he'd released her, even though the kitchen was hot as ever. "Not right now."

Jane walked to her rooms with her head down, thinking how difficult the last few days had been. Her mother had always said God never gave a body more than they could handle, but she wondered if that was true.

She convinced Matilda to leave her alone to grieve, then stood at the window a long time, until it was well dark, and gazed out at the stars. Was there a heaven for animals? Surely there was. She imagined Bouncer in a field of grass and flowers, his twisted back foot finally healed. She believed in her heart Mr. Cuddles would go there too someday when it was his time, for he'd meant no malice in his actions. Bouncer had simply looked too tempting to resist.

It wasn't until a couple hours later, when she lay in her bed staring up at the canopy, that she thought again about forgiveness. Why, she'd forgiven Mr. Cuddles at once, understanding why he had behaved as he did. But she had not forgiven her husband in over a week, when he too had behaved as one might have expected. He had behaved as a husband who didn't wish to hurt his new wife's feelings. It was understandable, if not ideal.

She let out a long breath, lying very still. She'd been so shocked, so emotionally injured by those gossips at the ball, she'd probably overreacted to his actual trespass. Just like Mr. Cuddles, her husband could not help his nature. Just like Mr. Cuddles, he'd made a mistake, but instead of eating the wrong sort of rodent, he'd proposed to the wrong sister.

She threw back the covers and stood, and walked to the door that separated their bedrooms. She heard no sound when she cracked it open. He was sleeping. It was dark and late at night, but she didn't care because there was something she needed to tell him now, right now. She walked to the side of his bed and leaned over it, and traced a light finger over his prominent nose, his strong jawline. His eyes opened.

"Jane. What is it?" He blinked at her, coming to wakefulness. "Are you all right?"

She clasped her hands before her. "I forgive you, Edward. I'm sorry it took so long."

"What?"

"I forgive you. I should have before now. You did not mean to hurt me, even though you hurt me with your mistake. It is like Mr. Cuddles and Bouncer, you see. It was not done in malice. Well, malice toward Lord Wescott, perhaps, but not me."

He blinked again, then moved back and lifted the covers. "Come in, please."

She crawled into the bed beside him. "Oh, Edward. All this time my emotions have been in a tussle because I felt hurt, but you didn't mean to hurt me, did you?"

"No." His eyes were wide in the darkness, as full of emotion as her heart.

"I think now that I exaggerated your crimes against me. You did marry me after all, when you might have walked away from the whole misunderstanding. Do...do you forgive me for taking so long to forgive you?"

"My love, all is forgiven, everything. Thank God I didn't walk away, for I'm so happy now to have married you. I hope you're happy to be married to me."

His open expression was utterly truthful. "I am," she said. "I always have been."

"Perhaps my mistake was not even a mistake. Perhaps you and I were always meant to be. My heart knew it as I proposed to Jane, even though my brain was thinking June."

"Your brain was thinking of revenge, but your heart wanted saving. I like that. Let's think of it that way."

He reached to cup her cheek. "Do you know, I was dreaming of you just now? Dreaming of lying beside you just like this? How I've missed our closeness."

"I've been so foolish this last week." She turned her face away, overcome by his tender words and touch. "I always go about everything wrong. Everything!"

"What do you mean?"

"I think I'm an honorable, kind person, but I held an awful grudge against you." She leaned her head against his shoulder. "And I've certainly been a terrible pet owner. I wonder now if I'm as foolish and selfish as the people at the Exeter Exchange."

"In what way? How could that be true?"

"I see myself as some great naturalist, a rescuer of animals." She sighed. "What folly."

"You *are* a great naturalist, Jane. You cared for your animals, you saw to their needs as best you could. The Exeter Zoo captures animals and displays them for money. I don't see how it's the same."

"Because both of us take the animals away from where they should be. I told myself that I must take in Bouncer, that he would die otherwise, but now he has died anyway in this awful manner. Perhaps it would have been kinder to..."

"Leave him where you found him, to starve to death, or perhaps be torn to shreds by some predator in the wild? He had a good life while it lasted. You gave that to him."

She frowned, kneading her fingers at her temples. "Sometimes I think I should be a proper lady, not someone mucking about in gardens and forests. Perhaps it is none of my business, to be so interested in nature. Perhaps I shouldn't interfere in the lives of things."

"Listen to me," he said, taking her fidgeting hands. "You've just spoken about forgiveness, about meaning well even if things go wrong. Something awful has happened, yes, but it was accidental. You mustn't question if you ought to have done things differently. Sometimes things just happen, and you move on as best you can. Just as we are doing in our marriage," he added. "You make mistakes, you apologize. You try again. Look at me, Jane."

She forced herself to meet his gaze. It was stern but loving, an anchor for her in the quagmire of her guilt.

"I love you," he said, emphasizing each word. "I don't know how or why, or what myriad events converged to make our union happen as it did, but you are the best thing that could have happened for me. I used to place such importance in pointless things, in tradition and propriety and perfection, but my heart was cold."

As he said this, he placed one of her hands flat against his chest, over his heart. She could hear it beating, *thump thump thump...*

"Then you came into my life and turned everything on its head, and I couldn't be more grateful." He wound his fingers around hers and brought them to his lips for a kiss. "Now I love you more than I ever thought to love a woman, more than seems possible on this earth. I love you as you are, with dirt upon your hems and your hair in disarray. I love your fascinating flights of conversation. I love you more than Mr. Cuddles could ever love you, or Bouncer, may he rest in peace. You are so good, Jane, so generous and kind—"

She cut his words off with a kiss. She had to kiss him, for he was making her feel so warm, so loved. Not because she was living up to some lofty standard of propriety or behavior she thought he wanted, but because she was herself. As soon as her lips touched his, his hands were upon her, pulling her closer.

Perhaps he truly loved her as much as he claimed. As much as she loved him.

He took her face between his hands and she didn't resist his dominance. She welcomed it, opening for his onslaught of deepening kisses. His masculine scent, his force, his tenderness, his possessiveness stilled her racing thoughts and brought her back to a sense of calm. *I love you*, she thought. *Perhaps everything is all right between us after all.*

And oh, how I've missed this.

He drew back and pressed his forehead to hers. "I've missed this," he said, a perfect echo of her thoughts.

She grasped his shoulders. "More then. More."

He indulged her, brushing his lips over hers until she felt the thrill in her ears and her stomach, and her toes. She stretched against him, against his safe, familiar contours, and basked in the pleasure of his tongue teasing hers.

"May I stay here with you?" she asked when the kiss, and the next kiss, and the kiss after that ended. "I would like to stay with you."

"Of course you may."

She twined her fingers into his. "My eyes hurt from crying. I cried a great deal."

"Close them for a while, then."

Kissing her husband had awakened dormant feelings within her heart, and certainly feelings lower down in her body, feelings that made it hard to settle down. She only meant to sleep next to him where she could feel protected and safe, but then she began caressing his muscular arm where he held her. She moved her legs against his, unable to hide her restlessness.

"I'm sad but I want you to make love to me," she said. "Is that strange?"

"Not so strange. We've said a lot of things to each other just now, things that wanted to be said, but there's another, more direct way of speaking together."

"With our bodies."

"It's only natural," he said, with a secret smile. "How well you conduct yourself in all things natural, dear Janie."

He was already hard and ready. She could tell as soon as she pressed her hips against his front.

"I love when you call me Janie," she said. "I have always loved that."

"Show me how much."

She was ready for this challenge. After so many days of avoiding her husband, she found she ached for his possession. She teased him with tantalizing kisses and caresses, and wrapped her legs about him, rubbing against his hard member with sinuous pelvic moves. He shuddered as she stimulated him, the thin cloth of her nightgown the only thing separating her from his virile heat.

After a few delicious minutes of this teasing, he gritted his teeth and pulled her beneath him, gazing down with animal intensity. "There are a thousand things I want to do to you, things I've dreamed of doing while you've been absent from my bed, but I don't have the patience for leisurely play right now. I want to take you hard and fast."

"On my knees?"

"No, just like this."

He drove inside her the next moment, and she lifted her hips to meet his powerful thrust. They paused a moment, their gazes locked as he remained deep within her. It had been a long, difficult night but now that they were together, their connection felt like healing.

"Yes, more... Please, Edward."

He gathered her close and pressed inside again, so she felt every inch of his possession. He said he would take her hard and fast, but he interspersed his wildness with exquisitely gentle kisses.

"I love you," he said as his lips whispered across hers. "I love you, Janie. I do."

Jane squeezed his shoulders and closed her eyes, drifting on the scent and skill of his attentions.

"I love you too," she whispered when she could catch her breath. "And oh, that feels so good."

She'd been drawn to his bed for comfort, but for this too. She didn't feel alone anymore. She felt treasured, she felt supported, even when her emotions were not completely steady. She didn't doubt anymore that he loved her.

She released his shoulders as she neared her apex and buried her hands in his hair, giving some of his violent passion back as she twisted her fingers into fists. "Yes, yes, yes," she said. "Please, I'm so close."

So close to happiness. So close to love. So close to you.

She would always look back on this night with some sadness because of what had happened to her sweet pet, but there would also be this to remember, this forgiveness and reconnection. She locked her knees about him as she achieved her release, reveling in the sensation of fulfillment. As the waves of ecstasy ebbed, she came back to herself in time to realize she was still pulling his hair.

Naughty of her. Would she earn a spanking for it? Probably not, because his fingers were twisting in *her* hair now, holding her fast for a kiss even as he sighed in surrender. When he reached his crisis, he shuddered so hard the bed shook. She smiled at his agonized groan, for it was not true agony, but satisfied lust. It was the first time she'd smiled in a while and it felt nearly as good as her release.

It had been the right thing to do, coming to his bed to forgive him. She need not suffer sadness alone anymore. And what an earth-shattering realization, that she was *loved* by the mythic Lord

Townsend. She remembered how she'd admired him from across parlors and ballrooms before he even knew who she was, and now…

"Oh, my love," he said, gazing down at her and stroking her cheek. "My dearest love."

She bit her lip in shyness and joy and he kissed her right on the lip she'd bitten, and told her to rest easy in his arms that night because everything would be all right.

Chapter Eighteen: Naturalists

Townsend arranged a small memorial service for Bouncer a few days later, when Mr. Cuddles was nearly through with his digesting and Jane and the kitchen staff had recovered from their emotional upset.

He gathered the guests in the backyard gardens near Bouncer's pen, where a memorial cross had been erected. For a rabbit's funeral, it was a well-attended affair. The entire house staff was there, for Bouncer had been a favored pet to all of them, a sweet creature to spoil and pet. His friends also showed up to offer their support to Jane: August, Marlow, Wescott and Ophelia. June and Lord Braxton came, as well as his parents and Rosalind, all of them dressed in muted colors of mourning.

Even Felicity and Carlo attended, holding no hard feelings about Jane's disruption at their ball, so Bouncer had royalty at his funeral, an honor few rabbits could boast. Their children greeted his wife with sad, sympathetic faces, as she'd made great headway becoming their favorite auntie.

Jane worried she might cry if she spoke, so he offered to address the gathered mourners in her place. He held the notes she'd given him, so charming and raw with love for the late furball. *He was a good rabbit. He was kind and never bit a person even if he was startled. He never let his lame foot keep him from getting around, although it was usually in a circle.* Townsend couldn't help but smile at her neat, bold lettering. How strong she'd been these last few days, accepting Bouncer's loss as a consequence of science.

How humbling, that she'd trust him to speak this eulogy. He used to think her pets such a nuisance. He'd come a long way from the inflexible man he'd been when he offered for her hand.

"Dear friends," he began, looking out at their sober faces. "We are gathered today to remember Bouncer, who was a very good rabbit. He was the sort of rabbit who never bit even if he was startled. He was a great pleasure to the kitchen staff, who spoiled him relentlessly." He paused at the cook's shuddery sigh, and a faint sob from a maid. He looked to Jane, but she was keeping her composure and nodded for him to continue.

"Bouncer was exceptionally brave with a persevering constitution," he said, looking down at the small, white cross, "for he never let his crooked back foot prevent him from exploring his small enclosure. He loved to chew the grass and rest in the sun on warm days; Jane brought him outside to enjoy the weather whenever she was able. In fact, if not for my kind wife, he wouldn't have had nearly as many warm naps as he accomplished in his short life. He was rescued, tended to, and treasured because someone cared." He paused again, turning to meet Jane's gaze. "And if rabbits have the capacity to do so, I'm sure he counted himself lucky. I speak for all of us here when I say he will be sorely missed."

An awkward silence followed. What did one do at a rabbit's funeral? August saved the day, murmuring "Hear, hear, Bouncer." A few others took up the cheer to honor the beloved pet's life. After that, guests filed forward to lay sprays of flowers near Bouncer's memorial, except for the cook, who instead produced a handsome bunch of carrots to nestle by the cross. That was the moment Townsend nearly lost his composure, but he managed to stay strong for Jane's sake.

The kitchen staff had arranged an appetizing spread of salads, fruits, biscuits, and punch for the guests to enjoy now that the sad part of the service was over. As Bouncer's mourners milled about, he noticed a slight, auburn-haired, mustachioed gentleman speaking with his parents. The man was an old friend from his university days, now a Cambridge professor active in the National Zoological Society. Townsend had invited him today so he might introduce the man to Jane...and her snake.

"Pavenham," he said, greeting him with a handshake. "Thank you for coming."

"It's my pleasure."

"You must come meet my wife."

When he presented Sir Pavenham to Jane, he bowed over her hand with a sincere, admiring smile. "How wonderful it is to make the acquaintance of a fellow animal lover. I am so sorry, Lady Townsend, about your rabbit's demise."

"He was a very good pet," she said. "Thank you for your condolences."

"Jane," Townsend said, "you'll be interested to learn Sir Pavenham is a member of our nation's foremost Zoological Society, and every bit as fascinated by the animal world as you. In fact, he travels regularly to foreign lands to observe exotic animals."

"Do you?" Jane was immediately interested. "Where do you travel? What animals do you see?"

"My particular field of study is West and Central Africa. The sub-Saharas if you will. I study gazelle and antelope, along with their food chain and ecosystem." He glanced at Townsend. *Yes, you're doing well, friend.* "I must say, in my travels through the brushlands I've seen a great deal of snakes, and I hear from your husband you're in possession of a native African snake."

"Indeed I am, though I did not import him here from Africa to be a pet. I don't believe in such things. I believe animals should stay where they are most comfortable, and most natural, but he was brought over by some mercenary scoundrels to put on display at the Exeter Zoo. They had no idea how to tend him either. He nearly died."

"Yes, it's a bad business, importing animals. So you rescued this snake?"

Jane nodded. "I did. I could not leave him to expire. I tried my best with him, although as you see from today's memorial service, things have not always gone to plan. Still, I've learned a great deal about the *python regius* species in an effort to help him."

"Oh, he's a king python, is he?"

Townsend stifled a smile. Pavenham's enthusiasm wasn't feigned.

"Do you think I might take a peek at him, Lady Townsend? I've never had the opportunity to observe a python up close."

"Certainly you must see him," said Jane, equally enthusiastic. "If you study African animals, you must meet Mr. Cuddles."

Now it was Pavenham stifling a smile. "Mr. Cuddles, eh? I suppose it's an apt enough name for a python."

"Because they squeeze their prey, you see?" said Jane, smiling back at him.

Townsend felt like an idiot. He'd never realized the provenance of the name until now. Very poor naturalist he'd be.

"He is a beautiful pale snake," she went on. "An albino, they call them. They are very rare, which is probably why someone caught him and brought him to England. Most pythons are black and brown."

"Indeed, albinos are rare. Goodness, I would love to see him."

Townsend looked about the gathering. The guests seemed content, drinking tea and eating biscuits and fruit. "We can take a few moments to visit," he said at Jane's querying look. "The kitchen is just off the back of the house."

"I suppose he stays in the kitchen for the heat?" Pavenham asked. "What a clever solution."

"Perhaps," Jane said. "But it was not clever to put his cage next to Bouncer's. If I could go back and do it again..."

Pavenham and Jane had already fallen into step together and headed off, so Townsend had to tag along behind. He might be jealous of their easy connection if he didn't recognize it was based fully on their mutual love of exotic creatures. Pavenham only had room in his life for animals. Townsend was more handsome, besides.

He pushed the jealous thoughts from his head. Pavenham was here as a favor to him. The man frequently traveled to Africa, and king pythons were native to Africa...

Mr. Cuddles, still sluggish from his rabbit meal, had at last been moved back to his glass-sided cage. Pavenham peered in at him with a cry of delight.

"Goodness, look at this pretty lady. What a big girl she is, with an enclosure fit for a queen."

"Lady?" She frowned at him. "Mr. Cuddles is a lady?"

"Indeed. A male python would be smaller, don't you think?" He crouched beside the wood and glass box and studied her more closely. "Yes. With her size, I'd say she's a two- or three-year-old female, which probably explains her recent interest in larger prey. Begging your pardon," he said, a blush rising in his ruddy cheeks. "It is crass to remind you."

"That's all right. It's hard not to remember what happened," said Jane with a sigh. "I'm only glad no harm came to him. He—I mean, she—was very distended for a couple of days."

"She seems healthy enough now," he continued in a kind voice. "In fact, she appears quite hale and strong for a snake kept in captivity. You've done well with her."

"I tried my best," she said, clasping her hands together to peer into the cage beside him. "Lord Townsend helped too, along with his servants."

"I just remembered something." Pavenham looked over at Jane, considering. "I received a letter last year full of questions about reptile diets and behavior, including some specific questions related to pythons. No, it couldn't have been you. It was from a young man, Jonah or Josiah or some such."

"Perhaps someone from the Exeter Zoo," his wife suggested a little too quickly.

"You may admit it, if it was you," said Townsend. He winked at Pavenham. "I have my suspicions."

"If it *was* me—and I am not admitting it was—well, I probably wrote under a man's name because I thought I might be taken more seriously. Not that I'm admitting anything." She bit her lip, then shrugged. "All right, I believe it probably was me. You wrote back so kindly, Sir Pavenham, with so much helpful information. I'm grateful, and I'm sorry I wrote under a false name. It seemed the wisest thing to do."

"I can understand why you wrote under a pseudonym, my lady. The scientific field has historically been the dominion of males, although it needn't stay that way. We have not had women in the Zoological Society to this point, but we ought to, if they are adequately interested."

Jane turned to Townsend. He shook his head. "I don't think so, love. Not yet anyway. Let's take it one step at a time."

"Perhaps *you* could join the Zoological Society," she said. "And I could attend the meetings with you."

"Perhaps we can talk about it later. Why don't you give Sir Pavenham a closer look at your snake?"

Of course, he would eventually join the cursed Zoological Society because she wanted him to. He was learning that marriage was all about doing things you never intended for the simple reason that you loved someone so very much.

He watched as Jane opened the enclosure, affording Pavenham greater access to the still-groggy reptile. They spoke of the snake's digestion, her muscle tone, her typical eating schedule, her temperament and markings.

Again, Pavenham praised her caretaking skills, but she shook her head. "It is not enough just to keep the poor thing alive. I fear she is very unhappy. I often think how much fuller her life would be if she were living where she belongs, in those African wilds you study."

Townsend saw the idea come to her, as he'd hoped it would. She gave a quick gasp.

"Sir Pavenham, would it be possible for you to transport Mrs. Cuddles to Africa on one of your future trips?" She touched the side of the snake's enclosure. "This might be too large to travel with, but we have an excellent portable cage I use to take her in and out of the house. Mrs. Cuddles sleeps a lot and only eats every couple of weeks, so she would be a very cooperative traveler."

"Good lady, I would be happy to take your python back to her homeland." He made a laudable effort to look surprised by the request. "If you're willing to part with her, the change of habitat would be a boon to her longevity and health."

"Yes, it would be wonderful for her, wouldn't it?" Jane paused, stroking her snake's smooth coils. "Will she be safe there?"

"I believe so. She's young enough to adapt back to life in the wild. It will be a sacrifice for you, of course, but I believe she'd be happier there."

"Oh, how I would love for her to be happy. She'll be so glad to go home."

"A *python regius* like our lady here will be comfy as candlewick in the shrublands and grasslands of West Africa."

"Would you like that, Mrs. Cuddles?" she asked the snake, gazing into its dark pink eyes. "To slither free among warm, dry grasses, where you could meet other snakes just like you?"

Townsend watched all this with an ache in his soul. How good, how selfless his wife was. Mrs. Cuddles would be happier in Africa, so she would let the creature go to Africa even though it would be two pets lost so quickly.

She looked back up at Sir Pavenham. "Will you watch him—her—a while to be certain she isn't afraid or confused when you release her?"

"Of course, Lady Townsend. I'll scout out the perfect stretch of land with similar snakes, lots of sunshine, a bit of water and a bit of shade. I'll watch to be sure she looks content." He glanced at Townsend. "I imagine it'll be hard to track her though, once she takes to freedom and stretches her coils. In a blink, she'll be seeking out males, mating and laying a clutch." The man colored again, rubbing his temple. "Forgive me for being indelicate."

Townsend chuckled. "You can discuss indelicacies with this particular lady, at least the reptilian sort. She won't take offense."

"Well, that is how species continue to grow, isn't it?" said Jane with a smile. "I think Mrs. Cuddles will make an amazing mama. Well, to her eggs at any rate. Did you know pythons wrap around their eggs to warm them until the baby snakes are born?"

Sir Pavenham smiled at her indulgently. "I did know, my lady."

Jane turned back to her pet, gazing hard at him. Her. "I only hope she doesn't feel abandoned," she said after a moment. "We have grown so close."

"She will remember you with fondness, no doubt," said Pavenham, "though she will be too busy going about her snake business to be maudlin about it."

"Her snake business," Jane echoed. "I like the sound of that."

"We should return to the garden and our guests." Townsend nodded at his friend, thanking him without words. "You'll let us know when your trip is imminent, Pavenham, so we can convey Mrs. Cuddles to you in her traveling compartment?"

"Indeed. That will be excellent. My ship sails within a fortnight, actually. I'll send a note within a day or two with more specific plans."

Later that night, Jane lay in his arms and cried, sad tears mixed with relief. "It is for the best, isn't it?" she asked.

"Of course, my love."

He kissed and soothed her, and realized he also would miss Mrs. Cuddles when she left on her journey. The old Townsend had been horrified his wife communed with snakes. The new Townsend understood that exotic, unusual creatures could be a wonderful change from the proper and ordinary.

Love did change one, that was for sure.

Chapter Eighteen: Something Important

    Two weeks later they went to the docks to bid farewell to Mrs. Cuddles. Jane had already said her goodbyes to her pet snake at home, in private, so she might not have gone at all except that Felicity and her family were sailing back to Italy the same day, on the same ship. That seemed to Jane a fair harbinger, even if the travelers would part ways after the first leg of the journey.
    She knew she would see Felicity, Carlo, and their children again one day. That parting was sad but not unbearable. Parting with Mrs. Cuddles was a bit more unbearable, for she knew she'd never see her again.
    She rode quietly on the way home afterward, looking out the carriage window at busy streets and busy people. She did not wish to cry. Why, Mrs. Cuddles was even now starting an amazing journey to return to her true homeland. Not only that, but a more trustworthy chaperone than Sir Pavenham could not have been found.

"Everything all right?" Edward asked. "Feeling heartsick, my love?"

"No, I will not grieve. I should not." She lifted her head and met his gaze, attempting to smile. "Why, I'm excited that everything has worked out so well for Mrs. Cuddles. Will you be sad that your sister's gone?"

"Of course. My mother will be very sad for a while, for she dotes on the grandchildren, but Felicity writes to all of us regularly. I imagine you'll receive letters now as well."

"I hope so. I'm glad I got to meet her and her family."

They rode a while longer in silence, before Jane burst out emotionally. "It's only that...I feel like a mama whose birds have all left the nest. Bouncer is gone, and now Mrs. Cuddles. I suppose I will feel like your mother does, pining for her grandchildren. I did love having my pets around."

"Of course." He took her hand. "But you will find other things to do with your time. Perhaps by next year we'll have a baby in the nursery."

Jane had not told him yet that her courses were late. Well, they were only a day or two late, but they'd always been so regular. A baby in the nursery...what a thing to imagine.

"Babies must be at least as difficult to care for as pythons, don't you think?" she asked.

"I'd never thought about it in quite that way. But I believe babies take a great deal of care, and for many years."

She hesitated a moment. "I suppose then it would not make sense to amass any new pets right now. Perhaps I should just reapply myself to gardening or..."

"I think gardening would be a good hobby for you now, yes. The groundsman was telling me of your assistance in the greenhouse, forcing flowers. He says you have a special talent for it."

"I find flowers endlessly fascinating. Do you know they mate to reproduce in much the same way people do? Well, not the *same* way, but there is pollination that must happen. Fertilization between male and female parts."

Edward grinned at her. "Male and female parts, eh? But not *quite* the same as what we do?"

She gave him a playful swat and looked back out the window, blushing. Why did she have the worst gift for conversation? Thank goodness her husband loved her anyway, despite her interest in awkward and strange things. She'd hoped he might encourage her to adopt some other pet, but if he thought gardening would be better for now, she was willing to spend her time on things that didn't hop or slither. She would miss the petting and cradling and hugging, but if a child came to them soon, she could do all the cradling and hugging she wished.

When they arrived home, she felt a bit tired and was all for taking a midday nap, but Edward asked her to accompany him to the front parlor instead.

"I have something to show you," he said. "Something very important that's arrived from Somerton."

"From Somerton?" She took his hand and let him lead her down the hall. "Are they bulbs? Are the iris bulbs blooming already?"

"It's not bulbs."

"Is it Matilda's favorite hairbrush? She wrote to Mrs. Loring last week to say she'd forgotten her preferred hairbrush at Somerton."

"That was returned to your maid a few days ago, I believe," said Edward.

"Excellent! Well, what is it, then?"

He opened the door and smiled at her. "Something you will very much like."

At first, she couldn't fathom what he was talking about. The parlor was quiet, and she couldn't see anything important except for an embroidering maid next to a sleepy fire in the grate. Then the maid smiled and looked down, and Jane saw what her husband meant to show her. A small, furry head lifted from the soft nest of a blanket.

"Oh, my goodness," she cried.

It was a dog, a little puppy. Well, not little. When the animal stood up from its bed, she saw it was a half-grown puppy in that awkward stage between babyhood and adulthood, when its ears and feet were too big and its limbs gangly. It was a black and white border collie with a twitching nose and ears that stood straight up in question.

"Oh, my goodness. Oh, my dear word!" She dropped her husband's hand and hurried across the room to the adorable creature. "Whose dog is this? What is its name? Is it friendly, may I pet it?"

"You may."

Edward caught up with her and knelt beside the dog's bed. As the maid slipped away, he picked up the wiggling animal and placed it in Jane's arms. The poor thing trembled as it sniffed her face, his large, dark eyes wet and curious.

"To answer your questions, Jane, this is your dog if you want it. He hasn't a name yet. He is friendly but skittish, and you ought to pet and cuddle him so he will bond with you as his owner."

"He's mine?" She'd always loved puppies, but her father believed dogs ought to be working animals who lived outside or in kennels. "Edward, does he have to stay in the kennel?"

"That, too, is up to you. I rather thought you'd want an inside pet."

"Oh, I do, I do!" She held the soft pup against her chest, against her heart. "I can't believe you've gotten me a puppy. It's the most wonderful, important thing, you were right about that." She looked up at her husband, flushing with pleasure. "You've made me so happy. How amazing you are."

He shrugged, downplaying her praise. "It's almost as if it was meant to be. I was wondering how to help you feel better after the loss of your pets when I received a letter from one of Somerton's tenants. He breeds herding dogs for Berkshire farms, and happened to have a dog that is a bit..." He paused, ruffling the pup's floppy, black ears. "Well, apparently this little man was a bit too shy and...well, he didn't specifically say stupid..."

She hugged him tighter. "No, he is not stupid. He is sweet. I'm sure he'll be the sweetest dog ever."

"He did say he was sweet-tempered, but perhaps not up to the task of training and work. The man remembered Somerton's mistress, Lady Townsend, was known for rescuing pitiful creatures, so he wrote to me asking if you might like to have him, and here he is."

"Oh, I'm so glad he thought of me." She cradled the puppy, touching her nose to his nose. "Who wants to do herding anyway? I think you're the wise one. Who wants to run around with smelly, woolly sheep? You'll be much happier as my pet. We'll go exploring outside sometimes, and take naps together, and play fetch with sticks and balls." The puppy gave her a tentative lick, which she took as agreement. "And when Edward and I have children together, you shall have playmates who'll love to laugh and play with you."

She turned to her husband, overcome with gratefulness for her pet. Overcome with love. He smiled back at her.

"You like him."

"I love him." She held the puppy close, already memorizing his smell. "And I think..." She bit her lip, looking shyly at her husband. "I think maybe we might have a baby soon."

His smile turned to a stare, then a different sort of smile. A wondering, surprised, delighted smile. "Really?"

"Well, I don't have much experience in the matter personally, but I have studied a great deal about reproduction in general and there are definitely signs."

He embraced her so the sweet puppy was sandwiched between them. The little dog squirmed as Edward kissed her forehead, her nose, her lips. "A baby," he whispered. "I hope he or she is as kind and intelligent as you."

"And as caring and generous as you." She felt suddenly close to tears. She blinked them away and touched the puppy's paws. "He has white socks, Edward. Look. Oh, this adorable thing." She held the furry bundle to her cheek. An eager pink tongue darted out to lick her a bit more enthusiastically as little paws scrabbled on her shoulder. "He's not trembling anymore," she said. "He's growing used to me."

"Indeed, he is. He knows he's in excellent hands. What is this adorable little man's name? What shall we call him? You ought to choose."

Jane thought about typical dog names. Charger, Spot, Rover, Laddie. Her dog needed a special name, because he was more special than the other dogs of his type, who were content to run around barking and herding livestock. Her dog would be a beloved companion, a real member of their family. Their growing family.

"He looks very wise," she said, gazing into the puppy's luminous eyes. "I don't think he is stupid at all, just given to daydreams rather than herding. Perhaps we should name him after a famous philosopher. Since he has socks for paws…how about Socrates?"

"Socrates, for a dog with socks." He patted the pup's soft head. "I like it."

"Do you remember the first day we met, when we walked in the garden and you quoted Socrates to me?"

He thought a moment, then said, "'*An unexamined life is not worth living.*'"

"Yes. I was so happy when you said that. I knew if you liked Socrates that we would get along."

His lips quirked in a half smile. "It took a bit of time for us to get along. But my parents also had tension early in their marriage, and look at them now, supremely happy after thirty years."

"Think how happy we'll be in thirty years."

He kissed her again. "I adore you, Jane. Every day, you make me examine my life in ways I never thought."

"Good ways, I hope."

"My sweet love. Of course, good ways." He smiled at her, stroking her cheek. How her heart pounded when he looked at her that way. She felt close to tears again, although she wasn't sad at all. Perhaps it was her pregnancy that was making her so emotional. Why, ewes were known for their fitful behavior while pregnant.

"Would you like to hold him a while?" she asked.

He took the dog when she offered it, collecting its gangly legs. "Hello, Socrates," he said to the puppy. "Do you know, my life was profoundly unexamined before I met your new mama? She changed me. Otherwise I probably wouldn't be holding you right now."

Socrates cocked his head in a comical way, as if trying to understand his words. They laughed together, then Jane pretended to frown.

"In the carriage, when I spoke of more pets, you said I ought to concentrate on gardening. I felt sad about it, but you were only toying with me, weren't you?"

"Well, I couldn't give away the surprise." He put Socrates back in his blanket, then leaned closer to her before the fire. "Goodness, Jane, I fully expect more pets through the years. As long as you'll still have time for me too."

"I will, I promise."

Socrates let out a soft snort and turned in a circle, looking for a comfortable place. He came to rest with his head against Jane's knee and his tail lying against Edward's thigh. His clumsy puppy paws curled against his body and he sighed in contentment.

"I love you," said Edward quietly. "I love you for giving me this."

She scratched behind one of Socrates's floppy ears. "But you gave him to me."

"That's not what I mean. I love you for giving me this, right now." He scratched Socrates' other ear until Jane looked up at him. "Love isn't obsession. It's not some quest for perfection. It's moments like this, isn't it? A cozy parlor, a snoring pup, and the most beautiful, caring wife one could ever hope to be married to."

She reached to take his hand, her heart full to bursting at his words. "We are so lucky, Edward. Let's never forget how lucky we are."

"We won't. I need only see you smile, and I remember."

As their puppy snoozed, as Mrs. Cuddles began a journey to a new life, Jane leaned into her husband's embrace and thought how mistakes could become opportunities, and imperfections an irresistible invitation to love.

THE END

A Final Note

I hope you enjoyed this second book in my Properly Spanked Legacy series, featuring "uptight" Lord Townsend and his wonderfully natural bride. This story takes place in the winter of 1822 through to the spring of 1823, nearly forty years before Charles Darwin's seminal book, *The Origin of Species*, was published. I like to think of avid zoologist Jane devouring it in her mid to late 50s, surrounded by pets, children, and grandchildren, and of course her beloved Edward, who would have bought it for her as soon as it became available, as an anniversary gift, perhaps.

It's also interesting to note that Transcendentalism, a popular movement celebrating the divinity to be found in nature, became popular around the 1820s-30s in the United States. Was Jane aware of Transcendentalist philosophers like Ralph Waldo Emerson, Henry David Thoreau, and Margaret Fuller? I believe she would have been, though I didn't make the Transcendentalist connection until after I'd finished writing. Jane loved libraries, books, and nature, after all.

I apologize that this story took so long for me to write; I think that might be because it unfolded in the fashion of one of Jane's hothouse flowers. It started as a tight bud, and it wasn't until it opened and showed all its petals that I saw what a beautiful tale it was. The book I meant to be a severe spanking novel became about a bungled engagement and a snake named Mr. Cuddles instead. It became about comfort, acceptance, mistakes, love, and forgiveness, and I was glad, because we all need a bit more of that in our lives.

I'll close with heartfelt thanks to Wendy, Carol, and author Renee Regent, who always make sure I don't put out a bad book. Stay tuned for the final two books in this Properly Spanked universe, which are coming…eventually. The best way to stay up to date with all things Annabel Joseph, including sales and new releases, is to subscribe to my email newsletter. I only send them out for important announcements, so you won't be spammed. You can find the link at my website or on my Facebook page (just search for Annabel Joseph.) Thanks for reading!

Other Historical Romance by Annabel Joseph

Lily Mine

When Lily wends her way down the country lane to Lilyvale Manor, she hopes the coincidence of names bodes well, for she is in dire straits. She's been disowned by her London family and finds herself desperately in need of a job.

Lord Ashbourne is equally at ends, his fiancée having jilted him for a commoner and run off to the Continent. Her powerful society family is determined to delay the breaking scandal in order to save the younger sister's prospects. When a servant leads Lily to his parlor, James is astonished to discover how closely she resembles the missing lady of the manor.

He hatches a plan, convincing Lily to play his absent "wife" to keep the gossips at bay. He reassures her it will be in name only, but soon enough, playacting turns to real attraction, and friendship to aching, mounting desire. The strictures of society and unforeseen tragedy combine to test the pair's forbidden love, even as they are driven ever closer into one another's arms…

About the Author

Annabel Joseph is a multi-published, New York Times and USA Today Bestselling BDSM romance author. She writes mainly contemporary romance, although she has been known to dabble in the medieval and Regency eras. She is recognized for writing emotionally intense BDSM storylines, and strives to create characters that seem real—even flawed—so readers are better able to relate to them. Annabel also writes vanilla (non-BDSM) erotic romance under the pen name Molly Joseph.

Annabel Joseph loves to hear from readers at annabeljosephnovels@gmail.com.

You can learn more about Annabel's books and sign up for her newsletter at annabeljoseph.com.

Printed in Great Britain
by Amazon